Trouble
Don't Last Always

Also by Francis Ray
in Large Print:

Someone to Love Me
I Know Who Holds Tomorrow

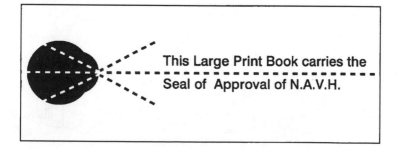

Trouble
Don't Last Always

Francis Ray

Thorndike Press • Waterville, Maine

Published in 2006 by arrangement with St. Martin's Press, LLC.

Thorndike Press® Large Print African-American.

The tree indicium is a trademark of Thorndike Press.

The text of this Large Print edition is unabridged. Other aspects of the book may vary from the original edition.

Set in 16 pt. Plantin.

Printed in the United States on permanent paper.

Library of Congress Cataloging-in-Publication Data

Ray, Francis.
    [Turning point]
    Trouble don't last always / by Francis Ray.
       p. cm. — (Thorndike Press large print African-American)
    Previously published as: The turning point.
    ISBN 0-7862-8259-2 (lg. print : hc : alk. paper)
    1. African Americans — Fiction. 2. Caregivers — Fiction.
    3. Louisiana — Fiction. 4. Large type books. I. Title.
    II. Thorndike Press large print African-American series.
    PS3568.A9214T87 2006
    813′.54—dc22
                                         2005028018

This book is dedicated to those who walk by faith and to those who are almost there.

As the Founder/CEO of NAVH, the only national health agency solely devoted to those who, although not totally blind, have an eye disease which could lead to serious visual impairment, I am pleased to recognize Thorndike Press* as one of the leading publishers in the large print field.

Founded in 1954 in San Francisco to prepare large print textbooks for partially seeing children, NAVH became the pioneer and standard setting agency in the preparation of large type.

Today, those publishers who meet our standards carry the prestigious "Seal of Approval" indicating high quality large print. We are delighted that Thorndike Press is one of the publishers whose titles meet these standards. We are also pleased to recognize the significant contribution Thorndike Press is making in this important and growing field.

Lorraine H. Marchi, L.H.D.
Founder/CEO
NAVH

* Thorndike Press encompasses the following imprints: Thorndike, Wheeler, Walker and Large Print Press.

Heartfelt Thanks and Gratitude

First of all, I want to thank God. With Him in my life all things are possible.

My gratitude also goes to the following:

LaRee Bryant and Angela Washington-Blair, who were with me in the beginning, two years ago, when the idea for this book came to me. I'm blessed to have you as my friends.

Bessie Lassiter, who called her son, Wright Lassiter Jr., who called Dr. Michael Harris, ophthalmologist, who answered question after question for over a year with keen insight and patient understanding.

Dr. Susan Parks, ophthalmologist/retina specialist, University of Texas Southwestern Medical Center at Dallas. A macula hole in my left eye could have meant permanent blindness. You and God deemed otherwise. Thanks also for the encouragement to write this book.

Dr. Eugene George, neurosurgeon/head trauma specialist, University of Texas

Southwestern Medical Center at Dallas. Thanks for the medical expertise and the laughs.

David Ondick, vocational specialist, and Shelly Smith, caseworker for the Texas Commission for the Blind. Thanks for giving me invaluable insight into the lives of those who view their loss of sight as an inconvenience, not a handicap.

Trisha Chandler, supervisor of Orientation and 'Mobility for the Dallas Lighthouse for the Blind. Thanks for the O & M lessons.

Glenda Howard, my editor. Your intuitive instincts are phenomenal. Thanks for helping me turn my dream into reality.

As always, to the home team, William and Carolyn Michelle Ray, husband and daughter, my biggest fans and supporters, thanks for not complaining about the house or uncooked meals. You make life meaningful. I love you.

Chapter One

"Death is inevitable. You can't hide from it, run from it, bargain with it. Each one of us has to accept that sobering fact. The best thing you can do is be ready."

Pastor Hezekiah Fowler's deep bass voice reached every person within the packed frame church without the help of the failing PA system. In the front pew, Lilly Crawford sat with her long legs demurely crossed at the ankles. Her hands clutched a flowered, tear-stained handkerchief as she stared at the white casket draped with a spray of white gladiolus. More sprays were at the head and foot and clustered around the casket and podium.

So many flowers, Lilly thought, *and so utterly useless. Mother Crawford couldn't smell them now.* She had loved flowers of any kind, loved to spend time in her garden, but she'd been bedridden for the past six months as her body fought a losing battle. Yet the only person who had thought to send her flowers while she could enjoy them was the one person who couldn't be here for her home going. If Rafe had come, there might have been two caskets instead of one.

To Lilly's left sat her husband, Myron, in his best black suit, his usually straight shoulders slumped, his callused hands clamped between his legs, his proud head bent in submission to a power greater than his. Next to him sat his daughter, Lilly's stepdaughter, Shayla, draped in black and misery, sobbing loudly. To her right was David, her husband, a shy, earnest young man with a nervous eye tic but, according to Shayla, a computer genius. Since David had been to his in-laws' house only a handful of times before their marriage three years ago and twice since, Lilly couldn't be sure.

"Hear me now; I said you can't run from it, hide from it, bargain with it," Pastor Fowler continued, and Lilly respectfully gave him her attention. "Each one of us in God's appointed time is gonna have to give an accounting of our sins and look God and death in the face. The best thing you can do is be ready."

Pastor Fowler's hands, work-worn from thirty years at the bottle plant lifting twenty-pound crates of beverages, clamped around the scarred wooden pulpit. Out of his mud-brown, heavily lined face his brown eyes sparkled with the fervency of his message as he leaned his robust torso over the worn, open Bible.

Shouts of "Amen" came from around the

church. Lilly knew if she were to turn around she'd see heads nodding in agreement as well. The pastor was in top form. Mother Crawford would have been pleased, but a little sad as well. She had always said no one preached more earnestly than Pastor Fowler when trying to win lost souls; his fervent prayers could wrench tears from the eyes of the boldest sinner. Too bad, she'd once commented after a particularly powerful Wednesday night prayer meeting, that he didn't seem to be able to save himself.

Lilly hadn't asked for an explanation. She had lost faith in too much to add Pastor Fowler's sins, real or imagined, to the list. Besides, she knew how frightening and helpless it felt not to be able to save yourself.

"Our faithful sister, Minnie Faye Crawford, was ready," Pastor Fowler said, assurance in every syllable of his voice. "At eighty-one she had lived a long time. Was blessed with a loving husband who preceded her in death, a loving son and granddaughter who gave her countless moments of joy and blessings in her declining years. The Lord saw fit to take her first daughter-in-law, but He blessed her with another fine Christian woman in Sister Lilly."

"Amen" flared up again. Lilly closed her

eyes against the looks she knew would be cast upon her. No one except Mother Crawford and Rafe ever let her forget she hadn't been the first Mrs. Crawford. To everyone else Lilly was still trying to measure up, still failing. Just as Rafe had failed.

"So, brothers and sisters, I come to you today asking this question." Pastor Fowler paused, his hard, piercing brown gaze sweeping over the gathered crowd again. "When it's your time to lie in the arms of death as our beloved Sister Minnie Faye Crawford now rests, when it's your time to close your eyes and wake no more, when it's your time to lie in front of the pulpit, when it's your time to take that last final ride, will you be ready?

"Will you be able to look back on your life with no regrets as this sister did, to count your blessings instead of your woes, or will you bow your head and weep for all that is lost, for all that should have been done and wasn't?"

Lilly's head snapped up. Wide-eyed, she stared at Pastor Fowler. Had he guessed?

No, he wasn't looking at her. He didn't know that she lived with regrets, that her blessings were few, her tears many.

Lilly didn't know she was sobbing until she felt the brush of wind on her face and opened her eyes. Standing in front of her, in her starched white usher's uniform and black armband, was Sister Lawrence waving her fan. "Mother Crawford wouldn't want you to weep for her."

Tears rolled faster down Lilly's amber cheeks. She shut her eyes again. Guilt pressed against her chest like a heavy weight.

If only they knew.

Stepping back from the pulpit, Pastor Fowler lifted his hands and beckoned. "Undertakers in charge."

"Grandma! Grandma!"

Lilly shut her eyes tighter against the wailing sound of her twenty-one-year-old stepdaughter. No matter how unchristian it was, Lilly couldn't help thinking that Shayla should have come to see her sick grandmother. Houston was only a three-hour drive away from Little Elm, but Shayla always had an excuse.

"Grandma!"

The wail grew more plaintive, more demanding. As in the past, Shayla's father drew his only daughter and favorite child into his arms, murmuring words of comfort and reassurance.

"Hush, baby girl. Daddy's here."

"She's gone! Grandma's gone!" Shayla refused to be comforted.

Lilly turned to see Shayla being physically restrained by her father and her husband. David's eyes were wide behind his gold wire-frame glasses. He was as lost as Myron in his attempts to comfort Shayla, and just as concerned. No surprise there. Shayla wouldn't have married a man who wouldn't meet her many demands and go soft at her frequent emotional outbursts.

"Daddy! Daddy!" Shayla shouted as the spray of gladiolus was removed, the upper half of the coffin lid lifted.

Lilly faced forward thinking this was one time that Myron wouldn't be able to give Shayla what she wanted or what he thought she needed as he had done so many times in the past. The pain and heartache he had caused others hadn't mattered. No price was too high for Shayla to be happy. No one knew this better than Lilly . . . or felt the burden of it more.

The small white frame house on North Fourth Street was filled to capacity. The April day was unseasonably warm, with no clouds in sight. People spilled out of the eight-by-ten living room, cooled ineffectively by a window unit, onto the freshly cut grass in the front yard, careful of the borders of newly sprouting tulips on either side of the paved walkway that stopped in the middle of the yard.

The mourners were content now to mingle happily beneath the undisciplined mulberry tree in the front yard. Laughter came often. Funerals were a social event. People took the opportunity to mourn, but they also renewed acquaintances not seen sometimes since the last funeral and gave thanks that they were still among the living.

Inside the scrupulously clean kitchen there was barely enough room for the women from the church's auxiliaries to fit. Mother Crawford, the eldest member of the church, had been well respected and loved. The food had been accumulating for days. Most of the women over forty were known for their special dishes and took pride in bringing them to the home of the bereaved.

Lilly stood over the huge roasting pan on top of the electric stove and scooped out corn-bread dressing onto a paper plate. Sister Madison had a touch with dressing that made you want to savor each bite. When asked what her secret was, she'd only smile in that serene way of hers. She never told. Some of the women at the church thought that was selfish, but Lilly knew that some secrets could never be shared.

"Sister Crawford, are you all right?"

Startled, Lilly looked up to find Sister Madison staring at her with narrowed eyes in her ebony-hued face. "Y-yes."

"Don't look like it." Sister Madison glanced at the plate in Lilly's hand. "I know my dressing is good, but don't you think whoever you're finding that food for wants more than dressing?"

Lilly jerked her gaze back to the plate in her hand. It was heaped with dressing and tilting dangerously. Flushing, she quickly scraped most of the dressing back into the pan.

"Maybe you should rest. Nobody would blame you." Sister Madison laid a broad, comforting hand on Lilly's thin shoulder. "You've been a good wife and stepmother to him and Shayla. Mother Crawford often said how blessed they all were that Myron found a good woman like you after Carol died."

Lilly flinched and grabbed the long-handled spoon in the green beans. Carol again. They didn't do it out of meanness, Lilly had finally decided, but as a compliment. Carol had been a fine, Christian woman. She'd worked tirelessly in the church. She never complained or had a cross word to say. Everyone said so. Myron most of all.

"Is that plate ready, Lilly?"

Lilly went completely still for the space of two heartbeats. Hands trembling, she quickly reached for the meat fork. "In a minute, Myron."

"Brother Small has a long drive ahead of him," Myron said.

"You go on out and talk with the men, Brother Crawford, I'll bring it to you," Sister Madison offered. "I don't think Sister Crawford is feeling well."

In the small kitchen, it only took Myron a few steps to reach Lilly. Sharp brown eyes studied her face. He took the plate out of her hand. "Go rest for a while. I'm sure the other women won't mind."

Immediately there was a chorus of agreement.

"I-I'm fine," Lilly protested.

He smiled in that old familiar way that used to make her heart turn over. "You've been on your feet enough. Go rest."

The words were spoken gently, but Lilly watched his eyes. They were cold.

Quickly untying her apron, she laid it over the back of the yellow vinyl-covered chair at the table. On her way out of the room she heard several of the women heap praises on Myron about how thoughtful he was and how blessed Lilly was to have him as a husband. They praised him for being a good Christian son, for the nice way he had put his mother away. He didn't bother to correct them.

If only they knew, Lilly thought, opening their bedroom door at the end of the short hallway. Mother Crawford had paid for her own funeral arrangements, and when Myron had learned she had paid cash he had acted so hurt that she hadn't trusted him that she had gone the next day to have his name added to her checking and savings accounts. By the time Mother Crawford died there was nothing left of the money she had done without to save.

Too nervous to rest, Lilly paced the carpeted floor and watched the luminous dial on the clock radio on the nightstand. When fifteen minutes had passed she returned to the kitchen, telling the protesting women she needed to keep busy. With looks of sympathy they let her stay.

Lilly was out of bed at first light the next morning. She never lingered. Before Mother Crawford's death it had been to check on her. Now it was to escape her husband. Easing out of their bedroom, she closed the door softly and went to take her bath. Walking down the narrow hall, she wondered how had she let her life come to this? How could she have been so wrong about a man?

She had had such hopes and dreams when Myron first asked her out. That he was sixteen years older, a widower with two children aged fourteen and sixteen, had made her feel somehow special that he had chosen her.

In the town of twenty thousand, he had a good job as a short-haul truck driver, and a neat little house, and was a respected deacon in the church. In everyone's opinion he was a good catch, and for the first time in Lilly's life women envied her.

She'd grown up being referred to as "that Dawson girl," and the reference had never been good. Marva Dawson, Lilly's mother, hadn't cared what others thought of her and certainly not what they thought of her daughter. To Marva's way of thinking, her life was her own to live as she pleased. It was her turn to have some fun after what she'd suffered. Her unwanted and unplanned pregnancy with Lilly had ruined Marva's life, just as her washout of a husband had.

Johnny Dawson was supposed to be the next great Jim Brown. Instead Johnny had been cut in spring training from the New York Giants. Marva had banked heavily on him being her ticket out of Little Elm.

If she hadn't been pregnant with Lilly, Marva could have stayed in New York and used her face and figure to be an actress or find a rich man. Instead she had to come back with a disgraced jobless husband who took off to parts unknown a year later.

Unemployed, Marva had used the face and figure she was so vain about to get "her due" from other men. She had no intention of standing in line for government cheese or having some social worker look down her snooty nose at her. If one man couldn't give her the things she thought she needed, she found another.

Lilly had grown up with people talking about her mother's lifestyle and speculating on how long it would take for her to turn out the same way. The girls of the good families didn't speak to her, and the boys who asked her out were mainly interested in how fast she'd take off her clothes. Even the girls with a reputation for being fast wanted nothing to do with her. Books became her friends.

At fourteen she lied about her age to get a job at the Dairy Queen in a wasted effort to help her mother so she wouldn't have to take money from men. Marva had looked at the fifty-six dollars Lilly had proudly handed her after two weeks of work and flatly told Lilly her perfume cost more than that. Lilly hadn't offered again.

She'd met Minnie Crawford when Minnie'd gone to JC Penney to buy a hat for Women's Day at Little Elm Baptist Church. Since Penney's was one of the few places to buy ladies' hats in town and elderly black women wouldn't think of setting foot in church without their hats, Lilly had waited on several women in her first three weeks of working in ladies' accessories.

However, Minnie Crawford hadn't looked at Lilly's name tag and stuck up her nose because some man in her family had biblical knowledge of Lilly's mother. Minnie hadn't taken her merchandise to another salesperson to ring up as a few of the women had. She'd looked Lilly in the eyes and asked her if she knew the Lord. Taken aback and sure Minnie was being condescending, Lilly had flippantly replied that He wasn't on her Christmas mailing list.

She'd always remember Minnie Crawford's reply: "Doesn't matter about your mailing list. I meant in your heart. Now, how much is this hat gonna cost me?"

Befuddled, Lilly had rung up the sale, thinking that was the last of it. It wasn't. Minnie Crawford kept stopping by, and before Lilly was sure how it had happened they were having lunch at the deli in the mall, then supper at Minnie's home.

Lilly had gone to church with Mother Crawford, as she liked to be called, out of respect for her and their growing friendship. Lilly went back because of the peace she'd found there — and because of Myron.

The first time she'd seen him, handsome and tall, in his black suit, his Bible clasped to his wide chest, her heart had beaten a mile a minute. She had been so nervous, she'd had trouble getting her words out. For the first time she had been conscious of people whispering about her and hadn't cared.

Myron had taken her home after Sunday dinner at Mother Crawford's and after prayer meeting that following Wednesday night. He and Lilly easily fell into a routine of him picking her up for church services and seeing her home. Always he was respectful and nice.

After a month of Lilly and Myron being seen together, people no longer whispered or speculated if she was as free with her body as her mother. They nodded cordially. Lilly could look people in the eye, hold her head up. Each time she was with Myron, she fell in love a little more and dared to dream that he loved her in return.

Thirty-six-year-old Myron Crawford was everything her naive twenty-year-old heart had wished for. He represented all the things she had never had: love, respectability, a family, and security.

Stepping out of the tub, Lilly grabbed a towel and rubbed it briskly over her body. She'd been starved enough for affection to believe he loved her, believe he wanted to share his life with her, believe he'd give her the children that, having been a neglected child, she'd always wanted.

Hanging up the towel, she stepped into

her plain white cotton underwear and hooked her bra. If Myron had felt any love for her it had disappeared fast. He'd wanted her as a caretaker for his children and a convenient bedmate. Pulling the slip over her head, she shot her arms through the shirtwaist dress. All her praying hadn't helped them to grow closer. Then Mother Crawford had suffered a stroke a year after their marriage and come to live with them.

That had been five years ago. Lilly had been trapped by her devotion and respect for the woman she had come to love dearly, a woman who had become her surrogate mother. Trapped by the two lost children who didn't understand why their mother had to die in a senseless automobile accident on her way to a meeting at the church. Trapped by her dream.

Making her way to the kitchen, she put on the coffee. Arms folded, she stared out the window at the red roses climbing the Cyclone fence in the backyard. She and Rafe had worked an entire morning on the project as a birthday surprise for Mother Crawford. Rafe, intelligent, proud, and determined to butt heads with his overbearing, tyrannical father at every turn. Rafe, the son that Myron now refused to acknowledge. The son Myron had tried to beat and cower into submission.

Rafe had stayed because Lilly begged

him to finish high school, but he had never come back to the dinner she had prepared after his valedictorian speech. His leaving had broken her heart. They were too close in age for her to think of him as her son, but he was the younger brother she never had. She wished she could have done more to shield him from Myron's anger.

She'd thought many times of leaving and taking Rafe with her before Mother Crawford's stroke, but since Lilly wasn't his legal guardian, it would have been considered kidnapping. Mother Crawford might have helped, but she had a weak heart and the doctors had already warned them that too much excitement wasn't good for her.

The first light heart attack Mother Crawford ever had was caused when Rafe and Myron's argument became physical shortly after he and Lilly married. Lilly had never seen that side of Myron, mean and hateful, spewing foul words meant to hurt as much as the belt in his hand. But Rafe had refused to bow down to his father's whipping because he hadn't mowed the lawn the way Myron liked. Mother Crawford's sudden illness had stopped that argument, but others followed.

Lilly did her best to protect Rafe, and when she failed it was as if her soul were being wrenched from her body. Before long

Myron's meanness dulled any love and respect she had for him. She couldn't leave Rafe, no more than she could leave Mother Crawford after Rafe left home.

Lilly understood Rafe's leaving; she just missed his easy smile, his laughter, in a house that had seen too much misery and hate. He'd been back several times in the four years since his graduation to see Mother Crawford but he'd always called first to make sure Myron wasn't there. Lilly understood that as well. After Rafe left Myron had turned his anger against Lilly. Just hearing the sound of his voice sent fear and loathing churning through her. She tried to hide her feelings, but apparently she wasn't always successful.

Mother Crawford wasn't blind to Myron's temper, but she was powerless to do anything about it. Lilly could see in her sad eyes the pain her son's behavior caused, but it was never discussed between them. Yet whenever she heard Mother Crawford praying and asking God to touch his heart, Lilly instinctively knew she meant Myron.

Although Mother Crawford never lost faith in God's power, she made sure Lilly went to the junior college in Little Elm to further her education. Myron hadn't liked it, but in that Mother Crawford had held firm. She'd known she wouldn't be around much longer and wanted Lilly to be able to care for herself. Mother Crawford had loved her son, but she had also loved Lilly.

Just as Lilly had loved her like a mother.

Hearing the coffee dripping, Lilly opened the cabinet for a cup. She didn't know how to contact Rafe to tell him about his grandmother. Somehow she felt he knew. The two had had a way of silent communication that had been as powerful as it was beautiful. Mother Crawford would say more than once, "Rafe's gonna call," and the words would barely be out of her mouth before the telephone would ring.

Their connection was something Lilly envied. She'd never been that close to her mother, a woman who was seldom home unless she was expecting one of her men friends. Lilly had never known the father who had walked out when she was six months old and never returned.

Sipping her coffee, Lilly stared back out the window, watched a bluebird light on the fence, then fly away. Wistfully, her gaze followed. Freedom. What a wonderful thing that must be.

Lilly was at the stove tending the bacon and sausages when Myron came into the kitchen. Immediately she went to pour him a cup of coffee. "Morning."

He rubbed his large hand over his unshaven face, then sipped his coffee, syrupy with sugar and enriched with condensed canned milk. "Morning. Anyone else up?"

"David came in a few minutes earlier. Shayla's hungry," she told him. "They're staying over another couple more days." Slowly she shook her head. "I'm so tired from caring for Mother Crawford. I wish I could just rest." The words were out of her mouth before she realized it.

He was across the kitchen and on her before she knew it, his large frame looming over her. "This was Shayla's house before it was yours. If she's hungry, you better cook her breakfast or anything else she wants."

"Good morning, Mr. Crawford," David greeted Myron from the kitchen door.

Myron swung around with a quickness that belied his six-feet-two height and 200 pounds, his posture relaxing as he did so. "Morning, David," Myron greeted him cordially. "I understand Shayla's hungry."

"Yes, sir," David said, worry in his voice and on his clean-shaven face. "She didn't eat much yesterday. I don't want her getting sick."

"Me, neither. Tell her to stay in bed today and Lilly will bring all her meals today on a tray," Myron told him.

"Thank you, sir."

Myron didn't move until David left. He

turned and stared at Lilly with dark narrowed eyes. "Don't make Shayla wait too long for her breakfast. You know what she likes. Cook it fresh. You know she don't like leftovers." Her orders given, he marched away.

Lilly was at the stove before he was out of sight. Removing the bacon and sausages, she placed them on paper towels to drain.

Rage almost choked her. Rage toward Myron, but also toward herself. She had been stupid and careless.

Rafe might have been his mother's and grandmother's favorite, but Shayla was her father's. Lilly had never understood why he felt that way unless it was because his daughter expertly played on Myron's need to feel important. He never seemed to realize that when Shayla fussed over him the most, she always wanted a new dress, a new pair of shoes, or money. Unlike her self-sufficient and loving brother, Shayla was usually out for Shayla. If it didn't benefit her, she wasn't interested.

Shaking her head, Lilly took down the plates. She had to remember Myron doted on his younger child and be more careful. She had to be as smart as Rafe until she left. And as God was her witness, now that Mother Crawford was gone, Lilly was leaving Myron.

★ ★ ★

"That will be three hundred and fifty dollars."

Lilly's jaw dropped. She stared in disbelief across the neat wooden desk at the lawyer she had hoped would take her case. Tied and tucked in her purse was all the money she possessed in the world . . . $394.33. "I thought it would be less."

His back straight in his leather chair, Kent Powell's expression didn't change. His long-fingered hands remained loosely interlocked on top of a manila folder with Lilly's name printed on it in neat black letters. "That's my fee. If you wish to seek another attorney for counsel, you're free to do so."

Lilly's flagging spirits sank lower. She had chosen Kenneth Powell because he was fresh out of law school and new in town. She'd hoped he would be hungry for business and charge less. She'd seen his sign hanging in front of the once-vacant house and memorized his phone number. Although his fee was twenty-five dollars less than the two other lawyers she'd contacted, it was more than she had allotted.

She moistened dry lips. "Can I pay half now and send you the rest?"

"You can, but I won't start proceeding with your case until I have the full retainer."

Hands clamped around the edge of her

patent-leather purse, Lilly's stomach knotted. She had to leave today. As soon as Myron had left for work that morning, she'd thrown a few clothes in Mother Crawford's old suitcase, packed some food, and paced until ten minutes before Kent Powell's law office opened.

"I don't want to go back." Her voice sounded high-pitched and frightened to her own ears.

"A restraining order doesn't cost anything."

Her head snapped up. "It would be his word against mine. The pain and scars are on the inside."

"Don't you have a friend or relative you could stay with?" he asked, leaning forward in his seat.

Lilly shook her head. Five years ago her mother had finally hit it rich with a man who owned a furniture store in Dallas. Lilly hadn't seen her since she had stopped by her house briefly to show off her diamond ring and the Mercedes he had bought her. Lilly hadn't been invited to the wedding or to their home. As for the people at church, they were Myron's friends before they were hers.

"I don't want to be here when he's served," she finally said.

"Then pay half and send the rest when you find a job."

That would be the sensible thing, but Lilly was already opening her purse and picking loose the knot in the handkerchief. She didn't want to be married to Myron one day longer than she had to be. Counting out the full amount of money, she laid it on the desk. "I want my freedom."

Powell barely glanced at the crumpled bills. "If he contests the divorce, the cost will go higher."

Despite the fear and worry, she said, "I'm getting a job as soon as I reach New Orleans."

For the first time a flicker of doubt ran across the lawyer's young face. "New Orleans can be a difficult place for people unfamiliar with it."

"My stepson is there." At least that was the last place Rafe had said he lived. The telephone operator hadn't found a listing in the phone book. But New Orleans was as good a place as any to stay until her divorce was final. Myron would never think to search for her there. And look he would. Not because he cared, but because he saw her as a possession, just like the house or his dogs.

Standing, she held out her trembling hand. "Thank you."

"You have my card to keep in touch." The handshake was brief.

"I'll call you when I'm settled."

Lilly walked from his office and got inside her car. Fear and uncertainty dogged each step.

Forty-four dollars and thirty-three cents wasn't much to reach New Orleans and start a new life, but it was all she had. Worse, finding a job to earn more would be tough. Myron had never wanted her to work after they were married. Initially he'd used the excuse that he wanted her to stay at home to get Shayla off to school and be there when she came home. In reality, he'd used it as a way of controlling Lilly and keeping her dependent on him.

Lilly had been blinded by his true nature, a nature he hid so well from others that they believed he was just a proud man. What he was, was manipulative and possessive.

But she hadn't seen that. She'd only seen that finally she had a family she could love and who would love her in return.

She had been determined to show her appreciation for Myron's faith in marrying her, to show the people of Little Elm she was a decent woman. She had succeeded in gaining respectability but failed in her marriage. She'd stayed these last miserable years because she hadn't wanted Mother Crawford to spend her last days in a nursing home.

Starting the car, Lilly put it into gear. There was one last stop she had to make.

After parking on the shoulder, she wove her way through the stone markers to the fresh mound of black dirt. A double granite marker was already in place. Minnie Faye Crawford, beloved wife and mother, would rest forever beside her husband, Effraim.

Kneeling down, Lilly placed her hand on the withered gladiolus.

"I'm sorry, Mother Crawford. I tried to make the marriage work, but I couldn't. I know you understood and tried to help me and Rafe. That terrible fight between Myron and Rafe brought on your stroke. I wish I could have spared you that heartache and pain." Tears welled in Lilly's eyes, trickled down her cheeks.

"I'm going now, but I'll never forget you. I promise, just like I promise to always love you and never forget you were the first person to love me."

Standing, she walked to her car and drove away fighting tears, fighting fear.

Chapter Two

The car died without warning.

Over the faded grayish-blue dashboard that had once been an electric, eye-popping blue, Lilly's brown eyes widened in alarm as a thin spiral of gray smoke curled from beneath the battered hood. Clutching the steering wheel, she wrestled the aged Ford onto the short-cropping of weeds beside the two-lane blacktop on the outskirts of Shreveport, Louisiana.

Her heart thumping, she watched in growing fear as the smoke blossomed into a thick black cloud. This couldn't be happening to her. It couldn't.

Damp work-worn hands clamped and unclamped around the steering wheel. Why did her life always have more misery than luck? She tried to do right. She was a good person.

In despair, she slumped back against the seat. She was still a good six-hour drive away from New Orleans. She didn't have money to fix the car. After paying the lawyer she barely had enough money to buy food and gas. Closing her eyes, she dropped her forehead onto the back of her clutched hands and fought against panic and the useless tears forming behind her lids.

No matter what, she had to stay strong. She only had herself to depend on. "You can do this, Lilly. You can do this."

Opening her eyes, she lifted her head and brushed the heel of her hand against the outer corner of her eyes. Bone-dry. Feeling steadier and a bit more in control of herself, if not the situation, she got out of the car. There was no use opening the dented hood to look at the engine; she knew next to nothing about cars.

Shielding her eyes against the hot midday sun, Lilly stared ahead of her and behind. All she saw was the black winding two-lane road bordered by dense green trees, tangled weeds among waist-high bushes, and a creek filled with murky green water that snaked beside the road.

Reaching through the open window, she took out the three-state map that con- nected Texas, Louisiana, and Arkansas and studied it. The blunt tip of her unpainted nail raked over Shreveport, Louisiana, then paused. Obviously she'd taken the wrong exit off the freeway for New Orleans, but she had no idea how close she was to an- other town.

She bit her lower lip. Reading maps was something else she wasn't good at.

"I always told you you were worth next to nothing."

Myron's often-spoken words came out of nowhere, seeping into her brain, shaking her newly emerging confidence. For a long moment, as she had always done, she drew into herself, bowing her head, accepting her husband's accusations.

A gentle breeze tugged the map in her hand, reminding her of her promise to never let him dictate to her again. Her head lifted; determination instead of defeat shone in her narrowed brown eyes. To-morrow or the next day he'd be served with the divorce papers and she'd be one step further to having her freedom from him.

"You're wrong, Myron."

Lilly spoke aloud the words she never could say before. There had to be something in this world she was good at. God gave everyone a special gift; she just hadn't found hers yet.

So, she'd taken a wrong turn off the freeway and ended up on some back road with her car now smoking like a freight train. She was a grown woman, wasn't she? She could figure out what to do.

But nothing came to her as one hour ticked into the next. A truck passed, fol-lowed by a late-model Chevrolet with three wide-eyed children in the back. Neither slowed despite her frantic waving. Doubt tinged with an escalating fear began to creep into her mind. Glancing back down the road from which she had come, she tucked her lower lip between her teeth. Nothing.

And if another car did pass, would they stop? People weren't as quick to help strangers anymore. Woman or not.

Opening the car door, she rolled up the windows, then slung the narrow black strap of her purse over her shoulder and locked the car. She'd do what she had done most of her life: rely on herself.

Without further hesitation, she began walking the way she had come. At least that way she knew she'd eventually reach a service station. If she continued, she wasn't so sure.

Less than two miles down the road she glimpsed the red slate roof of a house peeking through towering oak trees. With excitement rushing through her, her pace increased. When she stood in front of the wide arms of an intricately scrolled black iron entry gate, she realized why she hadn't seen the mansion when she passed. The two-story house sat at least 500 feet from the road at the arch of the curve. Her attention had been on maneuvering the sharp turn, not her surroundings.

Nestled beneath moss-draped oaks, the

immense home was breathtaking. A balcony ran the length of the second floor. To Lilly it looked like something out of a movie of days gone by when the plantation owner took his ease while the slaves worked the fields.

As she walked closer, she saw that the house had a stucco exterior and was painted a pale yellow with white trim. Chastising herself for her wayward imagination, she continued up the tree-lined path. Her mother had always said she kept her head in too many books. But books had been her salvation then and now. Closer, she realized the house hadn't been here in the 1800s and the owners were probably very friendly toward black people.

But what if they weren't? Her steps slowed. She hadn't dealt with many rich people, black or white. In Little Elm the teachers and the funeral home owners were the rich black people and, although they went to work every day, they were in a different social group from Lilly and her truck-driving husband. She couldn't imagine the owner of this place having a nine-to-five job or worries about the mortgage.

Stepping off the paved road onto the thick green grass, Lilly cut across the yard to the back of the house. Some people didn't like the hired help or service people coming to the front door. She wasn't either, but she wasn't an invited guest, either. One thing Lilly knew was how to keep her place. Another lesson courtesy of Myron.

Rounding the corner of the house, she pulled up short. Two well-dressed black women stood at the bottom of the wooden steps leading into a side entrance to the house. They were deep in conversation. The older woman was of average height and appeared to be in her late fifties. She wore a cream-colored blouse and pants. Her stylishly short reddish-brown hair complemented her attractive cinnamon-hued skin. She kept wiping the corners of her eyes with a white handkerchief.

The younger woman's lips were pressed together as if she fought her own battle with tears. Model-thin and a head taller than the other woman, she wore a sleeveless black shell and trousers. Silver hoop earrings twisted with each movement of her head. Smooth bangs brushed the slim arch of her brows. The rest of her bone-straight hair fell to the middle of her back.

Behind them the screen door burst open. Both women turned. Out came a tall, beautiful woman in her early thirties wearing a tangerine-colored linen pantsuit.

The door banged shut. The wind had picked up, carrying with it the scent of magnolias, but Lilly didn't think it had caused the door to slam.

"He's impossible!" cried the woman coming down the white-painted steps.

The older woman clutched the handkerchief tighter. "Nicole, he still insists we leave?"

"Yes, Mrs. Wakefield." The answer was clipped and final.

Mrs. Wakefield's head lowered.

Wide-eyed, the youngest woman stared from one to the other, then back toward the door. "But we can't leave."

"Try telling that to Adam, Kristen," Nicole said, folding her arms, her heavily lashed eyelids blinking rapidly, her magenta glossed lips tightly compressed.

Mrs. Wakefield's mouth curved upward in a strained smile; then she took Kristen's agitated hand in hers. "Don't worry. We'll find a way."

"How?" Kristen cried.

The women traded glances, but none spoke.

"Excuse me. Maybe I can help," Lilly offered before she thought better of interfering.

Three pairs of startled eyes turned to her. Fear quickly gave way to other emotions in their faces. Kristen's was weary, Nicole's suspicious, Mrs. Wakefield's curious.

"Who are you and what are you doing here?" Nicole asked, stepping forward.

Lilly clamped her hands together to keep from retreating. This wasn't Myron using his size to intimidate and abuse for the simple reason that he could. This woman had a right to demand answers. Trespassing was bad enough, but Lilly had compounded her bad manners by eavesdropping as well.

"Lilly. Lilly Crawford. My car broke down about two miles from here. This is the first house I passed, and I wanted to see if anyone could help or if I could use the phone."

"Of course." The older woman visibly relaxed. "I'm Eleanor Wakefield. This is my daughter, Kristen. Ms. Ashe is a family friend." The nods of acknowledgment were brief. "Samuel, the groundskeeper, is off, but you can certainly use the phone."

"Thank you."

"I'll show you where it is," offered Kristen, quickly bounding up the four steps and opening the door.

Lilly clamped her hand around the frayed strap of her purse and pushed the words out. "I–I couldn't help but overhear some of your conversation." She knew what it was like to feel helpless and without anywhere to go or turn. The women looked as if they were well off, but

41

she was a living testament on how looks could be deceiving. "If I can get my car started and you need a lift into town, you're welcome to come with me."

Surprise flittered across Mrs. Wakefield's face; then it was gone, to be replaced by a warm smile that erased the lines of strain bracketing her mouth. "Thank you, Ms. Crawford, but that won't be necessary."

Now it was Lilly's turn to be surprised. It was a rarity for anyone to address her as "Ms.," let alone her betters. Nodding, Lilly went up the steps after Kristen.

The house was as magnificent on the inside as it was on the outside. Yellow was here, too, but the mellow color of butter was mixed with the palest blue and green. Highly polished oak floors gleamed beneath the worn soles of Lilly's sturdy flat black shoes. Persian rugs were scattered throughout. Tall, wide windows were draped in blue silk.

Beautiful antique furniture, crystal lamps, and brass accents gave the home an air of subdued elegance and warmth. Picture-perfect. It would be like living in a little corner of heaven to stay in a place like this. She briefly wondered if the man the women seemed afraid of appreciated the beauty of his home.

"Here's the phone. The yellow pages should be underneath."

"Thank you." Squatting, Lilly opened the door of the cherry drum stand and pulled out the telephone book. Standing, she heard the back door close. Her shoulders stiffened. Myron had taught her early to avoid confrontations at all costs. She quickly began flipping the pages. Nicole had looked at Lilly as if she had crawled on her belly out of the slimy water that pooled in the ditch along the road. Lilly wanted to be gone as much as the other woman apparently wanted her gone.

Lilly's hand paused. What was she doing? She didn't have the money to pay for towing or repair. She'd hoped she'd find someone to help fix the car.

"Is there a problem?" Kristen asked, her pencil-thin brows furrowed.

"No." Turning away from the concern in the young woman's heart-shaped face, Lilly flipped another page. Lying was easier than telling the truth.

"Excuse me, then."

"Yes. Sure." She watched Kristen join her mother and Nicole in an adjoining room with a high ceiling and lined draperies that arched over the windows and pooled on the oak floor. It wasn't lost on Lilly that Nicole had positioned herself by the oak fireplace mantel so that she could see Lilly. She might be poor, but no one had ever questioned her honesty . . . until now.

Realizing she couldn't stand forever in the hall, she picked out a random garage number and dialed. If the towing cost was too high, she'd . . .

Her eyes shut. She had no idea what she'd do. She couldn't sleep in the car, not on a back road leading to who knew where.

She berated herself as she opened her eyes and punched in another number. Why hadn't she planned better? Why did she always make a complete mess of things?

"Did you decide what we are going to do?" Kristen asked as soon as she reached her mother.

"No, dear," Mrs. Wakefield answered, worry clear in her cultured voice.

"We can't just leave him."

"Don't worry. Adam won't be alone," Mrs. Wakefield promised. "If he doesn't want us, I'll find someone else to look after him."

"How will we do that on such short notice?" Kristen sought reassurance as she always had. She was twenty years old and still unsure of herself despite being eight weeks away from graduation from Stanford with a degree in art history.

"Jonathan may be able to help find a companion for Adam," Mrs. Wakefield said, her attractive face thoughtful. It was up to her to keep the family together. "After all,

Adam only needs a minimum amount of help with food preparation and cleaning his room. However, it will have to be someone who is completely trustworthy, someone who won't make him feel worse about his condition, and, of course, someone who is willing to live in."

"Finding someone to live here won't be a problem," Nicole said, glancing around the lavishly decorated room. "Adam has made this place a showcase. The problem will be keeping them."

"I know Adam has been difficult, but he has cause," Kristen defended hotly. "I get angry just thinking about what they did to him."

"I didn't say he didn't have reasons. But while we have an emotional connection to Adam, anyone we hire won't," Nicole replied. "People don't have the loyalty they used to have for their employer." She wrinkled her pert nose. "I know. They quit faster at my temp agency than I can hire new ones to replace them."

"Nicole's right, Kristen. We love Adam no matter what." Mrs. Wakefield laid a comforting hand on her daughter's rigid arm. "We love him now more than ever. We feel his pain as if it were our own. If we can't get a person to stay out of commitment to doing a good job, we'll have to offer them a financial incentive. For a thousand dollars a week, they shouldn't care if Adam is a bit cross with them."

The phone slipped from Lilly's hand, crashing down on the cradle and almost knocking over a small floral arrangement of sweet peas. She grabbed the phone and steadied the heavy cut-crystal vase.

Once again she found herself the focus of the three women's questioning gazes.

"I–I didn't mean to overhear your conversation," she stammered. "But . . . but I'm looking for a job. I'm dependable and hardworking, and since my car clunked, you don't have to worry about me leaving," she said, trying to make a joke out of the last comment, but none of the women smiled.

Since they hadn't said no, Lilly kept talking, "Up until a week ago, when she passed on, I took care of a woman after her stroke for five years. She was partially paralyzed on the left side, so I bathed her, read to her, took her for walks, her appointments, did her physical therapy. Dr. Mason always said I was the best caregiver he'd ever seen. I'm sure I could do a good job." She prayed she didn't sound as desperate as she was.

"We don't know anything about you," Nicole pointed out dismissively.

"She did offer to help us when she thought we needed it," Mrs. Wakefield said thoughtfully. "That showed a caring nature."

Nicole gaped, staring at the older woman in disbelief. "You can't honestly be considering her for the job?"

"We need someone immediately, and since she's here, why not let Adam decide?"

Nicole crossed her arms over her generous breasts. "He'll toss her out the same way he did us."

Mrs. Wakefield threw an irritated glance at Nicole, then crossed to Lilly. "Perhaps we should sit down and I can tell you about my son."

Lilly's eyes widened. "Your son owns this place!"

"Yes," Mrs. Wakefield answered, glancing around the high-ceilinged room as she led Lilly to the Chippendale sofa. "He bought it about five years ago. Although he's been back only occasionally, he always said he loved the beauty and peacefulness he found here."

Gingerly Lilly sat on the blue-green- and white-striped cushion, careful not to disturb the tapestry accent pillow by her elbow. "I can see why he'd never tire of being here. Everywhere you look there's beauty. Both inside and out."

Mrs. Wakefield's body jerked.

Nicole glared.

Kristen tucked her lower lip between her teeth.

"I'm sorry; did I say something wrong?" Lilly asked, apprehension sweeping through her: *Don't mess this up, Lilly. You need this job.*

"It's not your fault. You couldn't have known." Hands folded in her lap, her legs crossed sedately at the ankles, Mrs. Wakefield drew a deep breath as if fortifying herself and said, "Because of the senseless greed of others, Adam lost his sight."

"He's blind?" Lilly blurted.

"Oh, goodness." Nicole threw Lilly a look filled with derision and sank gracefully into a side chair. "I can see she's going to be fabulous."

Lilly flushed under the censure of the other woman. "I–I thought he was just sick." She gave her attention to Mrs. Wakefield. "If you're his mother, he can't be that old."

"He celebrated his thirty-eighth birthday just weeks before it happened."

Twelve years older than she was, yet he had accomplished so much while she had done nothing. Had nothing to show for her years but a broken-down car and a few pieces of clothes. "This must be hard on all of you."

"It is," Mrs. Wakefield admitted and

leaned back in her seat. "Worse because it didn't have to happen. Adam stopped at a red light and two men ran up to his car and demanded he give them the keys. When he refused they pulled him from the car and severely beat and kicked him." Hands trembling, her voice unsteady, Mrs. Wakefield visibly fought to continue.

"If you'd rather not go on, I understand." Lilly understood pain and despair.

"No, it's all right," Mrs. Wakefield said, her voice noticeably stronger. "You have to understand the kind of person Adam was to not think too badly of how this has affected him. One brutal act changed not only his life but also those of hundreds of others."

"My brother was a well-known neurosurgeon specializing in head trauma injuries." Kristen sat down on the curved arm of the sofa by her mother. "He had a thriving practice and was sought after by several hospitals across the country. But no matter how tired or how busy he was, he always had time for me and Mother."

"Adam takes his responsibilities seriously," Mrs. Wakefield said, pride in her voice.

Nicole's expression thoughtful, she said, "Month by month his reputation grew. He was interviewed the day before the accident by the Associated Press. When asked what

49

about his life he'd change, he said, 'Nothing. It is perfect.' "

Another silence stretched across the room until it was broken by Mrs. Wakefield. "The doctors aren't sure if the blindness is temporary or permanent. The X rays and other tests indicate a great deal of hemorrhaging. We're hopeful that, once the hemorrhage dissolves, Adam's sight will return to normal. If the doctors attempt to operate and remove the hemorrhage there is the possibility of causing other complications, including permanent loss of sight. The doctors thought it best to see if the hemorrhage will dissolve on its own."

"How long will that take?" Lilly asked, trying to figure out how long she'd have the job . . . if she got it.

The women traded worried glances again before Mrs. Wakefield answered, "At first they thought two to three weeks."

Lilly was almost afraid to voice the next question: "And now?"

Mrs. Wakefield reached up and clutched her daughter's hand. "They aren't sure. It's been almost five weeks and there's been no change in his sight."

Lilly wanted to ask Mrs. Wakefield if she thought the blindness could be permanent but didn't. From the worry in her face and the faces of the other women in the room, they were already dealing with that possibility.

"Adam is understandably having some difficulties adjusting," Mrs. Wakefield continued. "His medical training makes it more difficult, not easier. He's used to being active. Waiting has never been his strong suit. Now that's all he can do."

"Sometimes that's all any of us can do," Lilly murmured, thinking of her own problems. She'd waited and bided her time to leave Myron.

Mrs. Wakefield stood. "This way." At the foot of the stairs, she stopped and faced Lilly. "Adam's room is the third door on the right-hand side. He may not give you permission to enter, but go in anyway. I'd take you up, but my presence seems to upset him."

"Mother Crawford had bad days, too." Lilly felt compelled to try to ease the other woman's burden.

"Your mother?" Mrs. Wakefield questioned.

Lilly started to explain, then changed her mind. In every way that counted, Mother Crawford had been her mother. "Yes." Turning, she started to climb the stairs.

"Ms. Crawford?"

"Yes." Lilly paused, her hand wrapped around the mahogany newel cap.

"Adam is a wonderful man," Mrs.

51

Wakefield said, Kristen and Nicole on either side of her. "But he's used to having his orders obeyed. Being thwarted is not something he takes easily. He's striking out because he's angry at what's happened to him. Please remember that."

Not sure of how to answer, Lilly nodded and continued up the spiral staircase, her hand sliding over the smooth polished wood railing. With each step she fought the trembling in her body.

Remembered thoughts of Myron towering over her, his rage-filled face inches from hers, caused her stomach muscles to knot. A man could do a lot of damage with a cane. She hadn't seen any bruises on Mrs. Wakefield or the other women. Maybe she meant "striking out" figuratively. Or maybe they were good at ducking.

Wiping her sweating palms on her dress, Lilly stopped in front of the third door. Taking a deep breath, she lifted her hand and knocked.

"Dr. Wakefield. Your mother sent me. May I come in?"

"Dammit. Leave me alone."

Lilly jumped at the venom in the deep voice. "Dr. Wakefield, I want to help."

"Didn't you hear me? Go away."

She'd like nothing better, but that choice had been taken from her when her car died. Following Mrs. Wakefield's instructions, Lilly twisted the brass knob and slowly opened the door and entered.

She barely stifled a gasp. The room was in chaos. Chairs were overturned. Food littered the floor. And standing in the midst by the foot of the king-size four-poster, head bowed and his right hand clutching one of the thick, spiral-turned posts, was Dr. Adam Wakefield.

He was tall and elegantly built. The fingers holding the post were long and tapered. His body was lean, conditioned.

The hair on his head was shaggy and black. He sported an unkempt beard of the same color. His gray silk shirt and linen pants were stained and wrinkled. In no way did he appear to be a prominent doctor, related to the two immaculately dressed women downstairs, or owner of this beautiful house. He looked defeated, lost.

How many times had Lilly stood with her head down, misery pounding at her from all sides?

To have so much and then to have it taken from you because of the senseless cruelty of others would fill anyone with rage and despair. Hadn't she felt the same way after Myron had done a number on her? Empathy swept through her.

Abruptly his head snapped up, then tilted, paused, moved only to repeat the jerk–pause motion over and over as he moved his head in a semicircle around the room. Gold-rimmed shades were perched on his aquiline nose.

"Who's there?"

Lilly took a small step forward. "My name's Lilly Crawford. Your mother said I should come in. She wants to hire me to sit with you if it's agreeable wi—"

"Get out!"

She jumped, tucking her head as she had always done when faced with conflict. Then she remembered again her disabled car and little money. Her head came up; she took another halting step farther into the room.

"Please, Dr. Wakefield. I need this job. I've taken care of ill peo—"

"I'm not ill. I don't need you," he said, cutting her off once again.

"I could keep your room clean and make sure you eat," she said, her words as desperate as her face. "I promise to stay out of your way."

"I don't want you or anyone else here!"

"Please, I have nowhere else to go. I could read to you, take you on walks. I promise —"

"If you won't get out, I'll throw you out!" he threatened and started for her.

Lilly instinctively shrank back, throwing up her arms. A cry of rage caused her to

jerk her arms away from her face. Adam
lay sprawled on the floor. His left foot and
leg were hooked over the claw-and-ball leg
of an overturned armchair.

"Why! Dammit. Why?" he shouted,
pounding his fist repeatedly against the
area rug.

Forgetting her fear, Lilly rushed to un-
tangle his leg. She set the chair upright,
then reached for his arm. "Let me —"

Adam snatched his arm away, came to
his knees, and planted both hands firmly
on the floor. Head down, his lean body
trembled; his breath rushed out over his
lips as if he had been running. His shades
lay on the floor. "I don't need your help."

"I'm sor—"

"Get out," he ordered, finally turning his
face to hers.

She cowered from the rage she saw
there. Then she saw his eyes, black as onyx
but with none of its brilliance or fire. They
were . . . lifeless. The dramatic contrast
caused her throat to dry. The full depth of
what had been taken from him slowly sank
into her. In that instant Adam Wakefield
became a person instead of a job.

"I'm sorry. So sorry," she whispered, her
voice unsteady. "How could anyone be so
cruel?"

His shaggy head snapped back. His right
hand lifted toward sightless eyes, stopped

55

inches away, then curled into a fist. "I don't need your pity. Just leave me alone."

The soul-deep misery in his voice shook her as few things had. And she had put it there just as Myron had done so many times to her. Coming to her feet, she backed away, then turned and ran. From him. From herself.

Fumbling with the doorknob, she finally opened the door and raced down the hall. Rushing toward her were the three women and a distinguished-looking black man with wings of silver in his closely cropped black hair.

"What happened?" Mrs. Wakefield asked frantically.

Lilly moistened her lips. Guilt weighed heavily on her thin shoulders. "He — he tripped over a chair."

Mrs. Wakefield gasped and pressed the trembling fingers of both hands against the lower half of her face.

"Was he hurt? Did he hit his head?" the man asked. The drawl in his deep, authoritarian voice demanded an answer.

"No. I–I'm sorry. Forgive me."

Her back against the wall, Lilly quickly eased past them, then turned to run down the stairs and out the front door.

Chapter Three

On bended knees Adam found his glasses and slipped them on, then felt the cool, tufted cushioned seat of the winged leather chair that had tripped him. It was lying on the floor because he'd tripped over it earlier. She must have righted it. *Bully for her!* he sneered, coming unsteadily to his feet.

Could she possibly imagine how degrading it felt to flounder around, tripping over the slightest obstacle, while people stared at you as if you were on exhibit? No, she couldn't. No sighted person could. All she wanted was a job. Well, he didn't need anyone. He'd be fine until Samuel and Odette returned on Monday.

He had to be.

In the past he had always been able to overcome any obstacle he set his mind to, achieve any goal. He could do it again.

His anger turned inward. Why hadn't he given them the keys to the damn car? He'd just finished an emergency surgery on a young man with massive head trauma. Going in, the college student had had less than a 5 percent chance of survival. He might have been in a coma for the rest of his life. Thankfully, Adam's skill and that of his team had lengthened the odds. Once the marathon seven-hour surgery was over, the man's condition remained critical, but his chance of survival with normal brain function had increased dramatically.

When the unkempt man had come out of nowhere at a stoplight, Adam had first thought he was looking for a handout, a common occurrence in the San Francisco area. Adam had watched the man approach without apprehension. The night had been mild and Adam had the window down on the Porsche, unwinding with a Billie Holiday CD.

When he realized what was happening, he'd been tired enough after being at the hospital for almost twenty hours to tell the man and the one who suddenly appeared by his side to jerk off.

Adam would never forget the chilling sound of the windshield glass shattering. He'd thrown up his hands to protect his eyes. He had succeeded then. But he hadn't been able to protect them from steel-toed boots and fists.

His hands clenched. In one stupid, arrogant moment he had jeopardized everything he had worked most of his life to accomplish. He worried that the hemorrhage wasn't clearing up as fast as any of them had thought it would. But more so he was worried about possible damage to the optic nerve.

If the optic nerve was damaged, his blindness was permanent. He'd remain in a hell he had helped make.

Taking a sliding step, he felt the sole of his shoe smear across something soft and grimaced. Eggs from breakfast or mashed potatoes from lunch? He couldn't even feed himself without making a mess. He was as helpless as an infant. To urinate he had to almost get on his knees. Every waking moment of his life was filled with humiliation. Why couldn't they understand how it degraded him for the people he loved, people who had always seen him at his best, to see him at his worst?

The bedroom door opened. He pivoted. His hand connected sharply with metal. Frantically he grabbed for the object, only to hear it crash to the floor. Immediately he knew what it was: the solid brass trumpet lamp he had been so happy to find at an estate sale. His anger soared. It wasn't important. He'd find another reading lamp once his sight returned.

He straightened. "Enjoying the sideshow?"

"If you weren't blind, I'd knock you to hell and back," answered a heavily accented male voice that was just as biting as Adam's. "What if it had been your mother?"

His anger still high, Adam didn't back down. Jonathan Delacroix might be his godfather and a lifelong friend, but at the moment he was another reminder of what Adam had lost. "Get out, Jonathan."

"I'm staying."

Stalemate. Jonathan weighed in at 200 pounds and stood six-feet-two. He lifted weights to stay in shape. He was as solid as the trunk of an oak, and just as immovable if he wished to be.

In growing frustration, Adam ran his hand over his head and felt an inch of hair at the nape of his neck. He needed a haircut. Damn, he needed so much and was so helpless. His hand fisted. "Can't any of you understand? If I wanted company, I wouldn't have chartered a private plane to bring me here."

"It's a good thing you and your mother have the same travel agent and that she contacted her," Jonathan said, the words followed by a thudding sound.

Adam turned toward the sound. Another chair righted, probably the Chippendale armchair by the reading table. Leather creaked. Jonathan's heavy weight settling into the seat. Adam knew Jonathan had made both sounds on purpose. There wasn't a clumsy bone in his body. He might resemble a linebacker for the Forty-niners, but there the resemblance ended.

His gentleness and concern for his OB-GYN patients was almost legendary.

He was one of the finest doctors Adam knew. In the operating room, there was no hesitation, only precise, swift movements that amazed and awed those seeing Jonathan's large hands do such delicate work for the first time.

The unnecessary noise had been his way of making Adam aware of where he was. Talking to where you thought the person was, was another reason Adam didn't like being around people. Still, he wasn't in a mood to forgive the man he had looked up to and admired for as long as he could remember.

"My ex–travel agent. She won't get any more of my business when I start traveling again." He'd see again and when he did he'd find another agency. It was just a matter of time before the hemorrhage dissolved.

"I'm sure her concern wasn't monetary, Adam," Jonathan told him. "A great many people think highly of you and sympathize with what you're going through."

Adam's lips curved into a snarl. "They pity me."

"A few."

Adam's hand clamped heavily on the back of the leather chair. Those who didn't pity him felt uncomfortable in his presence.

They'd tried. He'd tried. But sooner or later a word would slip out and a thick pervading silence would hang in the room. A word he no longer could associate with. *See*.

He couldn't *see* the game, *see* to read the article in the medical journal, *see* a beautiful woman, *see* the curb.

He'd never noticed before how, in even casual conversation, gestures and expressions conveyed just as much as words. He was as lost in carrying on a normal conversation as he was lost in a world of darkness.

And it was all his own fault.

"I was about to lie down. I'm sure you'll understand if I don't show you the way out."

Jonathan's weight settled heavier in the chair. "Eleanor says you haven't been out of this room since you arrived three days ago. What do you say we go for a walk and get some fresh air?"

"I'm fine," Adam snapped, then said more calmly, "I'm just tired." If they realized the real reason he didn't want to leave his room, he'd never get rid of them.

"That's debatable."

"I appreciate your concern, but it's unnecessary."

Adam moved in front of the chair, guiding himself by the back of his knees against the edge of the seat. His hand securely on the arm of the chair, he sat down, then pressed his back firmly against the cushion. In the past he'd always liked space and the ability to move freely. Now it made him feel helpless and lost. "Please tell Mother not to bother with dinner."

"You aren't fooling anyone, Adam, and I think it's time the kid gloves came off."

Adam stiffened, a sense of foreboding creeping over him. The reasons Jonathan was such a good doctor were his unshakable concern for others, his dogged determination to help those in need, and his keen intelligence. Once committed, he was unshakable. "What are you talking about?"

"Your stubborn refusal to listen to reason," Jonathan told him. "You have to realize that there is no way you can stay here by yourself."

"Odette and Samuel will be back Monday." Adam tried to get his tense body to relax and his voice to sound normal. He knew he accomplished neither.

"Today is Thursday," Jonathan said.

From the closeness of his voice and the faint whiff of the spicy Oriental cologne he always wore, Adam knew Jonathan had stood and moved closer. His nearness was oddly menacing.

"What," Adam's godfather finally continued, "do you plan to do in the meantime?"

"I'll manage." Somehow he had to.

"I'm looking at the way you've managed for the past three days. Not only is this room in shambles; you're in pretty much the same condition. You need a haircut, a shave, clean clothes."

The painful words were like a slap in Adam's face. It took all of his control to remain seated. Giving full vent to his anger and coming to his feet to defend himself might make him feel better . . . until he stumbled over some object and proved Jonathan right.

Adam's fingernails dug into the soft leather armrest. "If I offend you so much, leave."

"If I didn't care about you and your family I would, but I do and you're stuck with me." Jonathan's sigh was long and deep and filled with frustration. "I was there with your father the night you were born. I watched you grow into a man to be proud of. You're the son that I never had. You've been hurt and it's not my intention to hurt you more, but I will if you leave me no choice."

"Stay out of my life, Jonathan."

The older man continued as if Adam hadn't spoken. "If you insist on staying here by yourself I have a lawyer ready to

64

start proceedings to declare you incompetent."

Fear came first, almost choking Adam before reasoning intervened. He eased back in his chair, dismissing the threat with a negligent wave of his long-fingered hand. "You'd need Mother's permission and she'd never give it."

"Don't bet on it, Adam. She'd fight until her last breath to keep you from the slightest harm, whether that harm was caused by you or another source."

Jonathan's deep bass voice grew quieter, yet infinitely more terrifying. "Insisting you stay by yourself in this huge house is insane. How the hell do you plan to find your way downstairs to the kitchen when you can't find your way around this room? What would you do if you were to fall and seriously injure yourself? I tell you what you'd do: not a damn thing, because you couldn't see how, and that's exactly what I plan to tell your mother."

Rage mixed with fear propelled Adam to his feet. "You bastard!"

"Never said I wasn't," Jonathan said calmly. "Your mother is outside this room worried to death. I don't care what you think of me, but she's suffered enough. She's not eating and Kristen tells me she's not sleeping."

"Once she returns to San Francisco,

she'll be fine," Adam said, aware of his mother's concern yet unable to reassure her. How could he when fear was his constant companion just as guilt was?

"You don't believe that lie any more than I do. Your mother hasn't ever been nor will she ever be that shallow. She loves with all her heart. And now her heart is breaking because of you."

A heavy weight on his chest, Adam slumped back in his chair. He and his mother had always been close. His father had been a busy gastroenterologist and raising Adam and Kristen had fallen to their mother. She'd never faltered or complained. Losing her husband, their father, five years ago was hard enough on her. Now this.

"I don't want her here."

"I can understand your reasoning, Adam." Jonathan's voice gentled. "Eleanor probably understands it, too. All she wants is to be sure you're taken care of. How that's accomplished is up to you."

Adam's head came up, hope surging through him. "Then why put her through a painful court battle?"

"You're slicing her apart. What's one more cut?"

Adam flinched. His mother loved deeply and completely. She was fond of telling one and all that her children were her greatest accomplishments. And she'd walk through fire for him and Kristen.

Head bowed, Adam braced both arms on his thighs; his wrists and arms dangled over his knees. "How long will it take to hire someone?"

"I don't know."

Adam was already shaking his head. He wanted the women gone today. Especially Nicole. Each time he heard her voice, the shame and humiliation of that night he came home from the hospital and they went to bed together came rushing back. "There was a woman just here."

"She left running."

"Find her; then all of you can leave."

"Aren't you forgetting one thing?"

Adam's mouth flattened into a hard, narrow line. "Please."

Jonathan laughed, a robust, hearty sound that easily rolled from his deep chest. "That was nice, but unnecessary. I'm used to your high-handed way of ordering other people around. Comes from being the top in your field."

Adam flinched again. Once he had been the best. *Once.* No more.

"I meant, aren't you forgetting the young woman may not want to come back?" Jonathan explained.

"Then you'll have to convince her otherwise, won't you?"

Adam couldn't see the smile on Jonathan's ebony-hued face but heard it in his voice. "I guess so."

Their questions tripping over one another, the women swarmed around him as soon as he closed the door to Adam's room.

"Is he all right?" Eleanor asked, pushing ahead of her daughter and Nicole.

"Did he hurt himself?" Kristen asked, her eyes teary.

"Can I go in?" Nicole wanted to know.

Jonathan's gaze stayed on Eleanor. Hope, fear, desperation shimmered in her deep amber-colored eyes. He'd give anything, do anything, to keep the hope alive.

"We'll talk downstairs."

"Jon—"

"Downstairs." Jonathan glanced meaningfully behind him to the closed door.

Without another word, Eleanor turned and headed downstairs, her heels clicking rhythmically against the hardwood floor. She had never been a patient woman, less when it came to those she loved.

In two long strides Jonathan caught up with her, his large hand closing around her upper arm. She never slowed or indicated in any way that she was aware of his touch. His fingers flexed out of his own perverse need for her to acknowledge him. The need no longer annoyed or disgusted him; it simply was.

The glance she threw him was impatient at best, but for the moment it was enough. His fingers relaxed, but not before he noted the fragility of the bones beneath the silk blouse she wore. His brows bunched as they started down the carpeted staircase.

Eleanor's once-svelte body had gently rounded as the years and the births of two children altered her shape. To him the change added depth and dimensions to her maturity, not detracting from it. He could still easily sweep her off her feet if the occasion arose, still admire the easy sway of her hips. What bothered him was her not taking care of herself. Mentioning it now would only be a waste of time. Her every thought was on Adam, her firstborn.

"Well?" she asked, rounding on Jonathan the instant she reached the bottom of the stairs.

"The living room." Steering her in that direction, he led her to the sofa. "Sit down, Eleanor. Please."

With ill-concealed grace she sat, then crossed her ankles and clasped her hands, preparing herself for the worst. For a brief moment he stared at the thumb of her right hand absently rubbing the diamond-encrusted wedding band on her left hand.

For a futile moment he wished she had reached for him.

Feeling every one of his fifty-nine years, Jonathan moved to the oak fireplace across the room. He stared at the woman he had always loved and could never have. "Adam will let the woman stay."

As Eleanor briefly shut her eyes, her shoulders slumped; her head fell forward. "Thank God."

Across from Eleanor, Nicole, her beautiful face a picture of disbelief, surged to her feet. She was tall, elegant, and, at the moment, enraged. "He can't do that!"

Jonathan dispassionately studied the beautifully polished woman in her early thirties. Not an auburn hair was out of place. She had flawless almond-hued skin and soulful hazel eyes. Once again he wondered why Adam never mentioned her name anymore. "It's his decision and he wants me to bring her back here."

"You can't seriously be considering letting that woman stay," Nicole retorted. "We know absolutely nothing about her. You can't forget she caused him to fall."

"Adam did that to himself," Jonathan said. He shifted his gaze to Eleanor. He'd expected Nicole's disapproval and outrage. Eleanor's opinion was the only one that mattered. "Even with my contacts in the medical profession, hiring another person on such short notice would be difficult."

"*We* could stay." Nicole glanced at Kristen for agreement.

Kristen, standing by the window, wrapped her arms around her waist. "It's Adam's decision."

Nicole's hazel eyes glinted; the lush, sensual mouth flattened in annoyance. "Adam hasn't been making the best decisions in the past weeks."

Kristen's slim body tensed. She stared at her mother as Jonathan knew she would. Adam was the strong, independent son; Kristen, the tender-hearted daughter who remained unsure of herself. Asthma as a child coupled with an overprotective family hadn't given her the opportunity to find her way as healthy, robust Adam had. Losing her father when she was fifteen had left her floundering even more. Just as she was beginning to come into her own, the brother she worshipped had to learn a hard lesson about invincibility. Regrettably, she had to learn with him.

"Uncle Jon?" Kristen asked, finally bringing her troubled gaze to him.

Despite his own doubts, Jonathan smiled. She'd been three years old when she announced to him and her family that she wanted him to belong to her, too, just like he did to Adam. From that day on he was "Uncle Jon." He loved her fiercely.

71

"I'd say it's about time for Adam to get one right."

The small smile that flitted around Kristen's mouth was worth hearing the inelegant snort from Nicole. Sitting down in the overstuffed wing chair, she crossed her long legs and swung her right foot impatiently.

From what Adam had told Jonathan, Nicole wasn't the type of woman who liked losing at anything. She was a self-made woman. With a college scholarship to Old Miss she'd been able to shake poverty and the red clay of Mississippi from her bare feet, and now she wore three-hundred-dollar shoes and thousand-dollar designer suits. Nannette became Nicole. She owned a successful temporary employment service in Marin County specializing in office skills.

She and Adam had been together six months before he was injured. With their busy schedules, he'd said they suited each other perfectly. The arrangement had sounded businesslike rather than loving to Jonathan, who, given a choice, would want the woman he loved with him even if it wasn't convenient.

But Adam had never been the romantic, sentimental type. Neither, apparently, was Nicole. Their loose relationship had suited them . . . until he lost his sight.

"You can go if you want," Nicole announced, her small nose tilted upward. "But I'm not leaving."

"Yes, and each time you go into Adam's room you send him deeper into depression," Jonathan bluntly told her.

Eleanor made a low, tortured sound of distress, but even so, it caught Jonathan's attention. Long strides quickly took him to her. Sitting beside her on the sofa, he gently took her soft, cold left hand into his large ones, inadvertently covering the wedding band. "Adam is a proud man."

"His father and I raised him that way." Eleanor managed a weak smile, her other hand coming to rest on top of their joined ones. "You helped."

Jonathan nodded. "That I did. He learned to go after and fight for what he wanted in life, but this time he's up against something he can't fight."

"He has to realize we don't think less of him," Kristen said.

"Kristen, he thinks less of himself," Jonathan told the young woman softly. He wished he could make this easier for all of them. "There's never been anything Adam set his mind to do that he couldn't do, and he looked good while he was doing it. He doesn't now, and he's aware of it more than you or I could ever be."

Folding her arms tightly, Kristen stared

down at her leopard-print sandals. "It's my fault he left Sausalito. If I hadn't told him I was going to change my plans and spend my spring break with him, he wouldn't have come here."

"Kristen, please don't blame yourself," her mother said. "We all did what we thought best for him, and it's not working."

"I don't want him hurt anymore." Kristen rubbed the heel of her palm across her eyes. "If having that woman is what he wants, then that's what has to be done. Please go bring her back."

"Yes, bring her back," Mrs. Wakefield agreed, finally pulling her hands free from Jonathan's.

Nicole was standing on her Italian slingback heels in seconds. "You can't do that! What's to keep her from leaving Adam or looting the place?" Her slim arm gestured around the antique-filled room. "Some pieces in this room are priceless."

"I value Adam more."

Nicole gasped, a tiny, horrified sound.

"I'm sorry if that came out badly, Nicole. I realize this has been difficult for you as well. You care for him, too, but I feel hiring Ms. Crawford, at least tempo-rarily, may be best at the moment," Mrs. Wakefield reasoned. "As she pointed out, her car doesn't run, so she could hardly leave."

"With the salary you plan to pay her, repairing her car or buying a new one shouldn't be a problem." Unrelenting, arms folded, Nicole remained stiff with indignation and disapproval.

Eleanor nodded. "I agree, and that's why I plan to stay in the cottage. I won't take any chances with Adam."

"I want to stay, too." Kristen crossed to the sofa.

"No, Kristen. Spring break is over tomorrow. You'll return to Stanford, finish your honors thesis, and complete your degree," Mrs. Wakefield said firmly. "Adam and I will be there as planned to see you get your diploma in June."

Kristen bit her lower lip. "I wish you could promise that."

"I promise to try."

For Kristen, whose mother had never broken a promise, that was good enough. "By the time we get through the baccalaureate, then the departmental ceremony afterward, you'll be bored to tears."

"Not a chance. We'll cheer just as loud as when you graduated from high school." Mrs. Wakefield turned to Jonathan. "By the way, how did you get Adam to change his mind?"

"Reasoning," he said evasively. Adam might be upset enough to believe his mother would start incompetency proceedings, but Jonathan knew she wouldn't. Too much had been taken from her son already for her to possibly agree to such a drastic and cruel maneuver. "Now, before she's picked up by a motorist I better go find her and convince her to return."

"You'll do it, Uncle Jon," Kristen said.

"Thanks for the vote of confidence." The light in her black eyes when she looked at him never failed to warm him. He was as proud of her as he was of Adam.

Standing, Jonathan quickly strode from the room. The women followed and watched him get inside his silver luxury sedan and drive away.

"I have a feeling you're going to regret this," Nicole said from beside Eleanor on the wide porch.

Despite the soaring temperature, Eleanor felt chilled and wrapped her arms around her body. "What's one more regret for this family?"

She had made a total mess of things. What if Dr. Wakefield had seriously injured himself? She'd be responsible, wouldn't she? But he looked all right, just angry. In any case, he had his family there to take care of him, which was more than she had.

Wiping the beads of perspiration from

her forehead with the flat of her palm, Lilly stopped for a moment to catch her breath. The breeze had died and the heat was oppressive. The thick, sultry air tinged with the smell of stagnant water made drawing in each breath unpleasant.

Hearing a car behind her, Lilly turned and waved frantically for it to stop. To her surprised delight, the big silver luxury car pulled onto the grassy shoulder behind her. She was halfway to the car when the driver's door opened and a man stepped out, tall, broad-shouldered, with streaks of gray at his temple. She immediately recognized him and halted. Fear clawed at her throat. What if he had come after her because Dr. Wakefield had injured himself?

"Ms. Crawford, we didn't get a chance to be introduced earlier." The man extended his large hand. "I'm Dr. Jonathan Delacroix, a close friend of the Wakefields and Adam's godfather."

Ingrained manners made her take the hand although hers was shaking. "He's all right, isn't he?"

"He suffered no ill effects from the fall, if that's what you're asking."

Pulling her hand back, she wrapped her arm once again around the bag, clutching it to her chest. "But he's still angry at me?"

"You. Me. Everyone, I'm afraid," Jonathan answered, his voice sounding tired.

She nodded, feeling only partially re-
lieved. "I didn't mean to make things
worse."

"You didn't. In fact, that's why I followed you. To ask you to come back and
care for Dr. Wakefield," Jonathan explained.

No matter how much she needed the
money or how much she wished she could
help, it wouldn't work. He was too angry
and she was too afraid of that anger. "He'll
be better off with someone else."

"He specifically asked for you."

"He did?" Lilly asked, her big brown
eyes widening in disbelief.

Jonathan smiled. He'd been soothing fe-
males for thirty-four years professionally
and longer nonprofessionally. He'd like to
think he was quite good at it. White teeth
gleamed. "I'm to bring you back to the estate immediately."

"I don't understand." The furrows in
Lilly's forehead deepened.

"I'd be happy to explain everything to
you if you'll accompany me back to the
house." Jonathan motioned toward his car.

She glanced at his car, then down the
road toward hers several yards away. She'd
walked enough for one day. She didn't
relish walking back to the car in the
growing heat if this didn't work out. "Why
don't you explain it here?"

A black convertible sports car zoomed recklessly by, causing them to step farther into the weeds away from the road. "My car might be safer and more comfortable."

Lilly studied Dr. Delacroix and said nothing. She didn't know this man with his expensive suit and good looks. But she had lived six long years with a man of similar build, a man who didn't hesitate when they were alone to intimidate and terrorize. The hand that she had shaken was soft and manicured, not rough and callused, but there was strength in it just the same. This man could inflict pain if he chose. Myron had hidden his meanness until it was too late.

"We can talk here."

If Dr. Delacroix thought her refusal strange he didn't comment. "Adam asked for me to get you to return, but he did it under duress. Unknown to his mother, I threatened him with declaring him incompetent if he refused to have help. I'm telling you this because he may take his anger at me out on you."

Lilly swallowed. "H-He's violent?"

"Never. But words can be just as harmful."

She shivered and glanced away. "I know."

Jonathan's shrewd eyes narrowed. "Do you live around here?"

She moistened her lips. "I was just passing through."

"Is there anyplace I could get a reference?" he asked.

Alarm swept through her. Her throat dried even more. "M-Mrs. Wakefield didn't say anything about needing a reference."

"I'm aware of that, but surely you realize she'll have to know something about you," Jonathan said reasonably.

Lilly shifted uneasily. She hadn't realized that at all.

"Is there going to be a problem with the reference?" he pressed, his brow furrowed.

Her gaze slid up to him, then away. "There might be."

Jonathan's voice took on a hard edge: "If you have a police record you won't be able to take care of Adam."

"It isn't that," she blurted, then realized she didn't know what else to say. Instead her gaze centered on the pristine white-shirted chest. Despite the intense heat, he appeared cool and unbothered in his tailored gray double-breasted suit. Perspiration ran in rivulets down her back. Her cotton dress was probably soaked. Nerves or heat, she didn't know. She only knew that she didn't want to admit to the biggest failure in her life.

"Well?" Dr. Delacroix prompted.

80

She swallowed and tried to think of a plausible explanation. "I recently lost my mother, and since we had no other close family I was traveling to New Orleans to start fresh. I took care of her, so I have no work history," she explained, silently telling herself the lie was necessary for survival.

Jonathan's expression cleared. "Determination in the face of adversity. That's Adam's mantra. He always had a privileged life, but never took it for granted. He worked hard, studied long hours. He was skyrocketing in his career when he was attacked. He thought he ruled his destiny, and then found out how tragically wrong he was."

"What happened to him was terrible, but I don't think he wants anyone's help, especially mine," she said softly.

"He may not want help, but he desperately needs it. At the moment he's feeling alone and desperate. In control of nothing." Jonathan studied Lilly's thin face closely. "I have a feeling you may understand a little of how he feels."

Tensing, she looked at Dr. Delacroix sharply. She didn't want him or anyone else probing into her life. "What if he changes his mind again?"

"As long as he thinks he's in danger of being ruled incompetent, he won't," the doctor told her, slipping his hands into the pockets of his tailored trousers.

"Isn't that rather cruel?" she questioned, unable to keep the distaste from her voice and face.

"Necessary," he corrected. "You saw the condition he and his room were in. He refuses to let anyone clean it or ask for help with any task. That's where you come in. Making sure he takes care of himself."

Indecision had her chewing on her lower lip and unconsciously shaking her head. "What you're asking is not going to be easy."

"We realize that," Jonathan told her. "You'll be in complete charge as far as Adam is concerned. Unknown to him, his mother will stay at her cottage in back of the main house. The couple who take care of the house will return from vacation Monday. However, Adam will remain your responsibility."

She dragged her hand through her hair, encountered the rubber band, and clamped her restless hand around her purse. "How am I to get him to let me clean him and the room?"

Jonathan sighed, withdrawing his hands from his pockets. "I have no idea."

Her mouth gaped.

"All I know is that neither Adam nor his mother or sister can go on this way," Jonathan said tightly. "Those of us who love him just have to be there for him until he can remember the man he was, and pray that his blindness isn't permanent. It won't be easy for any of us, especially Adam."

"He scares me," she said honestly. "I'm afraid I'll do or say the wrong thing and upset him again."

"We all are. We're all groping our way through this. We need your help, Ms. Crawford. Please stay," he asked quietly.

There was something else she needed to know. "You plan to do a reference check on me?"

"I have no choice."

"But I just told you I never worked outside the house."

"Then we'll check character references."

"You can't do that. If . . ." She trailed off, unable to finish the sentence.

" 'If ' what? Are you hiding from someone?" Suspicion entered his eyes and voice.

"No," she quickly said, trying with all her might not to look away from Dr. Delacroix's probing stare. "I'm just a private person. I don't like people probing into my life."

"If you want the job, I'll have to." His words left no room for discussion.

Lilly hugged her handbag tighter to her chest. His proposition would solve her immediate problems, but his investigation could also lead Myron to her.

Her stomach churning, she glanced at her car down the road. Every possession she owned, which wasn't much by anyone's standards, was inside. Although no smoke plumes spiraled from the hood, Lord only knew how much the repairs would cost. Repairs she didn't have the money to pay for. She didn't even know where she'd sleep that night.

She turned to Dr. Delacroix and despite the erratic beating of her heart heard herself say, "I give you my word that I'll work hard and do my best to care for Dr. Wakefield."

He shook his head. "That's not good enough."

"Then good-bye." Turning away, she started toward her car.

Chapter Four

"Didn't you find her?"

"I found her," Jonathan answered. He'd dreaded this moment since Lilly had turned her back on him.

"Then where is she?" Eleanor asked, peering around his broad shoulders as if Lilly Crawford might appear.

"I need a drink first." Stepping past an anxious Eleanor onto the marble tile in the foyer, Jonathan headed for the kitchen.

The room was large and airy, with sleek stainless-steel appliances, copper cookware, granite countertops, and white glass-fronted cabinets. Adam couldn't cook worth a damn, but he loved good food and, with the limited number of times he had to enjoy a meal without interruption, wanted the best.

Opening the cabinet, Jonathan couldn't help but remember Adam inspecting every nook and cranny of what he called his investment/retirement house. They'd been like two school kids, nudging each other every chance they got because the realtor couldn't hide the shock from her face that a black man who wasn't an athlete or musician or selling drugs had enough money to pay cash for the $3 million estate if he wanted to.

"Jonathan," Eleanor said in a voice that would not be denied any longer.

"The last time I saw Ms. Crawford she was sitting in her car." Jonathan jerked the slender glass from the shelf. Since he was on call tonight lemonade would have to do instead of the Jack Daniel's he wanted. As far back as he could remember, Eleanor always kept a pitcher of lemonade in the refrigerator in warm weather.

"Why didn't she come back?" Eleanor asked, stepping in front of the refrigerator door Jonathan opened.

Jonathan hated defeat of any kind. He hated worse to see the disappointment in Eleanor's face. He still found it difficult to believe that Lilly Crawford had turned him down. Not many had. "She didn't want me to run a character reference on her."

"I knew it," Nicole said triumphantly, leaning against the island countertop, her hair as shiny and bright as the copper pots overhead.

Eleanor's gaze remained on Jonathan. "Did she say why?"

"Just that she was a private person and didn't like people probing into her life." Jonathan stared pointedly at Eleanor. "Do you mind?"

Eleanor picked up the glass pitcher of

lemonade from the refrigerator. "What kind of car was she driving?"

From another woman the question and the withholding of his drink might have seemed incongruent or rude, but he knew better. He'd burned enough midnight oil in med school with Eleanor to know she had a sharp, analytical mind. She had been at the top of her class when she traded a promising career in medicine for marriage. He didn't think she'd regretted her decision for an instant in the years since. Eleanor had always known what she wanted. Now, she wanted what was best for her son and the answers as to why he wasn't getting what he wanted.

Jonathan sighed as he pictured the vehicle and a rumpled Lilly Crawford sitting inside as he had made a point of letting her see him turning around in front of her car. He'd hoped she'd try to stop him. She'd stared straight ahead, sipping clear liquid from a glass jar. "Twelve-year-old Ford, dented, rust spots."

"Then, it would appear that she could use the thousand dollars a week I offered."

"What!" he shouted. "Are you crazy?"

Eleanor sent him a look that had him blushing like an errant child. "Sorry."

The slight upward curve of her lips forgave him. "A thousand dollars, yet she chose to stay in a broken-down car on the side of the road," Eleanor said, her face thoughtful.

"I wouldn't want to do that," Kristen said, her hands jammed in the pockets of her black gabardine pants.

Eleanor glanced at her daughter. "Nor would most people . . . unless the alternative was worse."

"Now, wait a minute, Eleanor. You can't possibly think of hiring her without checking on her." Forgetting how thirsty he was, Jonathan lowered his glass.

"Adam wants her, Jonathan," Eleanor said.

The answer was so simple yet so complex. A mother's love always was. No matter how many times he witnessed it in his practice, it never ceased to amaze him. Perhaps because his mother had been more concerned with the success of her restaurant than her son.

To Eleanor, her family always came first. She was hurting. She couldn't give her child what he needed, so she'd give him what he wanted.

Eleanor loved unconditionally. Jonathan wanted to take her in his arms and remove the burden from her heart and shoulders. The only reason he didn't was that this time he didn't know if it would be more than friendship.

"He'd take anyone to get us to leave,"

Nicole said in the ensuing silence, coming to stand by them. "You can't hire her. She might be a criminal."

"Do you think she's a criminal or dangerous, Jonathan?" Eleanor asked, taking the glass from his hand and at last pouring the lemonade. Her hand was as steady as the eyes she lifted to his when she finished.

Instead of looking at Eleanor, he studied the cold beads of perspiration forming on the glass. His thoughts returned to Lilly Crawford. She had to be just as hot as he, hotter because she had walked to her car and she didn't have the luxury of air-conditioning. Yet she had turned him down. Stubborn, yes. Frightened, possibly, but dangerous or a criminal . . . . "No, I don't think she is," he finally answered.

"Neither do I." Eleanor returned the pitcher to the refrigerator. "Now, do I go get her or will you?"

"I'll go." Jonathan drained the glass in one gulp and handed it to Eleanor. "You're as stubborn as Adam."

"Where do you think he got it from?" Eleanor said, but her voice trembled.

"He'll come through this," Jonathan said, then left.

Nicole glanced from Jonathan's retreating back, to Eleanor. "Mrs. Wake—"

"Please, Nicole," Mrs. Wakefield said,

holding up her manicured hand. "I know you mean well, but my mind is made up on this matter."

"You want to trust her because she offered you a ride?" Nicole shook her head in a mixture of disbelief and disgust.

"Initially, yes, but I saw the regret in her face when she came out of Adam's room." Eleanor's arm swept the immaculate kitchen that would make any cook or thief rub her greedy hands together in anticipatory pleasure before finally stopping at the mint-condition hundred-year-old oak pedestal table and four ladder-back chairs in the breakfast nook. "You said it yourself. What person looking for a job, but especially a thief, would pass up a chance to stay here?"

Nicole's lush mouth tightened. "I don't like it."

"I understand that and appreciate your concern. Both Jonathan and I agree that she's not dangerous. If she's a thief, as you suspect, she can't run off without transportation. In the week it takes to earn her first paycheck I would have had time to be around her more, and if I get any indication that I'm wrong and that she poses the slightest threat to Adam, I'll take immediate measures to get rid of her," Eleanor finished, a hint of steel in her voice.

The frown on Nicole's face shifted into

the smile that invariably turned heads wherever she went. "Adam always said you were a lioness where your children were concerned."

"My children are all I have."

"I'd say you were both fortunate," Nicole told her, her voice wistful.

"Adam is lucky to have you," Eleanor said, meaning it. Love and family were worth any sacrifice. "Now, come on and let's get Ms. Crawford's room ready."

The three women were waiting on the front porch when Jonathan pulled up in the Mercedes. Mrs. Wakefield came down the four wooden steps, followed by Kristen and Nicole.

"Thank you, Ms. Crawford, for coming back to care for Adam. Your room is ready."

Nerves still jumpy, Lilly nodded. She couldn't believe it when Dr. Delacroix came back and offered her the job. She'd been suspicious at first, but as he had told her, with just her name he didn't have any means of checking on her. They'd waited for the tow truck in silence. Only when her car was hauled away did panic strike.

Dr. Delacroix must have seen it, because he'd said, "If you are telling the truth, you have nothing to be afraid of. If not . . ."

He hadn't finished; he hadn't needed to. Silently she had gotten into his car. Now, she was walking up the curved staircase again. She could only hope this time the outcome would be different.

"I put you in the room next to Adam." Opening the door, Mrs. Wakefield stepped aside and motioned Lilly to enter.

Beautiful. That was the only word she could think of to describe the bright room. The floral print pillows on the large bed matched the ties in the curtains. The room was almost as spacious as her entire house. "This is my room?" she asked in stunned amazement.

"Yes." Mrs. Wakefield walked around Lilly and opened another door on the far side of the room. "This is the dressing room and bath. You should be very comfortable here. The house staff, Samuel and Odette, take care of the general housekeeping and will be back early Monday morning." She returned to Lilly. "Later I'll show you the cottage where I'm staying, but under no circumstances is Adam to know I'm there."

"Yes, ma'am," she answered, glancing around the room again. She'd never seen so much luxury in one place. "Dr. Delacroix explained everything to me."

"Then we'll go say our good-byes to Adam and leave," Mrs. Wakefield said, then stopped at the door. "I think you should come also."

"Don't you want to be alone?" Lilly asked, trying not to show her nervousness.

"It will be less stressful on all of us if we get everything settled at once."

Without waiting, she left. Kristen immediately followed, as did Jonathan. Nicole stayed, her hazel eyes narrowed on Lilly as if she were back to studying slime that had crawled out of a swamp on its belly.

"If you do anything to harm Adam or his mother, I'll see that you pay for it the rest of your life," Nicole warned coldly.

"I'm not a criminal. I just want a job," Lilly said, barely resisting the temptation to back away from the animosity in the other woman's face.

Kristen reappeared in the doorway. "We're waiting."

With one last meaningful glare, Nicole walked out the door. Wondering why the other woman disliked her so intensely, Lilly slowly followed.

Mrs. Wakefield waited until they were all gathered, then knocked softly on the door. "Adam, Ms. Crawford is here as you requested. We've come to say good-bye, Adam."

Kristen sniffed. "I don't want to leave him."

Eleanor sent her daughter a small smile

of support. "I know, but it has to be done."

There was a thump, quickly followed by a curse. Nicole reached for the brass door-knob. Eleanor stuck her arm out in front of the other woman. "He wouldn't want us to see him."

Long seconds passed before the door cracked open. Adam, aviator shades firmly in place, stood in the narrow space no wider than the span of his hand. "Have a safe trip home."

"We will." Eleanor's voice trembled. "I don't suppose you'll change your mind and allow me to stay."

"This is best."

"All right, then give me my good-bye kiss."

Adam tensed, but he didn't move away as Eleanor slowly pushed the door wider, then palmed one of her son's unshaven cheeks and kissed the other. "I love you. Always remember that."

Stepping back, she shoved her knuckled fist into her mouth. Jonathan's arms curved around her. She leaned into his wide chest.

"I'd rather be here with you than studying for finals." Kristen took Eleanor's place and rested her trembling hand on her brother's chest. His hand lifted to briefly clasp hers, then returned to his side.

"You'll ace them as usual. I hate you

didn't get a chance to work on your honors thesis. I know how important it is for you."

She swallowed before speaking. "There's still time. I love you."

"Take care, Sis." He stepped back and started to close the door.

"Adam, wait!" Nicole cried, rushing to him. He turned his head around just as she lifted hers to his face. Instead of their lips meeting, the top of his head butted into her chin.

"Ooohhh," Nicole cried, slapping both hands over her mouth.

Adam froze. "What happened?" Silence reigned. "Dammit, what did I do?"

"It's nothing, Adam," Nicole said, her husky voice sounding strange and muffled with Jonathan's handkerchief pressed to her bleeding lower lip.

"Don't treat me like an idiot. I know I did something."

Everyone looked at one another, then away. No one spoke.

Stepping back, Adam slammed the door.

Nicole jumped. Tears glistening in her eyes, she stared at the closed door a long heartbreaking moment, then spun on her heels and ran back down the hall.

It was a good thing Nicole left when she did, Lilly thought, knowing the retreating woman couldn't hear the crash against the wall.

Eleanor Wakefield couldn't sleep. How could she when her children were in so much pain?

With her arms wrapped tightly around her waist, she stared at the light in the third window at the back of the house. Adam's room. He had insisted from the first that the light be kept on. He wanted to be able to see if his sight returned. Eleanor knew the last thing he did before going to sleep and the first thing he did on awakening was hold his hand in front of his eyes. The ritual was a daily torment he put himself through.

If she could, she'd gladly trade places with him. The choice hadn't been hers to make. Head falling forward on her delicate neck, Eleanor pondered the problem that was never far from her mind: was waiting for the hemorrhage to dissolve the right course of action? If they waited too long, the hemorrhage in the back of the eyes could cause permanent retinal detachment and blindness. If they operated now, they might damage the optic nerve and, again, cause permanent blindness. Until a short time ago hemorrhages were removed within two to three weeks, but recent studies had shown that waiting was the wisest and safest course of action.

What to do? Alex and his doctors had

chosen to wait, but at what price to her son?

Forcing herself to leave the window, she took a seat on the camelback sofa in the room she had lovingly decorated at Adam's insistence. He'd said the four-room cottage in back of the main house was to be her retreat, a place to do the painting she never seemed to have enough time to do. He'd surprised her on her first visit to Wakefield Manor. She could still see that quick smile of his, the twinkle in his onyx-colored eyes, when he opened the door where a decorator waited.

Adam was the kind of son any parent would be proud of.

Too restless to sit, Eleanor bounded up once again and found herself staring at the back of the house. Light now shone from the window next to Alex's. Lilly Crawford.

Eleanor hoped in this at least she had made the right decision. At the time there hadn't been much choice. As much as it hurt her, she had to come to terms with the fact that instead of her presence comforting her son, it had the opposite effect.

Adam had always been the strong one, the dependable one. Like most young men growing up, he had tested the rules and boundaries, but that was as it should be. He had a good head on his shoulders his father had said. How she wished her husband were still with her to lean on, to guide her.

Randolph Wakefield had been a kind, loving father and husband. Losing him so suddenly five years ago had devastated them all. Now this. If Adam's blindness weren't horrendous enough, the aftermath was tearing their once-close family apart, and she had absolutely no idea how to make it better.

This wasn't drinking or drugs or the influence of unsavory people you could discuss with reason. This was something far more insidious and destructive. She didn't know how to fight, only that she must. Not just for Adam's sake, but for Kristen's.

Eleanor's daughter's life had been shaken enough when her father died of a sudden heart attack while they were playing tennis. She had seen one man she loved and thought invincible succumb; now the big brother she had come to rely on even more since their father's death was struggling to survive.

Kristen had never been as outgoing or as strong as Adam. Eleanor knew that if Adam lost his battle it would have disastrous consequences on her daughter. There had to be a way to save her children from more heartache and pain.

The flash of headlights across the sheer curtain caused Eleanor to frown, then smile. Quickly she went to open the door to admit her late-night visitor.

"Hello, Jonathan."

Jonathan straightened from trying to balance the cardboard box in his hands and ring the lighted doorbell at the same time. "I hope you checked before you opened the door."

Used to his being protective and cautious where she and Kristen were concerned, Eleanor smiled and stood back for him to enter. "Only a few people know I'm here."

Stepping across the threshold onto the hardwood floor, Jonathan stared down at Eleanor's beautiful smiling face, caught as always by her beauty and charm. "Check next time," he said gruffly.

Leaning over, she sniffed appreciatively. "Is that Marie's gumbo?"

Realizing he had lost this particular conversation, Jonathan headed for the kitchen. Besides being independent, Eleanor was headstrong. "Kristen said you hadn't been eating."

The smile slipped from Eleanor's face as she followed. "None of us have."

Setting the cardboard box on the blue-and-white tile counter, he began to take the Styrofoam containers out. "That's going to change. I got Kristen to eat before I took her to the airport by promising I'd get you to eat." He reached into the cabinet and took down a soup bowl trimmed with clusters of ripe blueberries, Eleanor's favorite fruit. "So have a seat."

Eleanor sat, then propped an elbow on the table, her chin on top of her hand, watching Jonathan move around the small kitchen with such ease and economy of motion. No matter how many times she'd seen him, it always amazed her that a big man could move with such grace and elegance. "Thank you for taking her to the airport. She called to let me know she had made it back safely. Tomorrow she's going by my house and have my phone calls forwarded to the cottage."

"She called me, too."

Eleanor wasn't surprised. Kristen would know he was concerned. "Where's your bowl?" she questioned when he set the thick stew in front of her.

"Coming." True to his word, he dished up another bowl of gumbo, removed the foil from still-warm garlic bread, transferred the tossed salad from the plastic container into a clear bowl, then placed napkins and silverware on the table.

Hands on hips, he studied the table, then snapped his fingers and grinned. Reaching back into the box, he brought out a bottle of chilled chardonnay. "I figured we could both use this."

Eleanor lifted her glass. She seldom

drank strong liquor, but she loved wines and Jonathan knew the ones she liked best. "You always think of everything."

"I try." Half-filling her glass, he filled his, then set the bottle on the table.

"I thought you were on call?"

"Traded places with Maxwell for Saturday night." Jonathan took his seat. "He has a heavy date."

"You're a bachelor, too. Don't you have plans?"

"You know I tried marriage and it didn't work. Never again." Head downcast, he spread his napkin across his lap instead of looking at her, afraid she'd see the longing he wasn't sure he hid very well at times. Friendship was better than nothing.

"I liked Gloria." Eleanor sipped her wine, then studied Jonathan over the rim of the glass. "I was disappointed it didn't work out between you two."

"She's happy with her podiatrist in Arizona," he said lightly. The marriage had been doomed from the start. He had been unfair to Gloria by asking her to marry him when he loved another woman. What saved him many sleepless nights was that at the time he hadn't known it. He wished his ex-wife well.

"I suppose all marriages can't be as happy as Randolph's and mine." Eleanor's eyes became dreamy. "I considered myself the luckiest woman in the world to have found him."

Uncomfortable with the conversation and ashamed of his jealousy of the man who had been his best friend, Jonathan cut off a thick slice of bread and placed it on her plate. "Enough talk. Eat before the food gets cold."

The first taste was delicious, tempting her taste buds with forgotten pleasure. Eleanor closed her eyes and savored the rich flavors. When she opened them again, Jonathan was staring at her strangely. She laughed self-consciously. "What's the matter?"

Roughly he cleared his throat, then took a bite of gumbo to wash down the knot in his throat. He had to shake his head when it stuck. He reached for his wine and gulped. Thankfully it worked. Now wasn't the time or the place. "Nothing. It's just sometimes I find it hard to believe you have grown children. You look the same as you did when the three of us were in med school at Meharry."

Relaxing, the jittery feeling in her stomach gradually subsiding, Eleanor made a face. "Flatterer. As I remember, you had the silver tongue then also."

"Didn't seem to work with you."

Eleanor's gaze came up sharply, but Jonathan wore his usual teasing smile.

"Randolph and I always knew," she said softly. "I miss him still. I wish he was here to help me decide what to do."

"If it's any help, Eleanor, I'm here. I'll always be here for you and the children."

From somewhere she summoned a smile as she reached for his hand. His grasp was strong and steady on top of the hard surface of the table. "Jonathan. I don't know what we would do without you, and I sincerely hope we never have to find out."

"You won't." Ordering himself to let go of her hand, he picked up his spoon. "Finish your meal. I promised Kristen I'd call her tomorrow with a full accounting."

Eleanor dipped her spoon into the bowl, then put it down. "It's difficult to eat when I keep thinking of Adam alone and hurting."

"Not taking care of yourself is not going to help. And what about Kristen?" Jonathan stared at her across the table. "She needs you, too. By not taking care of yourself, you let them both down."

Fury flashed in Eleanor's amber-colored eyes. "You have no right to criticize me."

"Yes, I do. You're all they have. You love them more, but that doesn't negate my love for them or for you."

The anger rushed out of her as quickly as it had come. She leaned back against the high-backed cushioned chair. "You always could make me angrier than anyone else on the planet."

"It's a knack," Jonathan said mildly. Anger, but never the love he craved so desperately.

Eleanor tore off a piece of bread. "Well, don't overdo."

"Wouldn't think of it."

"What do you think of Lilly Crawford?"

Seeing Eleanor finally eating, Jonathan gave serious thought to her question. "I don't know. I wish you'd let me have someone do a check on her. A friend of mine in the police department can trace her through the car registration."

Eleanor took a sip of wine. "You gave her your word and that meant mine. If she were a criminal, she would have thought of that possibility. I'm going to go on instinct and hold off unless she gives us cause." She set her glass aside. "Nicole called as soon as she arrived home from the airport. She reiterated her dislike of Ms. Crawford caring for Adam, but as I explained to her, for the time being that's the way it's going to be."

"I don't think she wants any woman alone with Adam for an extended period of time, as he and Ms. Crawford are bound to be if this works out."

Eleanor raised perfectly arched eyebrows. She wasn't offended by his subtle reference to sex. Adam was very much a man. "But Adam isn't interested in that now."

Jonathan chuckled. "Spoken like a mother. Every man is interested in that, whether he can see or not."

Eleanor felt that hot fluttery feeling again and, for the first time in their relationship, wondered about Jonathan's sex life. She studied Jonathan the way another woman would who might be interested in him as a potential lover, not as a trusted friend of almost forty years.

He was certainly handsome enough, with glossy salt-and-pepper hair at his temples that made him look like the distinguished and successful doctor he was. His unending patience and soft brown eyes had probably comforted countless women in labor. She frowned slightly, remembering his gaze could also be piercing if called for.

The occasion had been shortly after Randolph's death. One of his associates had become pushy in his attention toward her. Jonathan had been in town on one of many trips from Shreveport to check on them and immediately set the man straight with a few terse words. The odious man had never bothered her again. Jonathan wasn't a pushover by any stretch of the imagination.

His broad shoulders and wide chest were strong enough to hold and shelter a woman and her problems, but he also had an ingrained goodness that made the entire package appealing. Why hadn't she noticed before?

"What?" he asked, frowning.

A bit embarrassed, she dipped her spoon into the gumbo. "Woolgathering. Nothing important."

Jonathan wasn't so sure. For one precious moment Eleanor had looked at him the way a woman looks at a man she is interested in. He couldn't have imagined it, but as time passed and she ate her meal, he wasn't so sure. Perhaps he had seen what he had waited almost forty years to see.

For the first time in memory, Lilly had nothing to do. After Dr. Delacroix left to take Nicole and Kristen to the airport, Mrs. Wakefield had shown her the location of the cottage. Once there, Mrs. Wakefield had given Lilly specific instructions regarding the care of her son, then said they'd talk in the morning.

Lilly had returned to find the double stainless-steel refrigerator and freezer and pantry well stocked, as Mrs. Wakefield had indicated they would be. Lilly had prepared Dr. Wakefield's dinner and left it outside his door on the table as Mrs. Wakefield had instructed her to do if he didn't answer. Then she went to her room.

106

Opening the door to the spacious bedroom done in salmon, slate blue, and yellow, Lilly still found it difficult to believe she was to sleep in the delicate-looking and distinctly feminine room. It was like something out of a dream.

Her fingers trailed down the intricately carved maple headboard that was as tall as she was, the double doors of the mahogany armoire, the pretty bench at the foot of the bed that was covered in the same sunny white-and-yellow fabric as the throw pillows on the bed and on the love seat. Everywhere her eyes touched there was beauty.

When she'd grown tired of looking and touching, she'd unpacked her few clothes and run a bath. She'd felt almost decadent in the white-on-white bathroom and a little impish when she sprinkled in the water some of the bath salts she found on the marble shelf over the immense sunken tub. Sinking into the rose-scented bubbles, she sighed with pleasure, then gasped as the unexpected buoyancy of the water lifted her. She laughed, enjoying the freedom to do so.

She'd played more than she had bathed and enjoyed it, instead of her habit of rushing to finish in case Myron needed her. Getting out, she'd pulled a large white towel from the heated towel rack to dry off. Wealthy people sure knew how to live.

Holding up her faded cotton gown, she could barely distinguish the tiny lilacs on the white background. She glanced at the mound of luxurious bedding. No problems this time distinguishing the plants. Large white hydrangeas were scattered across a ground of luminous yellow on the duvet, shams, and toss pillows. It seemed a shame to wear the old gown.

Grinning, she pulled on the gown and slid beneath the cool cotton sheets to snuggle in comfort. Overhead she caught sight of the detailed scroll around the ceiling of the room and the crystal chandelier. To live here every day, to own all this, had to be the most wonderful thing in the world. For a while, she would enjoy it, too.

The grin slipped from her face as she thought of Dr. Wakefield and the reason she was there. He could no longer see the beautiful house or the well-cared-for grounds. His world was one of darkness.

What if it remained that way?

Scooting down in the bed, Lilly turned over on her side and drew the covers up to her chin. Once she'd thought that her life had to be the most miserable in the world. Today she had learned different.

Mother Crawford had always said if you lived long enough you'd find someone in worse shape. The trick was to keep living.

Leaning over, Lilly cut off the light. Tomorrow she had to be at her best. She no longer thought Dr. Wakefield would harm her physically, but he'd defy her at her every turn. She just had to figure out how to get around him.

Like it or not, they were inexplicably tied to each other, for better or worse. She could only pray she had left the worst behind her in Little Elm.

The next morning she found out how wrong she was.

Chapter Five

"Dr. Wakefield, please unlock the door." Lilly twisted the brass knob again. The unsettling result was the same. "Please, Dr. Wakefield. I have your breakfast and I need to clean the room."

She heard the pleading note in her voice and briefly shut her eyes. A man used to having people jump when he spoke wasn't going to listen to her if she whined. The sad fact was that she was more used to taking orders than she was to giving them.

She glanced down at the untouched tray of food she had left outside his door last night. "You have to eat something or you'll get sick."

Her forehead fell against the solid oak door. "Very good, Lilly. Like he's concerned with getting sick," she muttered to herself.

Using the flat of her hand, she banged against the door. "I have to take care of you. Please."

Silence.

She banged again. "Please, Dr. Wakefield. If I could just come in. I'm supposed to take care of you. Dr. Delacroix and your mother will be calling tonight. What will I tell them?"

More silence. He wasn't going to open the door. All she was going to get was a sore hand. "I'll be back later."

Weariness in every step, Lilly went to the kitchen with the breakfast tray, then returned for the dinner tray. After all the thought she had given to preparing food he wouldn't have to worry about cutting or falling off his fork, he hadn't touched the veal cutlet or green beans.

Shaking her head over the wasted food, she fed it to the garbage disposal. There had to be some way to get him to open his door and listen to reason.

The ringing of the phone made her jump. Cleaning her hands on a dish towel, she slowly crossed the room and picked up the blue wall phone. "Hel— Hello — Wakefield residence."

"Good morning, Lilly. How are things?"

Lilly leaned heavily against the counter. She hadn't expected his mother to call so soon. Last night Lilly had asked Mrs. Wakefield to call her Lilly since she worked for the Wakefields. It might be the shortest job in history.

"Lilly, is everything all right?" Mrs. Wakefield asked anxiously.

She opened her mouth to say, "Yes," but the lie wouldn't come. Keeping her marriage a secret harmed no one. His mother deserved the truth. "He . . . he locked me out," she admitted, sure she was going to be fired.

"I knew my instincts were right."

"Ma'am?"

"If you had said things were fine, I'd have known you were lying," Mrs. Wakefield said bluntly. "Adam wouldn't have succumbed so easily."

Lilly was too overjoyed that she wasn't being fired to be concerned with Mrs. Wakefield's subtle bit of trickery.

"However, I didn't think he'd use his old tricks," Mrs. Wakefield continued, not sounding the least bit disturbed.

"He's done this before?"

"A couple of weeks after he came home from the hospital."

"What did you do?"

"Got an ax and broke his front door in."

Lilly smiled, settling on a padded high-backed stool by the phone. Picking up a pencil, she doodled on the notepad on the counter. She liked and envied Mrs. Wakefield's assurance. "I bet that got his attention."

"It did. You have to take a firm hand with Adam."

Her hand tightened around the pencil. "Dr. Wakefield has a mind of his own."

"I realize that, and unfortunately for you, he thinks he has the upper hand." The sigh that came through the receiver was long and deep. "He's aware what I'd do if that happened."

Lilly sat up straighter. She had to moisten her lips before she spoke: "You want me to take an ax to his door?"

"No. He has to feel he's in control of something. Besides, I don't think force will work this time."

"Then what?"

"I wish I knew. Love and patience certainly haven't. I'll let you try for another day. If you're unable to get him to open up, I'll have to hire someone else. Good-bye."

Slowly Lilly hung up the phone. She didn't want to leave. There was no way she'd find another job that paid as well and offered a place to live. Determination glinted in her eyes.

Adam Wakefield wasn't running her off. She'd run from her last man. Going back to the sink, she flipped the garbage disposal on. She'd figure out something. She had no choice.

Adam paced the floor at the foot of his bed. Five steps forward; five steps back. He was in a foul mood. His beard itched, he needed a bath, and his shirt would probably stand by itself. So would his linen slacks. He'd always been fastidious in his dress and in his person, changing shirts sometimes twice a day. His jaw tightened. How the mighty had fallen. He was afraid the fall wasn't over.

Nothing was working out as he had planned. He hadn't packed enough clean clothes. Worse, he hadn't had a decent bath since he came here. He sat in a couple of inches of water, afraid he'd slip trying to take a bath in the deep, oversize tub and further injure his eyes.

He'd yet to get the hang of adjusting the water temperature in the shower. Unlike the one-knob head shower at his house in Sausalito, this shower had two. Then there was the soap that he'd carefully put in the dish, then knocked out when he reached for it again. Down on hands and knees he'd go until he found it again. He'd chased his last soap!

He paused and scratched the stubbled beard on his face. He'd always been clean-shaven and preferred a regular razor to stay that way. After he'd come out of the hospital, he'd switched to an electric shaver when he kept nicking himself with the razor. It hadn't given him as close a shave, but now he didn't even have that. He'd packed in such a hurry he'd forgotten it, along with half of his other things.

All for nothing. His mother, Kristen, and Nicole had been on the plane. Of course, no one had said anything until it had taken off. Afterward none of them could understand how stupid or betrayed that had made him feel or how angry and worthless it felt to control so little of his life anymore.

He had thought once he reached the estate he'd be in control again. That had been his biggest mistake so far.

He hadn't calculated that he had been here only five times in the last five years, whereas he had lived in his home in Marin County outside San Francisco for six years. Since he was fairly neat, in his mind's eye he already knew the placement of furniture and his possessions there. Here he had to become acclimated with his family and Nicole hovering. In his anger, he had made things worse by barging in and overturning furniture. He should have planned better.

The sudden ringing of the phone startled, then annoyed him. It could only be one of four people. One of the four people he had sent hastily from here yesterday. He could almost detect who the caller was from the persistent ringing of the phone. Nicole. His mother or Kristen might have wished he'd answered the phone, but after eight rings they would have respected his desire for privacy.

Not Nicole.

Her aggressiveness was what had taken

her from an unsatisfying career as an accountant to president and CEO of her own temporary agency. That trait was what had attracted him to her in the first place.

In his profession he didn't have time for needy, clingy women. Nicole's assertiveness meant she wouldn't be dependent on him to make her happy, that she understood that there would be many times when his work would make him unavailable. When time permitted, they had enjoyed each other's company in and out of bed. Now he couldn't even give her that.

His mouth flattened as the phone continued to ring. "Let it go, Nicole. Just move on. Please, for both our sakes." Blessedly the phone stopped.

His pacing continued. How he wished he could be left alone. At the same time, he wished he could clutter his mind with so many thoughts that he couldn't think. His laughter was rough and rusty. Perhaps Jonathan hadn't been far off in wanting to declare him incompetent.

His stomach growled. In the midst of the turmoil his life was in, it seemed incongruent that he could be hungry, yet he was. Perhaps he should have eaten. Only the woman would see what a horrendous mess he had made. Food invariably ended up on his shirt or in his lap. He'd lost count of the number of times he had put an empty spoon or fork into his mouth.

He abruptly halted on step three, pivoted, sniffed. He recognized that smell. Fried chicken. An artery clogger if ever there was one. His stomach didn't seem to care, nor his salivary glands. His stomach growled. His mouth watered.

He'd never realized his sense of smell was so acute. If anyone suggested that it was because his other senses were heightened due to his loss of sight, he'd tell him that was a crock. There was nothing scientific to back up such a claim. Still . . . he smelled fried chicken.

She'd knock on his door soon, he was sure. Maybe he'd accept the tray this time. He'd already shown he was in charge by locking her out. Carefully, his hands outstretched, step by humiliating step, he made his way to the door, a straight twenty-one-step path from the foot of his bed.

Time passed. How much he couldn't tell.

Another irritating thing about his blindness was the complete lack of comprehension of the passage of time. The cuckoo clock Nicole had given him a week after he came home from the hospital had driven him crazy. He really had accidentally knocked it off his bedside table and broken it, just as he'd told her. He just wasn't sorry he had.

Becoming annoyed with the woman's tardiness, he pressed his ear against the door. The two-story house was built solid, but he was positive he heard some kind of droning sound. His stomach growled. Where was his dinner?

A thought struck. What if she didn't come back? What if she was downstairs taking it easy, watching the soaps, eating his fried chicken? What if she planned to do nothing, just pocket the money? What was the going rate to take care of a helpless man? Two hundred, three hundred dollars a week? Whatever it was, there was no one in the house to report her if she didn't do her job.

Except him!

Incensed, he jerked open the door. She wasn't getting away with it. "If you don't bring my lunch, you're fired!"

Lilly barely kept from clapping hands together. She did grin and turned over a drumstick in the electric fryer she'd been tending in the hallway. "You're sure you're ready to eat?"

His attention shifted downward. "What are you doing on the floor?"

She scrambled to her feet, almost knocking over the small electric fan positioned on the other side of the skillet to blow the aroma of frying chicken to Adam's room. "Your tray took all the space on the side table and I–I set mine on the floor."

"Well, bring mine inside. Now."

Lilly picked up the tray. "Certainly, Dr. Wakefield." Entering his room, she was prepared for a bigger mess than the day before. She felt a small measure of relief that it wasn't. The chairs and tables were upright; so were the lamps, their bulbs burning, their shades slightly bent. "I'll get the table from the hall and put it by the window. The sun is shining and you can hear the blue jays in the oak trees outside."

His mouth tightened a fraction. He hadn't moved from the door. "No, just put it on the bed. Then you can leave."

"I need to clean up your room." She paused, her hands firmly on the tray.

"Later. Now leave."

Somehow she didn't trust him. "You give me your word."

"Don't question me!" he bit out, but his growling stomach negated the force of his stern order.

Lilly caught back a chuckle. He was human.

His head jerked sharply toward her. "What was that?"

"Nothing, Dr. Wakefield. I'll be back later for the tray and to clean the room." Setting the tray on the rumpled bed, she started from the room, then made a quick detour. "I'll just grab your laundry from the bathroom."

A cursory glance in the room that was bigger than her bath told her she had her work cut out for her. Towels were strewn everywhere. The black tile in the shower could use a good scrub, and so could the tub.

His clothes in her hands, she edged past him. "Meat at twelve, potato salad at three, green beans at six, roll at nine, brow—"

The door closed firmly in her face.

Lilly jerked back, then went down the hall smiling. She had done something right. Gotten Dr. Wakefield to open his door.

Adam caught himself sucking on the chicken bone and tossed it in the direction of his plate. Since he heard a thump instead of a clatter, he set the tray on the floor beside him and felt around on the Persian rug until he found the discarded bone. This time he made sure it reached the tray.

With his back pressed against the footboard of the bed, he sipped his lemonade from the thermos spout. It wasn't one of the reds he would have chosen to complement his meal, but fried chicken wasn't his usual meal, either. However, he had to admit the food was good and so was the lemonade.

Ice cubes clinked as he lowered the thermos. Lots of ice, just the way he liked his beverages. This time he hadn't had to worry about knocking the glass over or ice sliding down into the glass and splashing the liquid up his nose as had happened in the past. Maybe she had possibilities. If she kept out of his way.

"Dr. Wakefield. It's me, Lilly."

Speak of the devil. He found his brownie again and took another generous bite. "I haven't finished."

"Did you have enough?"

Adam grunted. Four drumsticks, potato salad and green beans in little bowls so that he didn't have to chase the food over his plate, and three gooey but delicious brownies. She must be used to feeding truck drivers. "Yes."

"What would you like for dinner? I was thinking chicken-fried steak?"

Apparently she hadn't heard of the dangers of too much cholesterol. He took another bite of his brownie. "Whatever."

Outside the door, Lilly wrung her hands. Maybe she had celebrated too early. Although Mrs. Wakefield had been just as excited and had actually congratulated Lilly on her scheme. "I washed and ironed some of your clothes."

"What?" He scrambled to his feet. "Those shirts were silk and the pants linen."

"Not the ones I washed. I–I checked the labels in the shirts and washed them on Delicate. It's all right."

"Bring one to me now," he ordered. He didn't have any clothes to waste. He wasn't about to ask that traitor Jonathan to bring him more or admit that he wasn't prepared to care for himself. Getting his bearings, Adam went to the door and jerked it open. "Incompetent —"

"Here it is."

He jerked back. "I thought you went to get the shirt."

"I brought it with me. Here it is."

Adam extended his hand, hoping he wouldn't have to grope. He didn't. His fingers closed around soft-cotton material that smelled like sunshine. He barely refrained from lifting the clean shirt to his face. At the moment a too-small shirt was a small price to pay for clean clothes.

"Is it all right?" the woman asked anxiously.

"I suppose," he said, trying to keep the excitement out of his voice.

"I washed your jeans as well." She touched his hand with the denim.

Adam's fingers closed around the pants. "Is this all my laundry?"

"Er —"

"Well?"

He felt the additional weight and pressure of more clothes being added to his pile. He had a pretty good idea what. His cotton briefs. For some reason he felt oddly embarrassed by the situation, as she did. "You can take the tray now."

"You sure you don't want anything else?"

"Positive."

Crossing the room, she started to pick up the tray; then she saw the bed. The sheets were twisted. The geometric black-and-brown comforter hung halfway off the bed. "I'll just straighten up the bed a bit."

"That isn't necessary."

"It's part of my job." She quickly straightened the sheet on one side, then went to the other. "I'll just tuck in this sheet, put your comforter back on, and then I'll be out of your way and you can take a nap." A few more efficient movements and she was finished. "There."

Picking up the tray, she went to the door. As usual, Dr. Wakefield hadn't moved. He certainly guarded his domain. "I'll go start dinner."

This time when the door closed she didn't feel quite so shut out. But she still needed to clean his room.

Lilly expected Dr. Wakefield to open the door soon after she knocked with his dinner. What she didn't expect was to see him wearing the same soiled clothes.

"You can put the food on the bed," he instructed.

Unsure of how to delicately suggest he take a bath, Lilly did as instructed. "You said I could clean the room later."

"After I've eaten."

"But —"

"Later," he interrupted.

"Yes, sir." The door shut her out as soon as she stepped past him. Deep in thought, she stared at the closed door. Why hadn't he changed clothes?

She was still puzzled when she went back and found the empty tray outside his door. Somehow she knew if she tried the knob it would be locked.

Sitting on the side of the tub Saturday night, Lilly watched the water gush from the solid brass spout that gleamed like gold. Absently she sprinkled bath salts beneath the spout and watched the bubbles form and rise higher until they threatened to overflow. Time was running out. She had been on the job two days, and she still was no closer to getting Dr. Wakefield or his room cleaned.

Mrs. Wakefield, although pleased that Dr. Wakefield was eating, wanted her son and the room cleaned as well. She informed Lilly that Dr. Delacroix was already making inquiries.

If that weren't enough, the housekeeper and her husband were to return on Monday. If by some remote chance they could take care of Dr. Wakefield's needs, there would be no need for Lilly to remain.

She wanted to stay. The desire now wasn't so much because she had no place else to go but because of a sense of growing accomplishments. It had felt good to see the empty tray, to know that she had accomplished something others hadn't been able to do. Then, too, she had finally figured out why Dr. Wakefield made her uneasy.

She looked at him and saw herself. He was a victim just as she had been and, like her, unwilling to fight back. According to those who loved him, he hadn't been that kind of man in the past. There had to be a way to get him to be the man he used to be.

From all accounts, he had been a neat, clean-shaven man before his blindness. She didn't know if his sloppiness was because he couldn't see himself or because he just didn't care anymore. His mother and Dr. Delacroix were just as puzzled.

Cutting off the water, Lilly slipped off the white terry cloth robe she'd found in the bathroom and stepped into the tub. As soon as she sat down and took her hands from the side of the tub she felt the water lift her. Used to it, she didn't grab for the side of the tub. Instead, she stretched out her legs, leaned back, and reached for her soap, only to knock it out of the holder.

"Gracious, I'll never find —" Her eyes widened. "That's it." Standing, she stepped out of the tub. Without bothering to dry herself, she pulled on her robe, belting it as she went.

She found a ball of twine and a paring knife in the kitchen and raced back to her bathroom. Unwrapping a new bar of soap, she made a hole in the center, then looped the twine through and knotted the ends.

"Please, Lord, let this work."

Before she could let doubts creep in, she went next door and knocked on the door. "Dr. Wakefield. It's me. Please open up. Please."

Adam heard Lilly, then just as quickly dismissed her. He had few pleasures anymore. One of them was listening to baseball games, and he didn't want to be disturbed.

With radio, the great equalizer, every listener was on the same playing field, and the announcer recognized that. With television, the aptly named "boob tube," the announcer's comments were littered with visual expectations. Did you see that? What a great catch. Let's watch a rerun.

"Dr. Wakefield, please. It's important."

His inclination was to continue to ignore her; then he decided to see what had happened. Tonight her soft, southern-accented voice sounded breathless instead of filled with its usual uncertainty. In that, she reminded him of Kristen. Maybe she'd heard something downstairs and it had frightened her. Probably a tree brushing against a window. Kristen certainly hadn't liked being away from the bright lights of the big city her first trip here.

"Dr. Wakefield, please."

"I'm coming." Wishing Monday would hurry so he could send her away, he pushed to his feet and went to the door. He twisted the knob, then cursed under his breath when he realized he had locked it against the same annoying person who continued to annoy him. Unlocking the door, he jerked it open. "What is it?"

"I brought you a present."

"A present?" Had his mother hired an escapee from an insane asylum?

"Here." She grabbed his hand and put the bar of soap in it. "I made it. I was taking a bath and lost my soap in the bubbles and I thought how slippery soap can be. I saw this on television once."

He fingered the soap, then the cord. He honestly didn't know what to say.

"Your tub is bigger than mine, and the

127

first time I got in mine I felt like I was going to float off. I still feel like it sometimes."

He heard the girlish, unself-conscious laughter in her voice, then felt her brush past him. "Where do you think you're going?"

"To run your bath. Now you won't have to worry about finding the soap. While you're bathing, I can change your sheets."

"Come back here!"

"Or do you want me to adjust the water in the shower? I forgot men like showers."

She was talking too fast and confusing him. He wanted her to take her soap and get out of his room. He lifted his arm to fling the soap in her direction, but as his arm came up he gripped it instead. His nose wrinkled at his own odor. He needed a bath.

"Dr. Wakefield?"

"The shower."

A grinning Lilly turned toward the dresser. "I'll get your pajamas."

"I don't wear pajamas."

She stopped midway across the room, then slowly turned to gape at him. His mouth was curved slightly as if he had enjoyed the prospect of shocking her. She cleared her throat. "I'll just take your clean clothes from the foot of the bed and put them on the far right-hand side of the marble vanity."

Without waiting, she went into the bathroom, put his clothes on the counter, then stepped into the immense shower stall. Adjusting the showerheads away from her, she turned on the water. She laughed as it shot out, glad she didn't have any shoes on when water circled her bare feet.

Stepping out, she dried her feet, then went to the linen closet for fresh towels and bed linen. Placing the fluffy oversize gray towels on the warming rack, she took the maroon-and-gray-striped cotton sheets from the linen closet and left the bathroom.

Dr. Wakefield stood at the foot of the bed, his long-fingered hand clutching the bedpost.

"The shower is waiting for you. I put clean towels on the rack to the left as you leave the shower."

"I . . ." he began, then shoved his free hand through his long hair.

She frowned. In the short space of time she'd known Dr. Wakefield, he'd never been at a loss for words. Then another thought came to her: she had never seen him walk unassisted except for the time he had lunged at her and fallen.

"All this rushing around has made me thirsty. I'm going to the kitchen for a glass of lemonade before I start on the bed. Can I bring you one?"

"No."

"I'll be right back." Crossing the room, she opened the door and closed it with a crisp snap of her wrist.

Adam heard the door close. He toed off his loafers and moved cautiously toward the sound of the running water in the bathroom. She might be annoying, but she definitely had her moments. Shedding his clothes, he located a washcloth, put the loop of soap around his neck, and found his way beneath the warm spray of water.

With a minimum amount of effort, he managed to redirect the stream downward. Closing his eyes, he braced both hands securely against the tiled wall, leaned his head forward, and let the water run over him.

She definitely had her moments.

How had he thought he could do this?

The words hammered through Adam's brain. Head bowed, hands clamped around the edge of the vanity, anger swirled through him. He couldn't remember where his mother had said she had put his toiletries. She had repeated it to him as if he had lost his mind instead of his sight, and in his anger he had blocked out what she had said.

130

He was as helpless as he was useless.

Two knocks followed by two. "Dr. Wakefield, do you need anything?"

A new pair of eyes, he thought bitterly, anger surging through him again.

"Is everything all right?"

"Yes!" he shouted, his head coming up. If he wanted her gone, he'd have to prove to Jonathan and his mother that he could care for himself. There was nothing wrong with his sense of touch or smell.

Unclamping his hands, he slid them atop the cold marble, moving from one oval basin to the other. The heel of his hand hit an object, knocking it over. Glass clinked. He reflexively grabbed for it. More glass clinked and clattered.

The sound of glass shattering on the floor went straight through him. The strong smell of his after-shave filled his nostrils. Liquid tickled his toes.

"Damn!"

"Dr. Wakefield, are you all right?" Lilly cried, knocking on the door again. "Dr. Wakefield?"

"Can't you tell I'm just fine?" he hissed, balling his hands into fists to keep from sweeping the entire mess onto the floor. The main reason he didn't was that he remembered Jonathan's taunt that if he was injured he couldn't take care of himself.

"Well, come on in and clean up this mess," he ordered.

Moistening her dry lips, Lilly slowly opened the door. The sight of Dr. Wakefield with only a towel wrapped carelessly around his waist, water gleaming on his muscled back and shoulders, caused her to pause, her heart to beat a little faster; then she saw the slivers of broken glass scattered around his feet.

"Don't move," she instructed, rushing forward.

"I hadn't planned on it."

Reaching for the wastebasket beneath the counter, she picked up the larger pieces, then used a washcloth to pick up the tiny splinters. She didn't think Dr. Wakefield would wait until she went to the kitchen for a broom and dustpan.

"I'll go get your shoes." Coming to her feet, she rushed back into the bedroom. A quick search in his closet and beside his bed produced a pair of loafers. She guessed he didn't wear slippers, either. Grabbing the shoes, she went back to the bathroom. Seeing the taut way he held himself, she pulled his robe from the hook on the back of the door.

"Here's your robe." Although her hands were trembling, she draped the garment over his shoulders, then hunkered down. "Raise up your right foot."

"Just put them down."

"I might have missed some of the glass," she said quietly.

After a tension-filled moment, Adam lifted his right foot, then his left.

Standing, Lilly rubbed her hands on her thighs. Indecision and a small flicker of fear held her still. She'd seen Myron's body tremble the sane way when he raged at her. Afraid the slightest movement on her part would cause him to tear into her, she'd learned to wait until the danger passed.

In the mirror she studied Adam's hunched shoulders, the head turned away from her. Even with the unkempt beard and hair, he was a handsome man. He would have had a lot of women after him. She briefly wondered if Nicole was one of them. Unreasonable as the thought was, she hoped not. Lord knows she wasn't in any position to judge others, but Nicole, although beautiful, appeared cold and suspicious. And that would mean Adam was either like her or so blinded by his love that he didn't see her faults.

Like Lilly had been with Myron. The thought brought her up short.

She hadn't seen beyond Myron's smooth words to the cruel person he really was. All she'd seen was a man she thought she could love forever, a man who in return would love her and give her the children and loving family she'd always wanted.

She'd been wrong and paid dearly for her mistake. Just as Dr. Wakefield was paying for his mistake in not giving his keys to the car thieves. She had a chance to correct her mistake, and at the moment her chance was tied to another man who needed but detested her presence.

Had his blindness made Dr. Wakefield cruel or had he simply hidden his cruelty, as Myron had?

She studied his rigid reflection, wishing she knew the answer. Although his arms were taut, his body rigid, her fear wasn't as strong. The more time passed, the less likelihood there had been of Myron striking out. Like a rattler — if it didn't strike quickly there was always the chance that it would let down its tail and slither off on its belly.

Unless she wanted to face the possibility of Myron finding her and making her go back, she'd better get beyond her fear and do her job. Mrs. Wakefield didn't impress Lilly as the kind of person who bluffed.

She gazed at the heavy cut-glass bottles and tubes with similar shapes scattered on the counter. "What do you want next?"

Startled, Adam's head came up and around. She'd been so quiet he thought she had gone. "I don't like people lurking around."

"I wasn't — yes, sir."

The last two words were so soft, he caught himself leaning toward her. He jerked back. Even over the cloying scent of his after-shave he smelled roses. Maybe he was the one insane. "Put everything in the sink, then leave. That's all for tonight."

"Dr. —"

"Never mind; just leave!"

Lilly jumped, stepped back to leave, then stopped. How many times had she wished for someone to help, to understand? How many times had she been too ashamed and embarrassed to ask for help?

Both of them had been kicked in the teeth by life; maybe together they could fight back. "The bottle of after-shave must have been almost empty, because there wasn't much on the floor, and there's another bottle. Were you planning to shave?"

"Didn't you hear me?"

With trembling hands, Lilly placed the assorted bottles and tubes in the sink, ignoring the menacing voice.

"I've broken plenty of things. So has everyone, but it still gets you when it happens. I never thought of it before, but the cologne sprays and aftershave splashes. Your tube of hair cream is softer than your toothpaste. You ever notice how toothpaste falls off the toothbrush? A lot of times I bet

135

it would be easier to just squirt it in your mouth."

She stole a look at Dr. Wakefield in the mirror. What she saw wasn't reassuring. His face was set, his jaw clenched. The lean muscles of his arms were bunched.

"Your bed is made up and the covers turned back." She slid her hands into the pockets of her robe. "Good night, Dr. Wakefield."

She was at the door of the bathroom when he said, "What's your name?"

"Lilly. Lilly Crawford."

He turned and seemed to stare straight at her. "Well, Lilly Crawford, the next time you disobey my order, you're fired."

She was too stunned to speak.

Turning, he felt in the sink, picked up his toothbrush and the toothpaste dispenser. "And, Lilly?"

Scared, she wondered what else he was going to say. "Y-Yes, sir?"

Putting the bristles beneath the opening, he pushed down on the plunger. A mound of toothpaste rolled out on top of the bristles. "Keep your advice to yourself until it's asked for."

Chastised, she left. She didn't hear Adam curse when the naked bristles reached his mouth.

Chapter Six

Adam had a restless night. He wasn't very proud of himself. He hadn't been in a long time. His life had been hell since the carjacking and he had selfishly made everyone else suffer right along with him.

Last night he had reached a new low. He'd never been deliberately cruel, hadn't known he could be. Yet that was exactly what he had been.

Anger had clouded his judgment and he had said things to the woman he shouldn't. She'd tried to help, yet somehow she had made him feel utterly useless. Like a spiteful child, he had struck back.

Initially, her thin, unsteady voice had meant nothing to him, but as his anger cooled and he had time to think he recalled another voice that was just as unsteady and unsure, Kristen's. He'd heard the same uncertainty in his sister's voice too many times to count. Beautiful, talented, shy, and unassuming, she reached to the deepest part of him when no one else could.

He owed Lilly an apology, owed his entire family and Nicole one. The jury was still out on Jonathan, but that didn't mean

Adam had changed his mind about being left alone.

He'd regain his sight soon. They just had to give him space until he did.

Two brief knocks, followed by two more.

He stopped pacing in front of his bedroom door. She hadn't called his name and inexplicably he missed the breathless, hesitant catch in the soft drawl of her voice. Texas, he'd bet. She must be angry with him.

Good. It was better if she remained pissed and out of his way. An apology from him would be an open invitation for her to start giving him advice again.

Opening the door, he stepped aside. "You know where to place the tray."

"Yes, sir."

Silently she passed back by him. The only reason he knew was the hint of roses. Without thought, he leaned into the smell. Then he realized what he was doing and swung the door shut.

Over her shoulder Lilly glanced back at the slammed door, then continued down the stairs to the kitchen for her own breakfast. She detested cold eggs and usually waited until she returned from Dr. Wakefield's room before cooking hers. This morning there had been no need. He didn't want to talk to her any more than she wanted to be in his presence or be reminded of what had happened last night.

Picking up the stoneware plate, she took a seat in the breakfast nook in one of the ladder-back chairs facing the curtainless arched window. Absently munching on a strip of bacon, she watched two squirrels chase each other across the green lawn, then spring onto the trunk of an oak tree and disappear into the leafy foliage.

Beyond the trees she could see pink azaleas in full bloom beneath a cloudless pale blue sky. The day would be perfect.

But not for her. Her appetite gone, she dropped the bacon back on the plate and leaned back in her chair.

She had been so proud of herself, so hopeful that Dr. Wakefield had finally begun to accept her. She'd been wrong. Last night he had made that painfully clear.

"Keep your advice to yourself until it's asked for."

The harshly spoken words still had the ability to make her flinch. They were too much of a reminder of how Myron had treated her, what he might have said to her. Only, with him, she would have been too afraid to voice her opinion. From the mess she had made of things, maybe she should have dealt the same way with Dr. Wakefield.

She hadn't, and now she wasn't sure

how to proceed or even if she would have the chance. Mrs. Wakefield had been very clear; if Lilly couldn't do the job she'd have to hire someone who could.

Then where would she go?

She'd have money coming to her, but she wasn't sure how much, since she wasn't sure if Mrs. Wakefield planned to take out taxes. After paying for car repairs, she didn't know what she'd have left . . . if any at all.

Sighing, Lilly picked up her fork and dug into her eggs. She might as well eat while she had the chance. Her meals might become few and far between after leaving. As soon as the eggs settled on her tongue, she frowned and reached for the salt, then the pepper shaker. She was so upset she must have forgotten —

Her head came up; her hand paused. She had prepared Dr. Wakefield's eggs the same way. She was getting up with the salt and pepper shakers when she glanced back at her plate. The salt was indistinguishable, but there was a scattering of the black specks of the pepper.

People usually seasoned to sight just as she had. He wouldn't be able to do it. A simple thing . . . if you could see. Her hand clutched the small glass containers. What would it be like to live in a world of darkness? To be dependent on others?

If she'd been blinded, Myron would have kicked her out or put her in a home just as he had wanted to do to his mother. He hadn't because he didn't want to ruin his good standing in the community and because he just as badly wanted his mother's house and her rental property. Mother Crawford had come up in the Depression and could pinch pennies with the best of them.

Setting the shakers aside, Lilly closed her eyes, felt around on the table for her fork, then proceeded to eat. Two frustrating minutes later, she was on her feet heading for the stairs. If she couldn't last two minutes, how had a man of Dr. Wakefield's stature lasted five weeks?

"Dr. Wakefield. Dr. Wakefield!" she called through the door. "Don't eat the eggs. I left the seasoning out. I'll remake your breakfast if you'll wait. Dr. Wake—"

The door opened. He stood, shades in place, the plate in his hand, a hard frown on his face. "I believe you left something out of the biscuits as well."

"I'm sorry." She swallowed and reached for the plate. He didn't release it. She lifted questioning eyes to his. "I have it."

"Did you do it on purpose?"

"No." She shook her head wildly, then realized he couldn't see. "I . . . I was upset about last night and I wasn't thinking. I

141

didn't realize until I began to eat."

"You're sure it wasn't to teach me a lesson?"

"I wouldn't do anything like that to you or anyone," she said. "I was upset."

He didn't release the plate. "You've been upset before, and this is the first time the food has been unpalatable."

She threw a wild glance at the three perfectly browned biscuits with a bite missing out of one, the scrambled eggs barely touched. "I didn't mean it."

"You meant it, and I got the message." Finally he released the plate and stepped back to close the door.

"Wait!" she yelled, using the flat of her hand to keep the door open. His jaw was clenched, his body taut. "I promise I didn't do it on purpose."

He stopped but didn't say anything, just slanted his head down toward her. Knowing he couldn't see behind his shades didn't lessen his power to intimidate. Lilly could well imagine he had been a formidable man before his accident.

"I have no place else to go if I lose this job," she told him, unsure if she should have admitted how vulnerable she was.

His dark head twisted to one side. "My mother hired a homeless woman?"

She shifted uneasily. "Not exactly. I was passing through on my way to New Orleans. My car broke down near here. She needed someone immediately and I needed a job."

"Serendipity."

"What?"

Two lost souls thrust together. "How much is she paying you?"

Lilly's other hand clamped around the plate. "I think you should ask your mother that."

"I'm asking you." He hadn't stooped so low that he'd fire her if she didn't have enough money to fix her car and leave, preferably getting as far away from him as possible.

"Please, Dr. Wakefield, ask your mother."

The slight tremble in her voice got to him. He wished she didn't remind him so much of Kristen, lost and trying to find her way. "Are you from Texas?"

"H-How did you know?"

"Lucky guess. Now go fix my breakfast."

"Yes, sir."

She was as skittish as a foal, probably had legs just as long from the sound of her running steps. For a brief moment, he recalled nurses and interns scurrying the same way to carry out his orders. They would again.

Thankfully the kitchen had plenty of

clean skillets and bowls. Lilly whipped the four eggs, then added the cold, crumbled bacon, chives, green and red peppers, and cheese to make an omelet. Myron had gone to Las Vegas with some of his hunting buddies and come back insisting she learn how to make them for him. For the first time, she was glad he had.

Sliding the steaming omelet onto a clean plate, she then buttered four slices of toast. Rubbing her palms against the sides of her dress, she stared at the tray. At least the chilled fruit was still good.

Picking up the wooden tray, she went upstairs and knocked. "Dr. Wakefield."

The door swung open. "What took you so long?"

"Sorry," she mumbled out of habit. She hadn't been gone over ten minutes. Rushing across the room, she put the tray on the bed, then came back to the door. "Your omelet is at twelve, your toast at six. The fruit is at nine and your juice is to the right of your toast. I'll serve lunch early."

"What's wrong with your car?"

She blinked. "Sir?"

"What is wrong with your car?"

He enunciated each word as if he were talking to a feebleminded person. She flushed and dug her hands into the deep pockets of the white bibbed apron she'd found in the kitchen. "I don't know. The

144

man who drove the tow truck said no one could look at the car until Monday."

"What seemed to be wrong with it?"

Lilly barely kept from hunching her shoulders and squirming. "I don't know very much about cars. It just died, then started smoking like a freight train."

Folding his arms, Adam leaned against the door. "It's irresponsible to operate equipment you know nothing about."

Her head came up at the chastising tone. It was on the tip of her tongue to say something pithy; then she remembered she needed this job. "Yes, sir. Is that all?"

"Yes." He straightened.

She was several steps down the hall when he said, "Call first thing in the morning to see how soon your car will be ready." The door closed.

A chill swept through her. Dr. Wakefield had just given her notice. Her time at Wakefield Manor was running out. She could wait until she was fired or try to figure out a way to ensure that she stayed.

To remain she had to be of some use to him. But how, when he didn't want her help?

With Myron he'd needed her to care for Shayla, to cook and clean, to slake his lust, and, oddly, to dominate. He'd felt power in her weakness.

That wasn't the case with Dr. Wakefield.

He wanted nothing from her.

Her spirits sinking, she descended the staircase. There had to be some way to prove to him that he needed her.

"Think, Lilly. Put yourself in his place. What do you want more than anything?"

Freedom! Her brain shouted the word. She'd hated being dependent on a man she loathed for the very food she ate, the roof over her head.

Freedom and independence.

Her hand on the newel cap, she stared back up the stairs. How much stronger was Dr. Wakefield's resentment against her, even though his condition wasn't her fault? She had nothing to do with Myron's meanness, but she'd suffered his wrath just the same.

The difference between the two men, she thought, was that Myron struck out of cruelty, Dr. Wakefield from fear. However, both men put her on the defensive and wanted her to keep her thoughts to herself.

In order to survive with Myron she had let him dictate to her and kept out of his way. If she allowed the same thing to happen with Dr. Wakefield, she might very well end up the homeless person he thought she was.

Like Daniel in the Bible, she had to be brave enough to enter the lion's den and pray that, like him, she came out unscathed.

★ ★ ★

He shouldn't have come.

Jonathan knew that, but he hadn't been able to convince himself to stay away. Eleanor had sounded so tired and defeated when they had spoken briefly on the phone Saturday night. He'd called her in between one of the four babies he'd delivered. Maxwell had certainly chosen the right night to switch calls. He'd only stay a moment. He just needed to give her something to bring back a hint of the happiness that was usually in her voice.

Reaching across the seat, he picked up the brightly wrapped rectangular package, climbed out of the car, and started up the brick walkway. As always, the red front door surprised him. That she'd chosen such a bright, sassy color amazed all of them and kept him awake at night wondering if beneath her quiet, reserved nature was a passionate woman whose needs matched his own.

The door opened and the object of his desire stood smiling at him. Dressed in a white blouse and black slacks, surrounded by an arched arbor of English ivy, she simply made his heart stop.

"Jonathan, good morning," Eleanor greeted him, wondering why her heart felt odd in her chest. Perhaps it was because of all the pressure in her life lately. "You're out early."

"I wanted to bring you this." Lifting the package, he handed it to her.

Her amber eyes widened, then went from him back to the plum-and-gold paper. "You shouldn't have."

He chuckled, enjoying the delight in her face and eyes. "How do you know if I should or shouldn't until you've opened it?"

Laughing, she sat down on one of the curved stone benches positioned on each side of the door and tore into the present to reveal a paint set. Her slim fingers reverently traced the sable brushes, the pots of oil and watercolors. "Oh, Jonathan, it's perfect."

All the time he'd spent trying to decide how to bring back her laughter was worth it. "I'm glad you like it."

"I do, but I don't have any canvases!" she cried.

"That's the third part of my surprise." He smiled down at her crestfallen expression.

"Third part?"

Unable to resist, he sat down beside her, trying to act natural when their thighs brushed together and the heat of her body mingled with his. "Brunch at Antoine's."

For some unfathomable reason she had trouble getting her thoughts together. "I–I can't leave."

He folded his arms over his wide chest, making him appear more impressive and magnificent. "Why?"

"Adam might need me."

"I need you," he almost blurted. Instead he stood, bringing Eleanor with him. "Lilly is here and you need to eat. I promised Kristen."

The lines of annoyance radiating across her forehead cleared. "I know. We talked this morning. You were a good friend to Randolph and now to us."

Randolph's name pricked something deep and sensitive within Jonathan's soul. He wanted Eleanor to see him as a man, not as the best friend of her dead husband. That she might never do so sent a deep shaft of pain and misery through him. Involuntarily his fingers tightened on her arm; his other hand closed around her free arm, bringing her closer to him.

The hardness that swept across Jonathan's face made Eleanor want to run away and, at the same time, lift her hand to the hard line of his jaw to soothe him. Confused, her hands closed more firmly on the paint set between them.

"Mrs. Wakefield, are you all right?"

Jonathan's and Eleanor's startled gazes jerked sideways. Lilly, her face full of anger, stared at Jonathan.

Dropping one hand, Jonathan said,

149

"Why wouldn't she be?"

Instead of answering, Lilly looked at Mrs. Wakefield. "Are you all right?"

"Why, yes," Eleanor finally answered, trying to smile, but her facial muscles were stiff. Not sure what had just happened between them, but realizing that whatever it was Lilly had picked up on it also, she stepped away from Jonathan and off the porch onto the paved walkway. "Is Adam all right?"

"Yes, ma'am." Lilly's gaze flickered to Dr. Delacroix, then came to rest on Eleanor, whose breathing was rapid and cheeks flushed. Then it hit Lilly. Fear wouldn't cause her cheeks to flush. Desire or embarrassment would. Lilly's own cheeks burned. "I'm sorry. I didn't mean to interrupt."

"You didn't," Jonathan answered, folding his arms and bracing his shoulder against the arbor. "I was just trying to get Eleanor to have brunch with me."

That's not all he was trying to do, Lilly thought. But since she didn't see fear in Mrs. Wakefield's eyes, it was their business. Lilly's business was keeping her job.

"I've been reading in one of Dr. Wakefield's medical books about patients' reactions to sudden blindness, their depression, their fear, how it's important to normalize their life as soon as possible."

Moistening her dry lips, Lilly shifted from one tennis-shoe-shod foot to the other. "I looked in the yellow pages and there's a Lighthouse for the Blind in Shreveport. I was thinking maybe they could help."

Eleanor briefly closed her eyes. When they opened they were full of pain. Her voice trembled when she said, "Orientation and Mobility was suggested to Adam to acquaint him with his surroundings when he was released from the hospital. He refused to have the training because he insisted he didn't need it because his vision would return."

Blinking tears from her eyes, she wrapped her arms around her waist. "I went along with him because I didn't want him to think I'd lost faith."

She peered over her shoulder at Jonathan. "I guess I should have listened to you."

Jonathan went to stand by Eleanor, his narrowed gaze on Lilly. "Very astute observation and ingenious on your part." He glanced down at Eleanor. "I guess you were right to hire her. But Lilly points up an important fact. Perhaps we need someone with experience to care for Adam."

Lilly's burgeoning happiness took a nosedive; then she did something totally out of character for her. "I may not be experienced, but I got him to eat and clean up. No one else has been able to do that."

Jonathan lifted a heavy brow at her defensive tone. The gesture was enough to make Lilly remember the influence he had with the Wakefields.

Her voice softened, but the conviction remained. "With the right help, I can do more."

"I'll contact the Lighthouse tomorrow," Eleanor said, excitement in her voice. "Anything else?"

"Maybe you could send for some of his clothes. Washable pants and pullover shirts. It would be nice if there was a table in his room for him to eat on, a way to tell time, books on tape, and one of those battery-operated tape recorders with big control buttons. Puffy paint?"

"Puffy paint?" Eleanor and Jonathan repeated in unison.

"To mark the tags in his clothes and his toilet articles so he can distinguish them." She ordered herself not to fidget under their intense stares. "That's how it was done in the textbook."

"I'll call Kristen and ask her to send his things overnight." Eleanor shook her head. "He said his housekeeper was sending the rest of his things. I'm beginning to wonder since they aren't here."

"Then he'll be happy when they arrive,"

Lilly said, straight-faced.

Eleanor's lips curved. "Won't he? Thank you for caring, Lilly. Excuse me; I'll go call Kristen." The front door closed behind her.

Lilly turned to go.

"Lilly?" Jonathan called softly.

Clutching the book to her chest, she made herself face him.

"I want what's best for Adam. If that's you, good. If not, then we get someone else. Are we clear?"

"Very." Turning, Lilly started back to the main house, her mind troubled, her steps slow. One hurdle down, one to go.

Odette and Samuel were returning tomorrow.

Eleanor was nervous.

In all the long years of her association with Jonathan, she'd felt many emotions while with him, but nervousness had never been one of them. As she sat beside him while he maneuvered the Mercedes through the surprisingly heavy Sunday traffic at the shopping mall in Shreveport, her thoughts were troubled. She kept her gaze forward.

When she'd gone inside to call Kristen, she'd actually felt relief to be away from Jonathan. If there had been any way of getting out of him taking her shopping for

Adam, she would have grabbed at the chance. As it was she was trapped in the car beside him, unsettled and unsure.

What had happened between them just before Lilly arrived at the cottage?

Hell, Eleanor, she chided herself, as she seemed unable to keep from looking at Jonathan's strong, chiseled profile as he patiently waited for a woman to store the several packages scattered around her feet in the trunk of her car so he could park in her space, *you are not that naive.* There had been a spark of awareness between them. Sudden, sharp, and powerful.

And totally unexpected. It had rattled her, and her stomach had yet to settle.

Obviously it had meant nothing to him. On the drive from Adam's house to the shopping mall thirty minutes away, Jonathan's easygoing demeanor was the same as it always was. He remained the same good old reliable Jonathan she had grown to depend on more and more over the years.

Leaning back against the smooth leather seat, Eleanor was grateful he had chosen to ignore whatever it was that had caused them to react so strongly to each other. No doubt it was due to the stress they both were under. Whatever the reason, it couldn't be allowed to happen again. Adam and Kristen had to be her main concern, her only concern.

Finally the woman got in her car and backed out. Jonathan pulled into the parking space, cut the motor, then unbuckled his seat belt. "I'm glad she wasn't shopping with another woman or we might have been waiting until the mall closed."

"Women are selective. Men just grab," Eleanor said. The instant the words were out of her mouth, Eleanor felt the slow roll in her stomach again and quickly busied herself with her seat belt. "It shouldn't take too long to get the things on Lilly's list; then I want to return."

"What about lunch and your canvases?"

"Maybe another time." Opening the door, Eleanor got out of the car.

Eleanor was a master shopper and she used her skill to quickly purchase the list of items for Adam. But always, always she was aware of Jonathan's presence, the heat from his body, his disturbing gaze. By the time they returned to the car, she was even more on edge and not looking forward in the least to the thirty-minute drive back to Wakefield Manor.

He'd done it now.

Eleanor was skittish and nervous around him, and it was his own fault. She'd jumped each time he had even casually brushed up against her while they were shopping. He hadn't dared try to take her

155

arm as he usually did when they were out.

He had already guessed that the only reason she'd consented to letting him take her shopping instead of driving herself was that she hadn't been able to think of a gracious way out. In all things, Eleanor was a lady. At the moment, the lady wanted nothing to do with him.

All his fault.

He shouldn't have grabbed. It hadn't been the right time. Hell, he didn't know if there would ever be a right time, but at least he'd had her friendship. Now, he wasn't sure if he'd still have that.

Turning into the driveway of Adam's house, he tried to think of something to say to break the silence that had plagued them since they had gotten back into the car, but nothing came. As before, as soon as he braked, she was out of the car. He watched her practically run up the walkway.

Gritting his teeth, he got out and reached in the backseat for the bags. She was waiting for him at the door, her smile overly bright and strained. "Thank you, Jonathan, for taking me shopping. You must have a million things to do on a Sunday. I'll take the packages so you can be on your way."

He stared down into Eleanor's tense face, seeing the narrow line of her compressed lips, the nervous fluttering of the pulse in her neck as she stood in her doorway strategically blocking his entrance. One at a time, he handed her the two bags. "Anytime."

"I'll just go put my purse down and take these straight to Lilly."

Jonathan knew a brush-off when he heard it. "If you need me, call."

"I'll be fine. I shouldn't bother you so much."

His eyes narrowed. It was all he could do not to snarl. "Adam is your son, but he's my godson and I love him, too. Call if either of you need anything."

The bright smile wavered, firmed. "I will. Good-bye."

The door closed with a quiet click. As he walked to his car, Jonathan had the distinct impression that there would be no calls. Eleanor had just shut him out of her life and he had no one to blame but himself.

Eleanor waited until she saw Jonathan drive off before she left the cottage. She wasn't proud of herself. She'd never run from anything or turned her back on a friend before. Today she'd done both.

Nearing the house, she stared up at the window to Adam's room and wondered if she might have to amend her earlier statement. Had she run from the truth that

Adam's blindness might be permanent and, in doing so, let him continue to cling to a false hope that was destroying him day by day?

"Mrs. Wakefield."

Eleanor glanced around to see Lilly sitting beneath one of the huge oak trees near the back door to the kitchen. *She's too thin,* Eleanor thought, noticing with a discerning eye the way the wind shaped the cotton dress to Lilly's slender frame. The possibilities were there. Waiting. She just needed a touch of makeup and the right clothes to bring them out, just as the right words were needed to bring Adam out of his shell.

"Is everything all right?" Lilly asked.

"Yes." Eleanor continued across the lawn. "Here are the things you wanted."

Automatically Lilly took the bags. "Would you like to come inside for a cup of coffee?"

"No, thank you. I told Adam I was leaving the house and technically I am, since he gave me the cottage. A minor point, but one that I feel is necessary. So unless something is extremely important, we'll keep in touch by phone," Eleanor said.

"Yes, ma'am."

Eleanor nodded toward one of the bags. "Adam is a big mystery fan. I picked up a

158

couple of books on tape he should enjoy. If you think of anything else, please let me know."

"I will."

"Odette and Samuel should arrive early tomorrow morning. I've left a message on their answering machine to call me tonight no matter how late it is when they arrive home. I'll explain the entire situation to them."

Lilly's fingers dented the paper sack. "You don't think they'll mind me being here, do you?"

"No. From my experience with them, there's not a mean or territorial bone in their bodies. From the first, they've been wonderful to Adam. He trusts them so much they have a household account so they don't have to call him about every little thing they need to ensure the house is cared for."

"How long have they worked for him?"

"Five years. They were here when Adam bought the house. He bought it shortly after his father's death."

"You're widowed?" Lilly asked.

"Yes." Eleanor fingered the diamond ring on her finger. "Randolph and I shared thirty-nine wonderful years together. I miss him still."

"You're one of the lucky couples to have found love," Lilly said, wondering what being loved by a man you loved must feel like.

"Yes, it was. Were you ever married?"

"No." Lilly didn't consider it a lie. Whatever there had been between her and Myron, it certainly hadn't been a marriage.

"Well, I guess I'll get back; I want to call Kristen." She started to leave, then paused. "I wish you could have known Adam before. He was arrogant, but fair. He demanded the best of himself and those who worked with him. He loved life and did everything in his power to ensure that those he cared for were given the best possible care. He had a wicked sense of humor and a mean backhand on the racquetball court."

Lilly had already met the arrogant side of Dr. Wakefield. "Maybe I'll see that side of him one day."

"Yes. Good-bye." This time when Mrs. Wakefield turned away, she kept going.

"Good-bye."

Lilly watched her disappear around a large evergreen shrub. If she didn't know better, she'd think Mrs. Wakefield had more on her mind than her son. Adam's mother had appeared distracted, and although Lilly had known the older woman for only a short time, she didn't think that was usual. Lilly hoped the reason wasn't Dr. Delacroix. Now there was another arrogant man, and if he had his way, she might be looking for another job soon.

She just had to make sure she stayed.

Chapter Seven

Lilly was about to face another hurdle.

Standing in front of the high arched window in the entryway a few minutes before eight Monday morning, Lilly nervously rubbed her hand against the side of her leg. Despite Mrs. Wakefield's growing confidence, Dr. Wakefield's and Dr. Delacroix's warnings had kept Lilly up most of the night.

Mrs. Wakefield might keep her on despite the men's objections, but they could make her life miserable. She wasn't sure she could work where she wasn't wanted. Being subjected to Myron's scorn for six long years was enough for a lifetime. The best thing that could happen was that the men wanted her and approved of her staying. If Samuel and Odette liked her, their support would go a long way in helping her stay.

She had to keep this job and remain off the highway. She'd already called the garage and received the very bad news that the oil pump needed replacing. The bill was already $600, and the man had said it was likely to go up if they found any more problems.

She'd been fuming when she'd hung up the phone. The car had had no oil. Myron had said he'd taken the car in for an oil change three weeks ago. She should have known he was lying. He'd been angry about the car since Mother Crawford had told him that she was giving Lilly her Ford Taurus and putting it in her name.

Myron was an accomplished liar and manipulator. There was no telling what story he might have cooked up to get the police to look for her. He'd be filled with rage at her for leaving, but even more so for her putting him in a bad light in the church and community.

As usual, it would be her fault and not his.

If she could manage to stay for two weeks, surely she'd have enough money to find a job and a place to live. Maybe even in Shreveport. Little Elm was barely a dot and it had a junior college. In a city as large as the one she had passed through there had to be a host of colleges where she could finish her associate degree in business administration.

She'd always be thankful to Mother Crawford for getting Myron to let her attend classes at the junior college while Mother Crawford was at the community center with the other senior citizens.

Lilly's mother-in-law had believed in education and in women being able to care for themselves. She'd had to struggle with Myron and his two older brothers after their father died from complications of diabetes. Mother Crawford had learned firsthand what it was to have a low-paying job and hungry children to feed.

When she saw a late-model car turn into the drive, Lilly's heart rate increased. What if they didn't like her? Mrs. Wakefield and Dr. Wakefield had spoken highly of the couple. If they didn't like her, Lilly might be out on her ear today.

Taking a steadying breath, she opened the beveled door and stepped out on the porch just in time to see the big black Buick pass. Tentatively Lilly walked to the edge of the porch by the rattan swing, debating if she should wait or go meet them. A car door slammed, quickly followed by another.

Hands clasped, she waited for the couple to come around the front of the house. When minutes ticked by and they didn't appear, she realized her mistake. They had gone through the side door just as she had the first time she entered the house. Reentering the house, she saw a man and a woman climbing the staircase. The man wore a denim shirt and overalls, the woman a white cotton uniform. His right hand cupped her elbow.

Lilly hurried after them. "Mr. and Mrs. Tucker?"

The couple turned, their brown faces lined with worry.

"Yes, ma'am," the elderly man answered. "I'm Samuel Tucker and this is my wife, Odette. You must be Miss Crawford. Mrs. Wakefield told us about you when we called last night."

"We've been expecting you," Lilly said, then added hopefully, "I was hired to take care of Dr. Wakefield."

Silent tears ran down Odette's plump cheeks. "I still can't believe that terrible thing happened to Dr. Wakefield."

Samuel's long arm circled his wife's shoulders. "Don't start up again. Mrs. Wakefield said we were to act natural."

Odette shook her turban-covered head. "I don't know if I can. The doctor was such a good man. He never did nothing for this to happen to him."

"You got to try, Odette." Samuel looked at Lilly. "Ain't that right, Miss Crawford?"

Lilly didn't know what to say. They were both staring at her as if she were the expert when she was struggling herself. Knowing *what* should be done wasn't the same as knowing how it should be done. She gave them the only truth she knew: "Dr. Wakefield doesn't want to be treated any differently than before."

Dragging a crumpled white handkerchief from her pocket, Odette dried her eyes, then shoved the cloth back inside. From the rumpled appearance of the handkerchief, it had been used many times that morning. "If that's what Dr. Wakefield wants, then that's the way it's gonna be. We'll just go on up and pay our respects."

"You can't do that," Lilly blurted.

Both frowned down at her. Samuel spoke first, "You think he wouldn't want to see, I mean . . . I meant . . ." he floundered, glancing at his wife for help. Dragging out her handkerchief again, she wiped away fresh tears.

Seeing the misery on their faces, Lilly admitted her failure. "His room's not clean. He won't let me clean it."

Odette stared at her as if she had lost her mind. "But that man is one of the neatest men I know. Always wants things just so."

"Never seen a man change clothes so many times or take so many baths," Samuel recalled. "He didn't mind hard work, but he'd always come inside afterward to clean up."

"It's different now," Lilly told them, searching for the right words much as Samuel had done earlier. "It's like playing blind man's bluff, and you're turned around and around with the blindfold and it's hard to keep your balance and get your bearing. Only Dr. Wakefield can't remove the blindfold."

Odette nodded. "Brother Callahan was the same way when he went blind after that accident. Stays inside now. Never see him at the store or at church anymore, and he used to be an usher you could always depend on."

Lilly didn't say a word, but she couldn't help but wonder if Dr. Wakefield would end up the same way if his sight didn't return. The thought made her feel sick.

"If I had known the doctor wasn't doing well we would have cut our trip short and come back early," Samuel said. "I mentioned that to him last week when he called, but he wouldn't hear of it. Said we deserved the vacation."

So Dr. Wakefield could be kind and considerate, just not to her. "His family cared for him until they hired me. There was nothing more you could have done for him."

"I suppose, but I kinda still wish we had come back. If it hadn't been for Dr. Wakefield we might not have had a fiftieth anniversary." Samuel again curved his arm around his wife's shoulders.

Odette's hand covered his and gently patted it. "I got sugar. Went to three or four doctors and they all thought I was

167

some crazy black woman going through the change." She snorted and shook her head in disgust. "Dr. Wakefield came home when I was at my wits' end, thinking I had cancer. Samuel thought the same. Dr. Wakefield drove us to the emergency room and told the doctor he thought it was my sugar. The blood tests proved he was right. I took great pleasure in sending the lab results to those other quacks."

Lilly tried to reconcile the irate man she knew now with what she was hearing from a woman who had no reason to paint him in a good light. "I understand he was a very well-known doctor."

"I'm alive today because of Dr. Wakefield," Odette said emphatically. "There ain't nothing I wouldn't do for him."

"Same here. Come on, Odette; let's go on up." Samuel grasped his wife's arm, then glanced back at Lilly. "You're coming, Miss Crawford?"

She didn't want to, but from the way they were looking at her, they expected her to accompany them. If she wanted them and Dr. Delacroix to see her as Dr. Wakefield's caregiver, she had to act that way. "Of course."

Lilly's legs felt as if her shoes were made of lead as she followed the Tuckers up the staircase. The kind, caring Dr. Wakefield they knew was gone, and in his place was an angry, unpredictable man who wanted to be left alone. She'd be lucky if he didn't fire her on the spot.

The Tuckers paused in front of their employer's door and turned in unison toward Lilly, who was several steps behind. Since they gave no indication that they were going to knock, Lilly realized they were waiting for her to do so. Apparently they had accepted her as Dr. Wakefield's caregiver and planned on following her lead.

Giving the worried couple a wan smile, Lilly stepped in front of the door and knocked, praying Dr. Wakefield wouldn't ignore them or, worse, open the door and fire her. "Dr. Wakefield? Mr. and Mrs. Tucker are here. They came up to say good morning." Silence.

Dread slithered down her spine. "Dr. Wakefield?"

"Coming."

The gruff voice surprised Lilly. He'd spoken only once through the door. Either he couldn't wait to greet the Tuckers again or he couldn't wait to be rid of her.

The door opened by slow degrees. Dr. Wakefield stood to one side, revealing only a hand-span width of his face and body. He wore what could probably pass for a smile in bad light, one of the shirts Lilly had washed and pressed and the jeans he had on Sunday. His hair was combed, but his beard badly needed shaping. "Hello, Samuel. Odette."

The couple's eyes widened as they took in the changes in the man they hadn't seen since his blindness. Uncertain, they glanced at each other, then back at Dr. Wakefield.

"Morning, Dr. Wakefield," Samuel greeted him, sticking out his hand only to snatch it back in embarrassment.

"Morning, Dr. Wake—" That was as far as Odette got before the tears started again. "I'm sorry." Her voice hitched. "I–I just can't help it."

Adam's fingers on the door frame tightened.

Lilly felt the situation deteriorating and jumped in to help. "Mr. and Mrs. Tucker came up as soon as they arrived," she said, trying to get the conversation going again.

"If we had known how much you needed us, we'd have come back sooner," Samuel said.

"Don't you worry about a thing, Dr. Wakefield. Samuel and I will take care of the place just like we always have."

Adam flinched.

"Why don't we go downstairs and get acquainted?" Lilly suggested.

Odette frowned at her. "Don't you need to stay up here?"

"No!" Adam shouted.

Odette jumped; her weathered face crumpled. She reached for her soggy handkerchief.

"Dr. Wakefield prefers his privacy. Besides, I need to start lunch and wash the bed linen," Lilly said.

"Don't worry about lunch. Dr. Wakefield has always loved my boiled shrimp." Odette beamed, sure of herself in this at least. "Won't be no bother to peel them for him."

Lilly helplessly watched Adam withdraw moment by moment. "How about a jambalaya? That way both of you will be saved the task I always disliked. Is that all right with you, Dr. Wakefield?"

"Yes. Excuse me." His face a rigid mask, he closed the door.

Odette teared up. "I said all the wrong things."

Lilly placed her hand around the trembling shoulder of the older woman. "Showing love and compassion is never wrong. It has to be difficult for you and his family. I didn't know him before, so I have no expectations."

"He was always up when we arrived and in the kitchen, coffee made, waiting for me to cook breakfast while he read the paper or one of his medical journals." Odette's round face saddened. "He was a fine man."

Odette's reference to Dr. Wakefield in the past tense, as if he were dead, disturbed Lilly. "His blindness doesn't make him less of a man. His actions do that."

"But he was a neurosurgeon," Odette reminded her.

"He can't perform neurosurgery, but that doesn't mean his life is over; it means it takes a different direction," Lilly said, thinking of the new direction in her own life. "The first step is regaining his pride and independence."

"How do we help?" Samuel asked.

"By letting him know he's not totally helpless."

"Like letting him peel his shrimp?" Samuel asked slowly.

"If it comes to that," Lilly said, then continued, "But I have a confession to make. I need help myself in fixing the jambalaya."

Odette immediately perked up. "You come with me, child, and I'll show you. We'll have Dr. Wakefield smacking his lips and asking for more." With that, Odette started back downstairs.

Samuel twisted his straw hat in his hands. "Can I speak with you a minute, Miss Crawford?"

"Of course," she told him, trying to keep the fear from her face. "Please call me Lilly."

172

The older man nodded his gray head. "Thank you for helping my wife."

The tension eased out of her. "I've stood in Odette's shoes," Lilly admitted ruefully. Unfortunately, she probably would be there again.

"All I can say is that I'm glad you're here."

She finally smiled. "So am I." She just hoped she could stay.

He was batting a thousand.

How many more mistakes could he make? How could he have forgotten how emotional Odette was? Perhaps because his housekeeper in San Francisco had been a practical woman whose only concern was that her paycheck be on time. Since she was efficient and trustworthy, kept his house immaculate, was a fairly decent cook, and left him alone after his blindness, they'd gotten along fine.

Odette was a hoverer and worrier. She meant well, but she'd drive both of them crazy within a day. There was no way he could let her care for him. She probably had it in her head to try to pay him back for his help in diagnosing her diabetes. There was no need. Doctors were dedicated to heal, but they weren't infallible. They made mistakes.

He prayed daily that his case wasn't one

of those mistakes, that waiting was the right decision, that the new studies on going past the three weeks and allowing the vitreous hemorrhage to dissolve rather than operating and possibly damaging the optic nerve or causing retinal detachment were sound. In the meantime, what did he do about a replacement for Odette?

He had a feeling that if Jonathan had anything to do with hiring a replacement, his choice would probably be a retired nurse who was inflexible, pushy, and a royal pain in the gluteus maximus.

Making his way to the window, Adam turned his face into the soft wind that carried with it the smell of magnolias and roses. There was no way of getting around it. He had to accept the inevitable. As much as it annoyed him, Lilly Crawford would have to stay. Better the devil you knew than the one you didn't know. At least he could control her. He'd just have to make sure it stayed that way.

Lilly could easily see why the Tuckers were so well-liked and respected by the Wakefields and Dr. Delacroix. The elderly couple quickly made Lilly feel accepted. While helping her fix breakfast for Dr. Wakefield, Odette told Lilly about her large family, which included seven children, all boys. The youngest of her fifteen

grandchildren was a seven-month-old pow-
erhouse named Cameron, the first male of
his generation and spoiled rotten.

This time, hearing about other people's
children didn't sadden Lilly. One day she'd
have her own. Once again she thanked
God that Myron had never gotten her
pregnant.

By the time Samuel finished his cup of
coffee and left to cut the yard on the riding
lawn mower, Odette had almost finished
assembling the varied ingredients for the
jambalaya. Telling the housekeeper she'd
be back shortly, Lilly picked up Dr.
Wakefield's breakfast tray, took it to his
room, and knocked.

"Dr. Wakefield, your breakfast."

The door swung open immediately. "It's
about time."

She opened her mouth to tell him breakfast was just a few minutes later than
usual, then snapped her mouth shut. Even
before reading it in the textbook, she had
figured out that blind people, like most
sighted people, had no definite sense of
time passing unless they had a clock. In
the times she had been in Dr. Wakefield's
room, she hadn't seen one.

"Yes, sir." Stepping past him, she set the
tray on the bed, then glanced around the
room. Beautifully decorated, but layered in
dust. The rugs scattered on the floor

needed to be spot-cleaned to get the food stains out. She peered closer at something small and black moving on the area rug.

Ants. "My goodness."

"What is it?" he asked, his tone sharp.

Her head came up sharply. "Your . . . your —"

"Spit it out. My food is getting cold."

"Your room needs cleaning."

His full, sensuous lips tightened. "That will be all."

"You have pancakes at twelve. Would you like light, medium, or heavy syrup on them?"

"I can manage."

"Pan sausage at six, sectioned grapefruit in a separate dish at nine. I'll pick up the tray later." This time when she passed, she didn't look back. Downstairs she strolled into the kitchen, proud of herself that she hadn't cowered; then she saw the worry in Odette's heavily lined face.

"What is it?"

"Mrs. Wakefield called while you were upstairs. She wants you to come to the cottage immediately."

She was going to be fired.

There was no other reason Lilly could think of for Mrs. Wakefield wanting to see her. For some reason she must have changed her mind. Hadn't they decided

176

yesterday they'd keep in touch by phone unless something very important came up? She'd classify getting fired as important.

Fighting the stinging moisture in her eyes, Lilly took the paved winding brick walkway through the gardens to the cottage. Scarlet impatiens and pansies led the way. Farther back, clumps of yellow jasmine and honeysuckle scented the air. Warm pinks, hot yellows, mellow blues, brilliant reds stood out in the lush green foliage.

The house came into view when the path straightened. Deep purple tulips lined the walkway to the house. Lilly felt like Little Red Riding Hood going to Grandmother's where the Big Bad Wolf waited. But Little Red Riding Hood had a home to run to. Lilly had nothing and no one.

Pausing, she heard the soft purr of an engine, then saw a black limousine come up the paved drive and stop in front of the cottage. The driver got out and opened the back door. A large gray German shepherd hopped out, then paused. Next came a slender white woman neatly dressed in a tailored navy blue suit and white blouse. Leaning down, she closed her hand over the harness on the animal's back.

The red front door opened before they were halfway up the brick walk. Eleanor came out of the house and quickly went to meet the woman, her slender hand out-stretched. "Mrs. Parker, I'm Eleanor Wakefield. Thank you for coming."

"Hello, Mrs. Wakefield, and thank Jonathan. Good obstetricians are hard to find."

Eleanor barely managed to keep her face impassive at the mention of Jonathan's name. No wonder she'd been able to set up an appointment with a representative of the Lighthouse so quickly. "You're expecting?"

"Yes." The auburn-haired woman beamed. "Three months and counting."

"Congratulations, and it's a good thing I planned on serving tea. This way, and please call me Eleanor."

"I will if you'll call me Harriet, although I've abhorred my first name all of my life."

Eleanor smiled, liking the woman immediately. "Eleanor wouldn't have been my choice, either. The door is directly ahead and up two steps."

"Got it."

As she turned to go up the steps, Eleanor saw Lilly on the other side of the limo, watching them. "Lilly, please come inside and meet Mrs. Parker."

Tension whipped through Lilly. She was about to meet her replacement.

Inside, Lilly's worried gaze immediately went to the visitor sitting on the sofa with a perfectly held and balanced cup of tea in

178

her hands, then dropped to the Seeing Eye dog on the floor beside her feet, his head resting contentedly on his large paws.

"Thank you for coming, Lilly. Harriet Parker, Lilly Crawford, the woman who is caring for my son."

"Pleased to meet you," Harriet said, extending her hand.

Lilly jumped to take the offered hand. "I — yes, ma'am."

Harriet laughed, a bell-like sound. "You don't sound that young and I'm not that old."

At any other time Lilly might have laughed with the woman, but her nerves were stretched too thin. Lilly sat on the edge of the armchair, her back straight.

"Would you like some tea, Lilly?"

"No, thank you." All she wanted to know was how long she had left to work.

Eleanor placed her delicate cup and saucer on the polished cherry table. "I've asked Mrs. Parker here to help us both understand what is happening to my son and to ask your forgiveness, Lilly."

"Me?" Lilly's eyes rounded.

"Yesterday after you left, I realized I put you in an impossible situation when I asked you to care for Adam," Eleanor admitted. "But, as you pointed out, you have accomplished a great deal with him, and with the proper help you can do much more."

"I believe that's where I come in." Harriet set her cup on the polished table.

Both women watched her smooth movements, and although neither voiced it aloud, they compared them to Adam's awkwardness. "Harriet is a social worker with the Shreveport Lighthouse for the Blind." Picking up a pillow, Eleanor hugged it to her. "I have to believe Adam is going to regain his sight, but he needs help in the meantime."

"He hates being blind," Lilly said softly.

"Would either of you feel differently in his place?" Harriet sat forward, her face serious.

"No." Their answers came in unison.

"Honesty without explanations. We're off to a good start. Let's get something out of the way. I lost my sight seven years ago after an auto accident. I wasn't happy about it. The doctors were stupid and incompetent. I was sure if I could find the right one, he'd fix my eyes. It took long, torturous weeks before I got mad enough to stop feeling sorry for myself and come out fighting.

"What I'm about to say may not be easy to hear, but it's necessary if you're to help Dr. Wakefield. The best scenario is that he regains his sight. The worst is that he doesn't. In the interim, each time he is forced to confront his blindness he's going

180

to strike out until he comes to terms with it and realizes his loss of sight doesn't make him less of a man."

"He studied so long and hard to be a neurosurgeon." Eleanor's voice quivered with strain. "How can you or anyone expect him to give that up without being angry?"

Harriet shook her head of short auburn curls. "I didn't say that. Anger is good. Directed in the right way, it can accomplish a great deal. From what Jonathan and you have told me, your son's anger is directed at himself and occasionally at those around him. Is that right?"

Eleanor shook her head, her lips pressed tightly together.

"Yes." The answer came from Lilly.

Harriet turned toward her. "Your job will be the toughest, because you'll butt heads with him at every turn. From what I've heard from Jonathan, Dr. Wakefield is a strong, determined man. He's had to be to get to the top of his profession at his age. Now, he'll use those same traits to thwart anyone who might oppose him. It won't be easy. I don't know how tough you are, but to help you will have to be."

Lilly swallowed her fear. "Dr. Wakefield can be intimidating, but I can manage."

Laughter bubbled from Harriet. "Good for you. I don't envy you your job. You'll have to push him and he'll push back. I'm married to a doctor, and they can be as arrogant as they come."

Lilly caught a flash of light as Harriet picked up her cup and took a sip of tea. A huge diamond ring glinted on her ring finger. Lilly had a band Myron later told her he'd gotten from the pawnshop for fifteen dollars. He'd said more than once that he'd paid too much. She'd left it on his kitchen table.

"Your wedding ring is beautiful."

"And ostentatious. Did I mention doctors are territorial?" Harriet's smile blossomed. "Men are strange creatures, doctors even stranger. The man who attacked Dr. Wakefield not only stole his eyesight, but his identity."

She looked toward both women before continuing. "I don't have to tell you that a neurosurgeon is one of the most esteemed of doctors. In their profession, they operate on the very essence of man. Now Dr. Wakefield finds it difficult, if not impossible, to do simple tasks a four-year-old would run through.

"Being blind isn't easy. Your senses are constantly on alert, your brain working to identify your surroundings. Initially, you may sleep a great deal to rest your brain from all the overload of activity." Placing the cup on the table, she lifted both hands

182

palms out. Her nails were neatly polished a delicate pink.

"The pads of your fingertips become your eyes. You can see the window behind me. I feel the warmth of sunshine on my neck, but if it were dark I wouldn't be able to do that. With the aid of my cane and the sound wave bouncing back from tapping the area around me, I'd know there was a solid object ahead of me, approximately how far away it was. But not until I touched it could I identify it."

"How long did it take you to learn that?" Eleanor asked, her tea forgotten.

"Six long, arduous months. But it depends how much time and effort you're willing to put into the process."

"Adam will be seeing by then," Mrs. Wakefield said, but her voice lacked conviction.

"In the meantime, how much quality of life is he having now?" Harriet asked.

"He's miserable," Lilly found herself answering once again. "He wants to be independent so badly and can't."

"He can't because he refuses to learn or because no one has shown him how?" Harriet asked, her question hanging in the air.

"That's probably my fault, because I didn't want to push the issue. I didn't want him to think I had lost hope," Eleanor confessed.

"That's understandable, but what about now? Shouldn't the idea at least be presented to him?"

"Lilly and Jonathan think so," Eleanor said slowly. "I just don't know. He's so angry and defiant. He doesn't want any of his family near him."

"Then you'll have to either defy him or get someone else to broach the subject with him or teach him without him knowing he's being taught. But I warn you, trying to teach a person who doesn't want to learn anything is next to impossible. I know; I've tried."

Eleanor glanced at Lilly. Although the older woman didn't say anything, the speculation was clear on her face.

"But if you get past the denial and the anger, you can open up a whole new world for him. There are optical scanners that can read print, all sorts of devices that will allow him to gain independence. Orientation and Mobility classes can teach him how to get around independently." Reaching into the bag, she pulled out a bright orange pocket folder and held it toward Eleanor. "Here's some information you both might find handy on devices and programs."

"Thank you." Eleanor briefly opened the folder, then passed it to Lilly, who hesitated only for a moment before taking it.

"I've probably given you more questions than answers, but each case is different. Just like some people prefer a cane and others a guide dog."

"He's beautiful," Lilly said, her slim arms wrapped around the folder.

Harriet patted the dog's head affectionately. "Thanks, and I heartily agree. He's quite undeserving of the name my husband insisted we call him."

"What name?" Eleanor asked.

"Killer." At the mention of his name, the dog lifted his head and stared at his mistress. "Lloyd wanted any would-be attacker to know beforehand what he might be getting tangled up with."

"That sounds sensible," Eleanor said.

"In case either of you are wondering, I met Lloyd two years after I lost my sight. He says he never worked so hard in his life to get a date." She laughed again, free and guileless.

Lilly listened to the sound and again wondered why she, with sight, hadn't chosen as well.

Lifting her fingertips to the face of her watch, Harriet stood. Killer rose with her. "I'm sorry to rush off, but I have another appointment at ten."

"Thank you for coming." Eleanor came to her feet.

"My pleasure. I haven't ridden in a lim-

185

ousine since my wedding. Don't hesitate to call if you'd like to talk. It's going to take tough love for Dr. Wakefield's wake-up call. He may curse you now, but he'll sing your praises later. Good-bye."

Both women walked Harriet to the waiting limousine, then watched it drive away.

"What do you think?" Eleanor asked.

Lilly answered honestly. "He'd be happier if he were more independent, but he's going to fight me."

Eleanor's gaze was probing and direct. "Underneath all that rage and self-pity is the proud, determined man I raised. Help me; help him."

"Does that mean you aren't going to fire me even if he or Dr. Delacroix asks you to?"

"Do you think I'd have asked you to meet Harriet if I was considering that alternative?"

Lilly felt fear and relief at the same time. "No."

Eleanor extended her hand. "Good. Then we're in this together for the long haul, no matter what."

Lilly stared at the brilliant colors surrounding her, the cloudless blue sky, and the colorful flowers and immediately thought of the black abyss Adam lived in. She lifted her hand. "No matter what."

Chapter Eight

She was a fraud. Dr. Wakefield knew it; she knew it.

The folder in her lap, Lilly sat on the stone bench beneath the lacy canopy of a lantern tree. Dumb luck had allowed her to make some inroads with Dr. Wakefield, but if Harriet Parker was right, and Lilly had every reason to believe she was, a good amount of cunning and skill would be needed to effect a change in Dr. Wakefield. Two things Lilly didn't have.

She was setting herself up for failure if she tried to do more than care for Dr. Wakefield's basic needs. Why had she told Mrs. Wakefield she'd try?

Because you're crazy, she thought, then closed her eyes and leaned her head against the coarse bark of the tree trunk. If only it were that simple. She couldn't forget the first time she saw Dr. Wakefield. Lost and lonely, defeated and defiant, and so very frightened.

She knew what it was to be lost and lonely, defeated and frightened. She was learning defiance. In some ways, Dr. Wakefield was her counterpart. Perhaps in helping him face his demons, she could learn to face hers.

Clutching the folder to her chest, she rose and went inside the house. There was a phone call she had to make.

Upstairs in her bedroom, Lilly stared at the white telephone on her nightstand. Fear almost consumed her. *Just make the call,* she ordered herself, but she made no move to do so. It wasn't as if Myron could trace the call. She was in control of her life now, and it was time she started acting like it.

Without further hesitation, she snatched up the phone and dialed. The drawling voice on the other end answered on the third ring, "Good morning. The law office of Kenneth Powell. Can I help you?"

Lilly licked her dry lips. "This is Lilly Crawford. Mr. Powell asked me to call him this morning."

"May I ask what this is in regard to, Mrs. Crawford?"

"To find out if my — my husband was served with divorce papers yet."

"Please hold. I'll see if Mr. Powell is available."

Lilly mumbled, "Yes." Eyes closed, she silently prayed, *Please let it be all right. Please le—*

"Mrs. Crawford."

Her eyelids flew upward. "Yes."

"Your husband was served the papers this morning."

"Thank God." Her trembling legs were unable to support her any longer. She sagged down on the bed.

"He also almost got himself arrested."

"What?"

"According to the officer who served the papers, Mr. Crawford became confrontational toward him after reading you had cited mental cruelty in your petition," Mr. Powell explained. "The only reason he wasn't taken in was because he appeared so distraught to the officer. Your husband kept saying how he'd lost his mother and now the woman he loved."

"He never loved me," Lilly hissed, coming to her feet.

"He filed a missing persons report on you when you didn't come home Thursday evening. Friday night, your church held an all-night prayer vigil for your safe return."

Lilly was stunned, then realized she shouldn't have been. Myron always seemed to beat her. No matter what she did, it was never good enough. "He won again."

"This isn't a popularity contest, Mrs. Crawford."

"Yes, it is," she said quietly. She didn't try to explain to her lawyer that she'd been trying to get the people of Little Elm to respect her for as long as she could remember. For a while she had succeeded, but now . . .

"He seems to think you ran off with a man."

Lilly couldn't think of an answer to that outrageous lie, so she said nothing. Myron was playing his role of the forsaken husband for all it was worth. She'd probably be stoned if she went back to Little Elm.

"Where are you calling from?" Mr. Powell asked in the lengthening silence.

She frowned. Was there a hint of distrust in his voice? "You believe him, don't you?"

"You're my client," he answered.

"That's not what I asked you."

"According to the officer I spoke with a short while ago, there were tears in Mr. Crawford's eyes when he came to the police station Thursday night. The officer understood how hard it was on him to be hit with the divorce papers while at work."

Lilly sat on the bed again. The worst possible way for Myron to find out was on his job. It would be all over the plant in a matter of hours that she'd filed for divorce, but Myron would keep the reason to himself. To save face, he'd do everything in his power to tarnish her reputation. It wouldn't matter that for the past six years there had not been one whisper of gossip about her, that she'd been a faithful member of the church, a faithful wife, a caring daughter-in-law.

Instead they'd remember who her mother was and, with Myron here to play the deserted, wronged husband, Lilly's reputation would be irrevocably ruined.

She'd lost again. She'd never felt so alone in her entire life.

"I remember the bruise on your face the day you came to make an appointment."

The statement caught her off guard and had her palming her left cheek. "You do?"

"Your husband has a volatile temper. It's a matter of record after his near-confrontation with the officer who served the papers."

Hope flittered through her. "Then . . . then you do believe me?"

"If I didn't, I wouldn't have taken your case. Are you in New Orleans?"

"I never made it," she said. "My car broke down, but I got a job outside Shreveport."

"Good. Give me the phone number. I'll keep you posted on how things progress. Since there's no community property, we're probably looking at forty-five to sixty days."

"I only want my freedom," Lilly said, then gave him the phone number.

"I'll be in touch."

Lilly hung up the phone, trembling not with fear this time but with fury. Myron had destroyed her dreams; now he wanted to destroy the reputation she'd tried so hard to build. This time she'd fight. He'd taken the last thing from her.

Picking up the folder, she started reading through it again. She could do this for one simple reason. She had no choice.

Pick your battles.

Mother Crawford had always maintained that people who were smart chose when to walk and when and if they took a stand. Lilly could only hope that she had chosen the right time because, before another day came, she was going to clean Dr. Wakefield's room.

"Where do you want your dining table?"

"What?" Adam asked, guarding the entrance to his room Tuesday afternoon.

"Your dining table," Lilly explained. If they were going to normalize his routine as Mrs. Parker had suggested, he needed to eat at a table, and not on the bed or floor. "It's about the height and width of a card table, except this one is inlaid and has scalloped sides. By the balcony would be nice so you can catch the breeze and hear the birds singing."

Adam's face turned mutinous. "I don't want any more furniture in here."

Lilly wasn't surprised by his answer. She hadn't expected him to like anything else getting in his way, but she had also thought of a way of getting around any objections. "Your mother sent it. I'm sure she's going to ask about it when she calls tonight or tomorrow."

"She's going to call?"

"Wouldn't you in her place? Where should I put it?"

Adam started to step back, then paused. Furrows raced across his forehead. "How heavy is the thing? Do you need to get Samuel?"

Surprised by his concern, Lilly blinked. "No. It's not very heavy."

"How heavy is not very?" he pressed.

"I've lifted grocery sacks that were heavier," she told him truthfully. "Now where would you like for me to put it?"

"There's an upholstered side chair by the door leading to the balcony."

"Good choice."

Placing the table in front of the chair, she left his room to get his tray. She set it on the table. "Roast turkey sandwich at twelve. Potato salad at six. Green salad at nine. Iced tea. I put your stereo control on the tray to your far left. The stereo is about forty-five degrees to the left of your table. Enjoy your lunch. Oh, yes, Odette said to leave room for dinner tonight. Chicken breasts stuffed with cornbread dressing."

Adam closed the door. Carefully he made his way to the table, circled it, then sat down. Using his hands, he ran them across the sides of the table, then moved inward to find his napkin and flatware. He picked up his sandwich, bit, and chewed.

He was halfway through his meal before realizing his neck and back weren't stiff from hunching over his plate and his butt didn't hurt. He took another bite and leaned back in his chair without worrying about balancing the tray or spilling food. Maybe he'd call his mother tonight to tell her he appreciated her trusting him enough to go home and thank her for the table.

"I saw ants this morning in your room," Lilly informed Dr. Wakefield the moment she picked up his dinner tray. She'd briefly spoken with Harriet by phone that morning, and the social worker had been very specific on being firm and consistent with Dr. Wakefield.

Folding his arms, Adam leisurely crossed his long legs at the ankles. He leaned back in his leather chair, more relaxed than she'd ever seen him. Stuffed probably. For the first time he hadn't stood guard over the door. He was probably too full to move after eating two huge stuffed chicken breasts, a tossed green salad, four corn-bread muffins, and a huge chunk of

German chocolate cake.

"There are no ants in here."

His smug assurance, sitting there all clean in clothes she had washed and ironed, his belly full, irritated her no end. She and Odette worked hard to fix his meals. Men!

Dishes rattled as she plopped the tray back on the table. Grabbing his hand, she drew it toward the floor.

Immediately he stiffened and tried to pull away. "What are you doing?"

"Proving I'm no liar."

He snatched his hand away. "Are you crazy or just sadistic?"

"You may want to live in an ant-infested room and I might consider letting you if I didn't have to come in here."

"That's what you're paid to do," he snapped. She aggravated him no end.

"I'm also paid to clean this room and it's not getting done." She tried a new tack. "First ants, then roaches. I remember when I was in elementary school and one crawled into Deloris' ear when she was in bed sleep—"

"There are no roaches in here!" he shouted.

More accustomed to his loud outbursts, she didn't move a muscle. "Yet."

"Well, clean the damn room." He waited for her to say something to aggravate him again, but nothing came. Neither had she gone out the door. He always knew when she came and went. The scent of roses trailed in her wake.

His head twisted to one side. "Say something. You're still there. I hear you breathing."

"You cursed me. I won't have that anymore."

"What?" She could easily give him a headache.

"You cursed me," she repeated, her voice trembling.

The hurt tone got to him if nothing else did. "I did not curse you."

The silence that came this time was longer; then he heard her footsteps and the opening of the door. "I haven't dismissed you yet."

The door banged shut. He was out of the chair before he knew it. He reached the door in seven steps instead of ten and jerked it open. "Come back here, Lilly." Faintly he heard the thump of feet running down the stairs.

He took another step toward the sound, then caught himself. He became disoriented too easily to leave the room. What if he fell down the stairs and injured himself worse?

Frantically he turned, his heart thumping loudly in his chest. The rhythm only abated when he was inside his room again with the door closed. She could go to the moon for all he cared. Save him the trouble of firing her.

Taking his seat, he leaned back in his chair, found the controls, and switched on the stereo, listening to an aria from the opera *Madame Butterfly.* Unconsciously he also listened for the sound of his door opening.

Lilly got as far as the garden on the north side of the house. Adam's room was on the south side. Her temper spent, she sat on a stone bench amid blooming azaleas and daffodils. She'd never been able to stay angry at people for long. That's how Myron had gotten by with so much. He didn't have to make excuses for his behavior; she made them for him.

She should have washed his favorite shirt. Should have fried the chicken crispier. Should have kept the house cleaner. She should have been better, smarter, prettier. Her best was never good enough. She'd bowed down without a word. She'd tried so hard not to be her mother's daughter that she'd let him take her self-respect and grind it beneath his feet.

Holding her head up, she closed her eyes and let her face meet the sun. Taking a deep breath, she let the clean air clear her head. She'd started out trying to persuade Dr. Wakefield to let her clean his room and ended up doing what she had always wanted and never had the courage to do, stand up to Myron.

Her head hung between her shoulders. She'd snuck off like a thief from Myron. The words she wanted to hurl at him burned her throat like acid. She detested him for what he had done to her and herself for letting him do it. He'd stolen her dreams and she had silently let him. She'd stayed for Rafe and Mother Crawford, but she'd never had the courage to stand up to Myron. Instead, she had let him make her life a living hell.

But she had a chance now, and she wasn't going to let anyone stand in her way . . . and that included Dr. Wakefield.

The knock caught Adam by surprise. He knew it was Lilly. He recognized the tentative two taps, pause, two taps. He thought if she returned, she'd storm back in the same way she'd stormed out. Too bad he couldn't tell her to storm right back out. "Come in."

"I've come for your tray." The door closed quietly. "What do you want for breakfast?"

"I detest women who sulk."

"How about oatmeal?"

He hated oatmeal, and since Lilly had never mentioned the ghastly cereal or cooked it for him before, she probably knew it. Reminding himself that the devil he knew was better, he said, "All right. I apologize if I offended your sensibilities."

"Now you're making fun of me."

From her affronted tone he could well imagine her frowning at him. For the first time he wondered what she looked like. "I wasn't making fun of you. I was thinking of what I've come to, discussing so trivial a subject as ants."

"You won't think that if they bite you."

"I guess not."

"I'll just get the tray and say good night if there is nothing else you need." The door opened again.

His head lifted from the back of the chair. "You're going to leave me alone again, with ants crawling everywhere? What if I'm allergic to them?"

"Are you?"

"I haven't been bitten since I was a child, but I could have developed toxins."

"Speak English."

"Become allergic to the bites. So . . . please clean up this room."

"All right," she said, trying to sound put out but silently overjoyed. She'd done it! "I don't want you swelling up like Herbert after his bee sting. His face was so tight and red he looked like a baked sweet potato before you stick a fork into it and let the air out."

"Lilly, you do have a way with words."

Adam's words lingering in her thoughts, Lilly left to get the cleaning supplies. She had no idea if he had complimented her or insulted her. Probably insulted her. She did talk more around him, but it was so he wouldn't feel so disconnected with his surroundings and could "picture" what was going on around him. She was still developing that steel in her backbone.

An hour later, Lilly surveyed Adam's clean room with pleasure. The air smelled faintly of lemon furniture polish and pine cleaner. Every surface, including the hardwood oak floor, gleamed. Not a particle of food remained on the area rugs.

"I hope you're finished," Adam said from his chair, scratching his beard-covered face. "The racket from the vacuum cleaner is aggravating."

"So are ant bites." Lilly picked up the bucket containing her supplies with one hand and the vacuum cleaner with the other. "Is your beard itching?"

Adam immediately stopped scratching. "No."

"Rafe tried to grow one once but gave it

up because he said it itched like a bear. You're sure you don't want to shave it off?"

It briefly ran through Adam's mind to ask who Rafe was; then he decided against it. "Positive. Now, how about an omelet for breakfast?"

The UPS truck and Samuel and Odette arrived the same time Wednesday morning. UPS had tried Monday and Tuesday but hadn't been able to find the house. They probably would have still been looking if Eleanor hadn't called Tuesday afternoon to see why the delivery hadn't been made. Now that it was here Lilly could only shake her head at the three large cardboard boxes on the porch. "His sister must have sent all of his clothes."

Samuel picked up a box before answering. "Doubt it. Dr. Wakefield had a lot of clothes."

Odette grinned, showing an overbite. "He's a good-looking man and he knows how to dress. Caused a stir wherever he went. The time he took me to the emergency room, I had so many nurses in my room you couldn't move." She picked up a box and ignored Samuel's narrowed eyes. "Whenever he was here, I didn't have any trouble getting extra help cleaning up the place."

Intrigued and remembering the muscles delineating his back, Lilly flushed and picked up the third box. "You don't say."

"You women put those back down. I can take these up myself," Samuel told them.

"Women aren't helpless," Odette said and entered the house.

"Stubborn woman," Samuel mumbled and followed.

Slowly Lilly trailed behind them. There had been annoyance in Samuel's voice, but concern and love as well. Two things Lilly had never known from a man and no longer particularly cared if she ever did.

Her current concern was more pressing: how to get Dr. Wakefield to accept the clothes without becoming angry. Lilly might have sounded confident to his mother, but she wasn't so sure as she climbed the stairs.

As she expected, Odette and Samuel set their boxes down across from the doorway, leaving room for her box . . . and for her to knock. Despite her trepidation, Lilly placed her box in front of Dr. Wakefield's door and did just that.

"Dr. Wakefield. Dr. Wakefield." Trying not to show her concern when there was no answer, she knocked again. "Dr. Wakefield. Dr. Wakefield."

The door jerked open. "I'm not deaf, although you could make a man wish he were. My breakfast won't get that cold."

Lilly's eyes widened. He stood in the doorway, his jeans unsnapped, a white towel around his neck. Moisture beaded on his muscular chest. Obviously he had been in the shower.

"I . . ." her voice croaked. She swallowed. Except in magazines, she'd never seen a more perfectly sculpted body. And even scowling with his shades on, he was a strikingly handsome man.

"Well, bring it in," he ordered, standing back.

Lilly bent to pick up the box, then straightened. "It's not your breakfast. There was a UPS delivery. Three boxes. Odette and Samuel helped me bring them up."

"Odette's here?" he said, quickly shoving the door partially closed.

Lilly frowned. What had gotten into him?

Behind her, Odette laughed. "I've seen a man's naked chest before, Dr. Wakefield."

"You should have said you weren't alone sooner. Let me get a shirt." The door snapped shut.

Lilly barely repressed a sigh. Would there ever be a day when Dr. Wakefield didn't reprimand her about something?

The door opened again. Dr. Wakefield had on a shirt, unevenly buttoned. "What's in them?"

"Let us put them down and get them opened first," Lilly answered. Samuel already had his pocketknife out slicing through the mailing tape. Lilly went behind him, pulling back the top and inspecting the contents. "Clothes."

"Clothes," Dr. Wakefield repeated slowly.

"Enough so that I won't have to wash for a long time. I'll come back later to put everything up," she told him.

"I'll help," Odette quickly offered.

"If you don't mind, I'd rather you cook me a peach cobbler instead," Adam said, slowly turning toward the direction the housekeeper's voice had come from.

Odette's flagging smile brightened. "Loaded with peaches and lots of crust, just the way you like it."

"As I recall, Samuel likes his cobbler the same way."

Pleased that Adam remembered, the older man nodded his gray head. "You have a good memory, Dr. Wakefield."

"I won't keep you then," Adam said mildly.

Realizing they had been dismissed even if the older couple didn't, Lilly said, "All right. The boxes are directly in front of your five-drawer dresser. The first box is short-sleeved knit shirts; the second box is jeans and slacks; the third box is suits with shirts and ties. The clothes in the first two boxes are pretty much mix-and-match in earth tones. The closet is about fifteen feet away to the left of the dresser. Your omelet will be served in thirty minutes."

Long after the door closed, Adam remained where he was. He knew who was responsible for the clothes. Making his way to the phone at his bedside, he picked up the receiver and punched in 0 for operator assistance. For the first time, he didn't feel as much animosity in explaining why he needed her to dial the number for him.

The answer came on the third ring. "Hello."

"Hello, Mother."

"Adam? What is it? Are you all right?"

The flurry of questions and love behind them caused him to tighten his hand briefly on the receiver, then briefly tuck his head in shame. He certainly hadn't acted like a loving son in the past weeks. "I'm fine. I just wanted to thank you for the table and the clothes. They arrived this morning."

"You aren't upset with me?" she asked, surprise obvious in her voice.

Adam felt worse. "I should be the one asking that question."

"I love you, Adam."

To his mother love meant everything. "I know leaving me here wasn't easy. Thank you for giving me the time and space."

"Oh, Adam," her voice wavered, hitched.

Adam fought the sudden lump in his own throat. "Don't cry. I'm going to come through this. It'll be all right."

"Of course you are."

He knew one certain thing that would cheer her up. "Kristen's graduation is coming up, and we have to be there, don't we?"

"Yes, we do," Eleanor agreed, her voice stronger.

"Good-bye, and thanks again."

"Good-bye, Adam." Eleanor hung up the phone, guilt battling with happiness in her heart. Not once since the accident had Adam called her. Now, the first time he had, it was because of her subterfuge.

Folding her arms, Eleanor leaned her back against the cabinet in the kitchen where she had been preparing a cup of coffee. She believed in honesty. She hadn't been honest with Adam, certainly not with Jonathan. Both incidents troubled her. With Adam, she had made the only decision possible. With Jonathan, she wasn't so sure.

Picking up the carafe, she poured coffee into a mug and sipped. In college she had quickly learned to take her coffee black and strong. Sugar and cream diluted the caffeine kick she needed to stay awake and alert to study.

Of its own volition, her mind returned to Jonathan. She'd met him her first year in med school. He'd never been dismissive of her as a woman studying to be a doctor, as some of the other male students had been. He'd been fun-loving, the complete opposite of serious Randolph.

Her coffee forgotten, Eleanor stared out the window. She hadn't a choice when Randolph was taken away from her. She had with Jonathan, and she couldn't help wondering if she had made the right decision.

She missed Jonathan's calming presence, his ability to make her laugh and not take herself too seriously. At any other time, she'd be on the phone telling him about Adam's call, sharing her happiness with him. She'd never realized how much he'd insinuated himself in her life, how much she looked forward to sharing with him, being with him.

But Sunday had changed things somehow. Until she was sure of how to handle the subtle shift in their friendship, she wasn't going to see him.

Of course he'd called, but she'd always told him she was too busy to talk. Taking the coffee with her into the living room, she looked around the beautiful, immaculate room. She's never been less busy in her life. In San Francisco she had a full calendar. Here she moped and worried.

Not anymore. Returning to the kitchen, she poured out her coffee and rinsed her cup. She should be celebrating, not moping in the cottage. And that was exactly what she was going to do.

Chapter Nine

Adam's progress was slow. More than one curse word had slipped past his lips as he'd unpacked the box of shirts. *How could one man have this many clothes?* he asked himself, then grimaced.

If he recalled correctly, he had four closets full. He liked to look nice and had always had the money to buy what he wanted.

A knock sounded on his door. He recognized it as Lilly's. He picked up another shirt before answering, "Come in." He didn't know why, only that it was important that she was aware that he didn't need help.

"A ham-and-cheese omelet at twelve, hash browns at six." The tray rattled slightly as she set it on the table. "You're doing a good job of unpacking."

Somehow her words bothered him. "You didn't think I could?"

"What I thought was that rich people didn't do much of that sort of thing." Her voice and the faint hint of roses moved closer, then away. "When you're finished, ring downstairs and I'll remove the boxes."

Adam listened to the door closing, then

moved the empty box out of the way. He reached into the second box, picked up a pair of what felt like khaki pants, and put them into the fourth drawer with a growing sense of accomplishment. Lilly hadn't tried to help or pat him on the head for completing a task a four-year-old could do. Instead, she'd acted as if she'd expected him to unpack by himself. And that was exactly what he was going to do.

Downstairs Lilly entered an empty kitchen. She didn't discover the reason until she looked out the window. Odette and Eleanor sat on the same stone bench Lilly favored, the bushel of purple hull peas Odette had brought that morning between them. Grabbing a bowl from beneath the cabinet, Lilly went to join them.

Mrs. Wakefield glanced up as soon as Lilly stepped out of the house. "Good morning, Lilly. How's Adam?"

Lilly didn't have to look at Odette to know she was waiting for the answer almost as much. It hadn't taken Lilly long to learn the jovial housekeeper was a worrier and protective of those she cared about. Dr. Wakefield was counted in that number. "He was almost finished unpacking the box of shirts."

"You don't think he needs help?" Eleanor asked, tiny lines radiating across her forehead.

Lilly was sure Odette was the cause of Eleanor's concern. "I don't think a man of Dr. Wakefield's intelligence needs help in unpacking a box."

"But he's blind," Odette blurted, then flickered a worried glance at Mrs. Wakefield.

To Eleanor's credit, she didn't flinch at the blunt statement. She simply waited for Lilly's reply.

"Being blind doesn't make him helpless or suddenly less intelligent," Lilly said gently, grateful for the literature Harriet had left for her to read. "More important, he hates being treated as if he were."

"Lilly's right." Eleanor picked up another pea pod and snapped the top. "Even as a child, Adam was self-sufficient and detested me helping him dress or tie his shoes. He's probably hated me hovering."

"He knows you love him," Lilly told her.

"Yes, he said so a little while ago when he called. I have you to thank for that." Eleanor's smile was warm. "He should have been thanking you for the clothes and table."

Lilly shook her head. "He was ready to toss the table back until I said you'd sent it."

"He was a willful child."

"Who grew into a willful adult," Lilly said. The older women laughed and Lilly with them. Then she plucked a handful of peas from the bushel basket and sank gracefully to the ground.

Watching her, Odette shook her head. "If I got down there you'd never get me back up."

Lilly smiled and crossed her legs beneath the full hem of her skirt. "It remains to be seen if I need help."

"You won't," Odette said with a shake of her head. "I've seen you go up and down those stairs enough to know. The extra cleaning women I hire dread those stairs."

"I don't." Lilly shelled a pod and reached for another. "They add to the beauty and charm of this place. It wouldn't be the same otherwise."

"You see the beauty; others see the work. Samuel and I have been here for over thirty years. Dr. Wakefield is the third owner." She paused, a pod in her hand. "When the previous owner's wife heard he was being transferred and they had to move, she cried for a week. Samuel and I were a bit worried that the new owner might not want to keep us. You could have knocked me over with a feather when Dr. Wakefield and Dr. Delacroix showed up."

Eleanor's hands stilled. "Adam and Jonathan were out for a drive when he saw the

FOR SALE sign in the front yard. Adam immediately decided he wanted the house. He calls it his investment/retirement house." Pain flickered in her amber-colored eyes. "Now it's his refuge."

"There's nothing wrong with a refuge." Lilly glanced around the immaculate grounds. "Most people want a place to go during bad times. I can't imagine one more perfect than this."

"But a refuge can become a cage. I don't want that for Adam," Eleanor said, her lips compressed tightly together.

"It won't. You said yourself that he called this morning. Has he done that before?"

"No," she admitted quietly.

Lilly nodded her satisfaction. "He's slowly getting there. You just have to keep believing and have faith."

"I know. It's just . . ." Eleanor's eyes misted.

Leaning over, Lilly placed her hand gently on top of the other woman's. "Walking by faith is never easy. Especially when it's being tested day after day. All I can say is that giving up is not the answer." With all the upheaval in her life, that was the one truth Lilly was sure of.

Eleanor's lips gently curved upward. "I'm glad your car broke down."

"I never thought I'd say so, but so am I."

"What's this about your car breaking down?" Odette wanted to know.

Lilly told her the entire story and, although Eleanor hadn't asked, told about the recent death of her "mother," as Lilly affectionately called Mother Crawford because that was the name she had grown up hearing. She finished by telling them of her intention of driving to New Orleans to start a new life.

"You got any more family?" Odette asked.

Lilly thought briefly of her stepson, Rafe, then shook her head. He had been more like a little brother than a son. "No. I'm all alone."

"Not anymore," Odette said firmly.

Lilly hadn't expected to feel the warmth the housekeeper's words gave her or the sudden stinging in her throat. "Thank you, Odette."

"Did you give Adam the tapes yet?" Eleanor wanted to know.

"No. I can't think of a way to get him to listen to them. As sure as I'm sitting here, if I just gave them to him he'd stick them in the closet and not listen to them, although I know he has to be bored in that room all day."

Odette's hands paused over the half-filled bowl of peas. "He never slept past eight, and after breakfast he'd be out with

Samuel in the yard, on that computer, or doing something else. He never stayed in his room."

"He had two offices, one in San Francisco and one in Sausalito near his home. He was always on the go."

The three women paused and pondered.

"You ladies sure look nice resting there. Morning, Miss Lilly, Mrs. Wakefield. Wish I could just sit around under a big tree and rest all day." Tipping his hat, Samuel smiled broadly and walked past them and entered the kitchen's back door.

"Men," all three women said simultaneously, then laughed out loud.

"But Lord, what would we do without them?" Odette asked.

"We wouldn't have to cook and clean, that's for sure," Lilly responded.

"But we also wouldn't have the love and companionship," Eleanor pointed out.

"Amen," Odette said.

Lilly remained quiet, then became aware that the two women were staring at her. She searched her mind for anything to say and could think of nothing good to say about men.

The back kitchen door opened and Samuel came out with a red thermos in his hand. "Don't either of you try to bring those empty boxes back downstairs. I'll get them when I come back."

Odette harrumphed. "That man thinks I'm helpless."

"Jonathan is the same way," Eleanor said; then she and Odette looked at each other and grinned. Eleanor turned to Lilly. "I think Samuel just helped solve your problem."

Pride was an awesome thing. It could defeat, challenge, inspire. At the moment Adam freely admitted that while unpacking the three boxes he had experienced all three emotions.

With a last, final pat against the suits hanging in his closet, he closed the door. Trying to get the three suits on hangers had nudged him close to defeat. Finally he had sat on the floor. Getting the crease straight and aligned in the pants had been long and tedious but satisfying.

He'd unpacked all three boxes by himself. He wasn't helpless.

Turning, he went to his chair and sat down in front of his tray on the table. The omelet was stone cold. So was the rest of his food.

He'd spent enough nights in hospitals to have more than a nodding acquaintance with cold food; that's why he detested it so much and enjoyed his food at the correct temperature and well prepared.

He leaned back against the chair. Of

course, he could always call the kitchen. If Lilly wasn't there, Odette probably was. A smile touched his face. She was probably busy cooking his cobbler. The smile vanished. He wished he'd told her he wanted it for lunch.

He straightened at the knock on his door. Lilly.

Rising, he stepped around the table and went to answer the door. "My breakfast is cold."

"I can take care of that if you can help me with this."

"What?"

"The battery won't snap in my tape recorder. I could go back down and see if Odette could help, if you're busy."

His hand flexed on the door. Sometimes he wondered about the woman. What the hell did she expect him to do?

"Here, I'll show you."

Before he could protest, she lifted one of his hands and curled it around one end of the recorder. The other hand she placed on top, then slowly moved his fingers over a round, solid rise. The battery.

"When I pop one in the other pops out. My finger is getting sore. I want to hear this book on tape while I clean up."

The pad of his thumb slowly raked over the battery.

"You're probably thinking I shouldn't

own this, either, since I can't operate it, but I'm trying to learn. And before you ask about my car, it won't be ready for another week. They had to order parts."

The relief he felt that she was staying was as disturbing as it was surprising. "What's wrong with your car?"

The sigh was long-suffering. Her warm breath gently brushed across his face. "I think it would be easier to tell you what's right with it. An old pump that has gone out is the major problem. At least at the moment."

"Are you sure? Some mechanics try to get over on women."

"Dr. Delacroix called them, so I guess I can trust them."

"Still, have Jonathan call the garage and speak to the mechanic for you."

"He doesn't have time."

"Don't you ever get tired of arguing?" he snapped.

"I'm sorry."

The tightness went out of his voice. "I didn't mean to snap," he told her, recalling the last incident when he'd upset her and she'd run away. "Let's get this fixed. What kind of tape is —"

"The killer was in the cave. Erin knew it just as surely as she knew she was next to die. The only question that remained was how long she had left to live."

218

"You fixed it!" Lilly cried.

"It's a book on tape?" Adam questioned.

"Yes. I like listening to them sometimes, although I'm going to have to pass on this particular one. I thought the tape was straight fiction. Mystery is all right when I'm with someone; otherwise I'll be looking over my shoulder and getting nothing done or up all night checking under the bed."

"That's childish."

"All right, then you listen to it and, if you don't get scared, I'll bring you a bowl of peach cobbler as soon as it's done."

Adam's hands itched for the tape. Mysteries were his favorites. He enjoyed pitting himself against the protagonist, trying to solve the crime first. Trying to keep the excitement out of his voice, he said, "Add a couple of scoops of vanilla ice cream and you have yourself a deal."

"Shake." Lilly's hand touched his. The handshake was brief.

"I'll go to my room and get the rest of the tapes. The recorder is one of those five-button, big old-fashioned ones. Button one is RECORD, two is REWIND, three FAST FORWARD, four PLAY, five STOP. Got it?"

"Just bring the rest of the tapes," he ordered.

"Be right back."

While she was gone, he returned to the chair. He'd had an antique like this in high

219

school. While taking some college courses his senior year and auditing others, he'd used the tape recorder extensively. It was better than taking notes and more reliable than asking for the notes of his classmates. His fingers felt the indentations in the buttons. He could do this.

"Here are the rest of the tapes. I'm putting the case on your table. There are twelve in all. Thirteen hours and twenty-five minutes of nail-biting listening. Remember button two will rewind."

"I remember."

"I'll be back with a hot breakfast. If you jump when I knock there'll be no ice cream." There was laughter in her voice. "I'm putting you on your honor."

He hit the REWIND button and heard the whir of the tape. "Just tell Odette to remember I like lots of crust."

"Like you said, I remember."

Adam didn't flinch when Lilly brought him another breakfast tray. He did show his annoyance at the interruption and shushed her. Lilly barely kept from shuddering as the narrator gave the gruesome details of carnage left by the unseen forces of evil. Unfazed, Dr. Wakefield forked his waffle into his mouth.

"Save room for cobbler," she said and opened the door.

"And the ice cream."

Lilly closed the door on a recorded scream. She might not have been untruthful about her reaction to murder mysteries after all. Her hand on the railing, she went to the kitchen and straight to the upright freezer. There wasn't a doubt in her mind that Dr. Wakefield would win the bet. She couldn't be happier.

However, a few minutes later she closed the stainless-steel door with a frown on her face. "There's no ice cream."

Odette glanced up from rolling out the crust for the cobbler. "Like I told you, I'm a diabetic, and that's the one food I can't resist, so I don't keep it anyplace I can be tempted."

Lilly walked over to her. "I promised Dr. Wakefield ice cream."

"I can send Samuel into town." Odette laid down the rolling pin.

"No, he was trying to finish cleaning out the azaleas beds. I'll go see if Mrs. Wakefield can go." Outside, Lilly quickly took the path to the cottage and knocked.

Eleanor frowned on opening the door and seeing Lilly. "Lilly, what is it?"

Lilly quickly explained the situation. "Samuel is cleaning out the azalea bed, and Dr. Wakefield is expecting his ice cream. I thought I'd ask you."

"Of course. Come on in; I'll get my

keys." Eleanor returned shortly with her purse. "Is there anything else?"

"There might be one thing. Has he always worn a beard?"

"No, just since the accident. Why?"

"He's always scratching at it," Lilly told her. "I think it bothers him. When I cleaned up his room, there was after-shave lotion, but no shaving equipment."

"I thought he had just decided not to bother with shaving. He always preferred a razor, but after his blindness he kept nicking himself. I seem to have missed something else." Eleanor's words were as forlorn as her face.

"Because you're too close to him. Everything is new to me, and I notice things you might not," Lilly consoled her. "Dr. Wakefield certainly isn't talkative about what he wants, except to be left alone."

"From what you've said, that has changed."

"Some, but he still has a long way to go."

"At least he's on the road. I'll be back as soon as I can. I'll pick up a razor while I'm there."

"The woman was dead. Her car had stopped and she had hitchhiked with a kind-faced man who turned out to be a serial killer. The boyfriend waiting for her at

222

the restaurant would never see her again. The killer had made sure of that."

Adam's fingers fumbled as he hit the STOP button. He rolled his shoulders to get the tension out. That story was fiction. The author had a vivid and grisly imagination. There was no reason to think the same thing would happen to Lilly when she left. He himself had been chosen at random because of the car he'd driven. The two addicts who attacked him wanted to sell the car to a chop shop — they'd needed the money for their drug habit. They hadn't gotten away with it, but he was living in a world of darkness nevertheless. Even their being caught and jailed didn't change that.

He hit the PLAY button and settled back. Fiction was not reality.

Adam thought he was doing fine until a hunter in the story accidentally stumbled upon the woman's remains. By the time Forensics made a positive identification and the boyfriend had been notified, Adam felt the tension seep back into his body.

Lilly would probably be just as gullible to offer a ride to a baby-faced hitchhiker. Kristen had. When Adam had found out, he'd read her the riot act; then his mother and Jonathan had raked her over the coals as well. Kristen had promised never to do anything so dangerous again. Young women alone were too vulnerable.

Adam hit the STOP button. Was Lilly young? He thought so, then wondered why. It didn't take long to recall the shy, hesitant tone of her voice, the quickness with which the angles of her voice would shift, the briskness of her steps. Plus he never remembered her being winded when she reached his room after climbing the stairs. Together these things pointed to a young, agile woman.

Getting up, Adam went to the phone. In less than a minute Jonathan was on the phone. "Glad you decided to speak to me again."

"Don't make me sorry," Adam quipped, realizing how much he had missed hearing the other man's voice.

Jonathan chuckled. "Straight to the point. I'm taking *Lady Lost* out this weekend. Want to join me?"

Lady Lost was Jonathan's thirty-foot speedboat. She handled like a dream. "A criminal name for such a sweet boat."

"Better than *Paradise*," Jonathan retorted, then added, "but we both know why you named her that."

Before Nicole, there had been a steady progression of women in Adam's life. He'd enjoyed making love as the boat gently rode the waves. Like his vision, those days might be gone forever.

"Look, I called about something else," Adam said, his voice impatient.

"I'm listening."

"I want you to call the garage and check on Lilly's car. Make sure she's not being taken."

"Pardon me while I shake the phone."

Jonathan's droll sense of humor could be funny or irritating. At the moment, Adam wanted to shake *him*. "Just do it. She plans on driving to New Orleans after she leaves here. I just want to make sure she gets there."

"You two seem to be getting along."

"She's irritating as hell, but she means well," Adam said.

"In that case, I'll call the garage."

"Thanks."

"Anything else you need?"

"Yes, but you can't give it to me." Quietly he hung up the phone.

Something was wrong. Lilly looked at the barely touched meat loaf on the plate for dinner. He hadn't eaten lunch, either. "You want something else?"

"No."

Lilly bit her lip. She didn't know what had happened to send him into this depression, unless it was the tapes. But Mrs. Wakefield had said he'd enjoyed listening to them in the past. So there had to be another reason, but what?

Her spirits plummeted. It wasn't likely he was going to tell her. "Odette is going to be disappointed. She enjoyed preparing meals."

"I'm not hungry." Slouched in the leather chair, he still wore his robe. His arms rested loosely on the armrest; his long legs were stretched out in front of him.

"You haven't been hungry for a couple of days now," she ventured.

"I'd like to rest now."

All he did was rest. Today he hadn't gotten out of bed until dinner. "Would you like me to turn the radio on?"

"No."

"Are you sure there's nothing else I can get you?"

"I'm sure."

"I'll check on you before I go to bed."

"Don't bother. I'll be asleep and won't hear the door."

Meaning he didn't plan on answering the door. "I'll see you in the morning."

His hands tightened on the armrests. "No doubt."

Leaving, Lilly went back downstairs. Odette and Samuel waited in the kitchen. It was almost six and they usually were gone by now, but both were concerned by the depression Dr. Wakefield had been experiencing since last Friday.

"Maybe if I fixed some more gumbo?" Odette said, looking at the barely touched meat loaf on the tray.

"He wouldn't eat it." Lilly scraped the food into the sink.

Behind her the phone rang. They all knew who it was.

Setting down the plate, Lilly reluctantly answered the phone. She had been hoping to have better news. "Hello, Mrs. Wakefield. There's no change. . . . Yes, I'll call in the morning." Hanging up, she went back to the sink, pressing her hands against the countertop.

"What happened? One minute he was gobbling food like there was no tomorrow, and now for the past two days he's barely touched his meals."

"He's got to eat," Samuel said, his dark brows furrowed in concern.

"Yes," Lilly said and faced the worried couple. "But I have no idea how to get him to do so."

She wasn't home.

The disappointment was sharp and deep when there was no answer to Jonathan's repeated knock on Eleanor's door. His broad shoulders slumped. He thought he finally had a reason to ensure that Eleanor face him and talk with him. This afternoon when Harriet had come for her appointment, she'd told him the talking clock Eleanor had ordered was in. He'd jumped at the chance to deliver it, sure that this time she couldn't evade him or put him off. No matter how things had deteriorated between them, she was too well-mannered not to answer her door.

And now she wasn't home.

Heaving a sigh, he went back to his car and took the circular drive that passed the main house. He might as well leave the clock and go home. There was no reason to wait. It was safe to assume that if Eleanor saw his car in her driveway, she'd leave.

Getting out, he saw the groundskeeper, Samuel, digging in the flower bed and waved. Adam couldn't have gotten anyone better to care for his home. Walking up the wooden steps and across the wide white porch, Jonathan rang the door chime.

A few minutes later the door opened. Lilly, dressed in a simple cotton dress that appeared freshly washed and ironed, stood in the doorway. Her hand remained on the doorknob.

Weariness flashed in her brown eyes. "Good afternoon, Dr. Delacroix."

Jonathan lifted a heavy brow. His opinion of the rightness of Lilly Crawford was another matter. "Good afternoon, Ms. Crawford."

"Please come in." She stepped back.

Jonathan noticed the reluctance in her movement and decided to ignore it. Once he was over the threshold, his gaze went to the staircase and beyond. "Is Adam upstairs?"

"Yes. Are you going up?"

"Not today. Do you know where Mrs. Wakefield is?"

"Yes."

He waited for her to elaborate. Nothing. Apparently she had picked up on the undercurrents between him and Eleanor and wasn't happy about it. He got the distinct impression that she was trying to protect Eleanor.

"Where is she?"

"She went for a walk."

"On the grounds?"

"Yes."

Jonathan worked to keep the annoyance from his face. The house sits on five acres. "Do you know when she'll return?"

"No, sir."

Was there satisfaction in her answer? Studying the slight upward curve of her lips, he decided there probably was. "Please give this to her. It's the talking clock you wanted for Adam."

Lilly had the clock in her hand in seconds. She looked from him to the cardboard casing. He could almost feel her anticipation. "I'm sure she won't mind," Jonathan said.

Opening the box, Lilly took out the fat, triangular object. "Now he won't feel so lost."

Although the words were mere whispers, Jonathan heard them. "You really care," he said in astonishment.

Her head jerked up; weariness was back, but so was a brief flash of anger. "Why does that surprise you?"

"Because Eleanor hired you out of desperation and I got the distinct impression that you took the job for the same reason," he said bluntly.

"But that doesn't mean I don't care about another person's pain and suffering."

"Adam can't have made caring for him easy," he returned.

Lilly's eyes narrowed. "Do you treat your difficult patients with less care?"

"No."

"Yet you expect me to." Her words were a statement, not a question. Before he could answer, her chin lifted. "If you're sure you don't want to see Dr. Wakefield, I have to get back."

He'd been dismissed. Expertly. He opened the front door. "Adam called me about your car."

"He called? When?"

He frowned at the excitement in her

voice. "Three days ago."

"What did you say to him? Did you threaten to have him declared incompetent again?" she asked, anger sweeping across her expressive features.

"Of course not. Why would you suggest such a thing?"

"He's almost stopped eating," she told him, biting her lower lip. "We don't know what to do."

Jonathan's eyes narrowed. "*Why* didn't she call me?"

"She —"

Jonathan didn't wait for an answer. Hurrying past Lilly, he hit the stairs at a fast clip. "Fix some soup and bring it up."

Lilly didn't question him, just went to prepare the food.

The knock was brisk and brief before the bedroom door opened. "Adam, what the hell are you trying to do to yourself?"

Slouched in his chair, Adam lifted one heavy brow. "Come with more threats, Jonathan?"

"I've come to knock some sense into your thick skull."

"Go on. I can't see it coming."

"You certainly are a bastard today. Having a good time feeling sorry for yourself, aren't you?"

"I don't know anyone who has more of a right."

"People love you, Adam."

"They pity me. Just like you do."

Adam suddenly found himself dragged up. He came out of his lethargy enough to shove at Jonathan's wide chest and found it immovable.

"I don't want to hear that crap. Hell, I admit life threw you a hard curve, but you still have hope; you still have life," Jonathan said tightly.

"Being blind! What kind of life is that?" Adam snarled.

"It's what you make of it, Adam. Last night I had to tell a husband his wife was dead and that he'd have to raise their twin girls by himself. A blood clot, a stupid blood clot. She was only twenty-four years old. She'd been laughing and planning to take her daughters home and spoil them. What do you want to bet she'd trade places with you in a heartbeat to be able to hold her children, hear their laughter, feel her husband's arm around her?"

The misery in Jonathan's voice penetrated Adam's own anguish. He'd lost his own share of patients. "I'm sorry."

Jonathan released the lapels of Adam's robe. "No matter how many times it happens, it still tears you up inside."

"Sit down."

"How do you know I'm not sitting down?"

"By the angle of your voice," Adam answered. "Now sit and tell me about her."

Lilly stood at the door with the tray in her hands, tears forming in her eyes and running down her cheeks as she listened to Dr. Delacroix. Mother Crawford always said each person always thought his heartache was the worst until he heard someone else's.

"You did all you could to prevent this from happening. I'm sure of that, Jonathan."

"Knowing that doesn't make it easier. Life is precious. Wasting it angers the hell out of me," Jonathan answered tightly.

Adam rubbed his neck where the collar of the robe had bitten into the skin. "I noticed."

Lilly knocked on the partially opened door and entered. "I brought you some soup, Dr. Wakefield."

"Is there a sandwich with it?" he asked.

"No, but if you give me five minutes there will be."

"Bring one for Jonathan. You haven't eaten today, have you?"

"No."

Lilly mouthed, *Thank you,* to Dr. Delacroix and hurried back downstairs. When she returned, Adam's dining table

233

was between the two men. Placing the pita bread ham sandwiches in front of them, she told Dr. Wakefield the position, pleased that before she left he picked up his sandwich and took a hefty bite. Whatever the crisis had been, it was over.

Lilly was waiting for Dr. Delacroix when he came downstairs. There was no sense beating around the bush. "Thank you. I–I didn't know what to do. I guess you were right about my experience."

"I was wrong. You have something infinitely better. Empathy. I thank you for that. Good night." He was almost to his car when the door behind him opened. He glanced over his shoulder.

"I forgot to ask how much the talking clock cost?"

He surprised her by answering without hesitation. "Sixteen seventy-eight. Tax and shipping included."

Lilly studied the well-dressed man whose very size made her wary. He obviously cared about the Wakefields. She'd been judged unfairly too many times in the past not to feel a little guilty about doing the same to Dr. Delacroix.

"By the way, Mrs. Wakefield returned while you were upstairs with Dr. Wakefield. I told her you had gotten him to eat. She's at the cottage."

Jonathan studied Lilly a long time before a slow smile spread across his handsome face. "Thank you. I think I'll drop by."

"I thought you might."

Chapter Ten

"Why didn't you call about Adam?" Jonathan hurled the words without preamble when Eleanor opened the door.

Her fingers clutched the doorknob. She'd known before opening the door that he was angry. She'd seen that side of him too many times in the past not to recognize what the set jaw, the narrowed gaze, the tense shoulders meant. She just hadn't correctly calculated the degree of his anger.

However, even if she had, after Lilly called a few minutes earlier with news of how he had gotten Adam to eat, Eleanor would have opened the door in any case. He'd gotten through to Adam when they were all floundering. She owed him that courtesy.

"Why?" he repeated.

Her accelerated heartbeat, the strange fluttering in her stomach, were the reasons she hadn't called, reasons she couldn't possibly share with him. "I didn't want to worry you."

His handsome face harshened. "That's a crock, Eleanor. I love him, too, and you damn well know it. Now why didn't you call?"

Eleanor felt the pounding in her head that had been a slow tapping for the past three days become the loud clang of an angry anvil. Her fingertips massaged her throbbing temples. She would have faced the devil himself if she thought it would help Adam, but she hadn't been able to call an old friend because his mere presence sent her heart skipping in her chest.

She moistened her dry lips before she spoke. "Thank you for helping, but do you think we could discuss this later?"

Jonathan's shrewd brown eyes narrowed. "What's the matter? You have a headache?"

"Yes. So, if you don't mind . . ."

"I do mind," he said and brushed past her into the house.

Incensed, Eleanor whirled around. "What do you think you're doing?"

Jonathan kept walking. Fuming, Eleanor closed the front door and followed. When she entered the kitchen he was bent over looking inside the refrigerator.

"What are you doing?"

Straightening, he shut the door. "You're not eating again."

She'd had enough of his interference, of her acting like a simpering fool. "You'll have to forgive me if I forgot to eat when my son wasn't eating."

"Would starving yourself help Adam?

Would going blind help?"

Her head snapped back. "You've gone too far."

"I haven't gone far enough." He began opening cabinets, then turned to face her. "Did you stock food after you decided to stay?"

Beside a few staples, she hadn't. "The main house has everything I need."

"Then why aren't they here? Why aren't you taking care of yourself?"

She couldn't answer. The pounding became worse. Her hands went back to her temples. "Jonathan, please. I really don't feel well."

"Be glad I can see that or you'd see just how upset I am," he said, advancing on her. Unsure of his mood, she cringed. Despite the anger in his face, the hand that closed around her forearm was gentle. "Come on."

Eleanor tried unsuccessfully to pry his unrelenting fingers loose. "Stop. What are you doing?"

"Making sure you eat. You need more than a sandwich."

"I'm not Adam!"

He stopped and stared down at her, his brown eyes blazing. "In some ways you're as blind as he is." He started toward the door again.

Eleanor didn't say anything. She didn't

think he meant physical blindness, but she didn't want to discuss it.

Opening the passenger side of his car, he helped her in, then went around and climbed inside. Instead of starting the car, his hands flexed on the steering wheel. His face looked hard, remote, but there was something else there that pulled at Eleanor. "Are you all right?"

He looked at her, his gaze piercing ice. "Would you care if I wasn't?"

The question was like a slap to her face. The hurt was overwhelming. "How can you say anything so cruel to me?"

"Is it any crueler of you to shut me out of your life, out of Adam's life, as if neither of you matter to me?"

Eleanor tucked her head. He was right, yet there was no way she could explain. Even now, she wanted to lay her head on his shoulder, have him comfort her the way he used to, but fear of how far she'd take that comfort held her immobile.

"Eleanor," he said quietly, and no power on earth could have kept her from raising her head. What she saw in his dark eyes was a misery equal to her own. "I missed you."

Tears pricked her eyes; emotion knotted her throat. "I missed you, too."

His sad smile almost broke her heart. "We've been friends too long to let anything come between us. What do you say we forget this week happened and start over?"

He was giving both of them an out. She'd been wrong. He had picked up on the currents between them. Thankfully both of them realized to act upon them might ruin their friendship. A risk neither was willing to take. "After we eat, I'd like to pick up a couple of canvases."

His hand briefly covered hers. "I'd like nothing better."

Lilly tidied the room and turned down Adam's bed. She felt the time was right for another nudge. Kneeling beside the leather chair he sat in, she said, "I've brought you something. Listen."

"Seven-thirteen P.M.," said an animated female voice.

He jerked upright. "What?"

"It's a talking clock. Give me your hands."

Slowly he extended his hands and she wrapped his long fingers around the squat, fat, triangular shape. "You can set the time for automatic or manual."

The three control buttons on top were the size and shape of the eyes on his computer keyboard. Adam thought of the cuckoo clock that had driven him crazy and asked, "Which one is for the manual control?"

"The second one. Here." She moved his index finger to the indented button and pushed.

"Seven-thirteen P.M."

Adam clicked the button again. Again it noted the time in its electronic voice. A frown worked its way across his forehead. "Where did this come from?"

Lilly crossed her long legs under her. She'd already decided what to say. "I asked your mother to get it for me. Dr. Delacroix dropped it off tonight."

"Why?"

"The clock will help me keep my job."

"How?"

She almost smiled. Dr. Wakefield certainly didn't take anything at face value. "By letting you know that I'm doing my duties in a timely manner."

His fingers closed around the bulky shape and he hefted the clock. "I thought you were low on funds."

"I am, but I consider the clock a necessity. If I don't keep this job, I won't be able to get my car out of the shop."

"You do realize that this may work against you?"

"How?"

"Now I'll really be able to tell if you're loafing." Sitting back, he pushed the MANUAL button.

Lilly rolled her eyes. No one but Dr.

241

Wakefield would say such a thing.

The itching beard woke Adam up. Scowling, he sat up in bed, his fingernails raking through the stubble. It was all her fault. He'd been doing just fine — well, almost just fine — until she had started talking about some guy's itching beard. She was strange. At times she was a motor-mouth; other times she was strangely silent.

Knowing the scratching only made the itching worse, he got out of bed and went to the bathroom to splash cool water on his face. He caught himself scratching in the bathroom and returned to bed. Frowning, he wondered what time it was, then almost smiled as he made his way to his clock and punched the button.

"Two-o-five A.M."

Setting the clock down, Adam picked up the phone and punched in the first two buttons. If he had to be up, then so did she.

A sleepy Lilly answered on the second ring, her voice husky with sleep. "Hello."

For some perverse reason Adam enjoyed the fact that he had awakened her. "My beard is itching."

"What?"

"My beard is itching and you have to do something about it," he told her, his hand

242

going back to his face.

"It's the middle of the night."

"Two-o-five A.M., to be precise," he answered, satisfaction in his voice. "You must have a razor of some type. Bring it." He hung up the phone and went to the sink in the bathroom.

Dressed in his bathrobe and jeans, his arms folded across his chest, his legs crossed at the ankles, Adam leaned back against the marble vanity. His chin was thrust out and he looked immensely pleased with himself when Lilly entered the bathroom.

"I have the razor."

"Good." With surprising agility, he hooked his bare foot around a stainless-steel stool to pull it from beneath the vanity, then sat down on the soft padded leather seat. "I'm ready."

"What?"

"I want you to shave me."

Her eyes widened. "I've never shaved anyone before."

"I've never let a woman shave me before, so I'd say we're even."

"You're sure about this?"

"I'd like to get some sleep before the next century." Pushing his shades back firmly on his nose, he lifted his chin.

"Remember, this was your idea." Her

243

hand unsteady, she turned on the hot water, then draped a towel around his neck. Wetting a hand towel, she wrung out most of the moisture and wrapped it around his face.

"You're standing wrong. You'll have to get behind me or between my legs."

"What!" she shrieked.

"Don't go woman on me. Come on; this thing is itching."

Not sure what he meant, she debated her choices. If she got behind him and had to lean his head back it would be even with her breasts. She was already shaking her head as she took a tentative step between his legs. Thank heaven she had taken time to put on her robe. With trembling hands, she removed the towel from his face, rewet it, then pressed it to his beard.

"Umm," he sighed, refolding his arms and relaxing against the vanity.

Her hand shook a little more. She tried not to think where his head would be if she had stepped behind him. "You're all right?"

"Yes. Use short, even strokes and I'll remain that way."

Removing the towel, she squirted the foaming white shaving cream into the palm of her hand, then quickly spread it over his face, around his mouth, beneath his nose.

"Here goes." The first swipe of the razor on his face sounded as if she were scraping sand paper, but hair, not skin, came off. Pleased, she repeated the motion, gaining confidence with each stroke.

Five minutes later, she straightened. "Finished. You can wash your face again. The sink is to your right. Your after-shave is next to the right of that."

Getting up, Adam wrinkled his nose, then rubbed his hand over his face. "Don't you ever get tired of badgering me?"

"Helping you," she said before she thought, then tensed as uneasiness swept through her.

"So you say." Slowly he stood and faced the sink. "Good night. I can finish from here."

Her relief was immense, but she wasn't home free yet. "Then I'll leave you with this for the future." Lifting his hand, she put a small black leather pouch in it. "Everything is marked with raised letters. Shaving cream is SC, moisturizer is M, face cream, although I'm not sure what you need it for, is FC."

"Marked?"

"Puff paint."

He twisted the soft leather case in his hands, then turned his head toward her. "You had this ready, didn't you?"

A lie was useless. "Yes."

"Then why didn't you just give it to me?"

It was now or never. "You don't take suggestions very well."

His long fingers flexed on the case. "The tape recorder was for me all along, wasn't it?"

She took a leap of faith and answered, "Yes."

"You tricked me."

Although there was no heat in the words, her nervousness increased. "I only did it to help."

He turned his back to her and faced the sink. "That will be all."

Feeling miserable, she turned to leave. "Good night, Dr. Wakefield."

"Lilly."

She stiffened. She was almost afraid to turn. "Yes?"

"Thank you."

Relief and happiness flooded her. The wide smile on her face carried over to her voice: "You're welcome."

"What time do you bring my tray for breakfast?"

"Eight."

"Don't be late."

At exactly eight the next morning, Lilly knocked on Dr. Wakefield's door. "Dr. Wake—"

The door opened, and Dr. Wakefield stood in the doorway. "Come in. I'm starving."

It took a few seconds for Lilly to get past how the yellow Polo shirt delineated the muscles in his wide chest, the clean smell of his spicy after-shave. Odette had been right: Dr. Wakefield was a good-looking man.

"Lilly?"

"Potato pancakes at twelve, link sausages at six, hash browns at nine." She placed the tray on the table and waited, hoping this time he'd come to the table while she was still in the room. He didn't. She tried another tack: "It's a gorgeous day outside. Would you like to take a walk later on?"

The pleasant expression on his face vanished. "No."

"You need exercise."

"Don't tell me what I need," he snapped.

Lilly saw all her hard-earned progress fading away. "I'm sorry. I just thought you'd like to get some fresh air."

"Why do you think the balcony windows are open?"

She shifted from one foot to the other. "Can Samuel drive me into town this morning to get my car?"

He took a step toward her. "You're sure it's fixed?"

"The mechanic said it was. He said it was ready yesterday, but he had to wait for an inspection." Lilly frowned. "He acted as if I knew what he was talking about."

"I had Jonathan check out your car."

"He told me. Why?"

"To make sure you reach New Orleans safely." Stepping back, he opened the door wider. "My breakfast is getting cold."

Dismissed, she started from the room, then stopped when she was even with him. "Thank you for helping."

She was out the door when he called her. "Lilly?"

"You aren't going to fire me now that my car is fixed, are you?" she asked, her voice shaky.

His mouth flattened. "Don't pick up any hitchhikers on your way back." The door closed.

"What has gotten into him?" she muttered, then started down the hallway. She stopped abruptly and stared back at the closed door. He'd been attacked when he'd stopped.

She continued down the stairs. Despite Dr. Wakefield's animosity and gruffness at times, he'd done what Myron never had thought to do, worry about her safety and ensure that she had a safe car to drive.

Shreveport, Louisiana, with its old red-brick buildings and streets in the downtown area, reminded Lilly a little of Little Elm. But there the similarities ended. In Little Elm there were no freeways to get lost on, no riverboats a short distance away to lure modern-day gamblers, no giant malls or billboards everywhere you looked.

And although Texas and Louisiana connected, there was a laziness about Shreveport that she hadn't found in Little Elm. It was easily distinguishable in the slow, almost thoughtful way people talked and moved. There was an open friendliness, with men tipping their caps and hats and women nodding and smiling.

Perhaps, she reasoned, that was because there she had been prejudged. In Shreveport, she was an employee of an important doctor, not the daughter of a woman who went through men like Kleenex.

"You need to go anyplace else, Miss Lilly?" Samuel asked, walking with Lilly to her car.

He'd already taken her to the bank to cash the check Mrs. Wakefield had given her. Her hands had trembled as the teller counted $1,500 into her hand. She'd almost cried when she had to pay $900.63 to the mechanic.

"No. I've spent enough money for today."

"Yes'm." He opened her car door. "But

I always figure it's better to have it to spend than not have it."

Pausing, she looked back up at his lined leathery face. "You're right. Thanks for reminding me."

"You follow me closely now. The freeway can be tricky."

She pulled the door closed, then rolled down the window. "That's how I got lost."

"Not this time. Dr. Wakefield called down to the kitchen and told Odette to tell me to see you got back safely."

"He did?"

"Yes'm. Dr. Wakefield takes care of his own, always has. You follow close now." With that last warning, he went to his car.

Lilly started the car. The engine ignited immediately and she pulled out behind Samuel's black Buick. The scent of strawberries filled the air. Lilly sniffed, noticing the high shine in the faded dashboard, the windshield free of the carcasses of bugs. They'd detailed the car. Then she noticed something else.

Cool air gushed from the vents and bathed her face. The air-conditioning worked for the first time in five years. Rolling up the windows, she eased to a stop behind Samuel. Maybe, just maybe, things were turning in her favor.

As soon as Lilly walked into the kitchen,

Odette looked up and rushed toward her. "Is he all right?" Lilly asked anxiously.

"Dr. Wakefield's fine, but some man's been calling you since you left."

She tried to swallow the dread clawing at her throat and couldn't. "Did — did he give a name?"

"Kenneth Powell."

Lilly sagged in relief. The phone rang again.

Odette's and Lilly's gaze met; then Lilly rushed to the phone. "Hello."

"Mrs. Crawford?"

"Mr. Powell, what is it?" she asked, recognizing the Southern drawl in his voice immediately.

"We got trouble. Your husband has decided to contest the divorce and the grounds of your petition."

Lilly glanced at Odette's watchful face. "I'll call back." Hanging up the phone, she started out of the kitchen.

"You remember, child, if you got troubles you got folks who care about you," the older woman said.

Nodding, Lilly rushed out of the kitchen. In her room she quickly called her lawyer's office. "This is Lilly Crawford. Tell me again."

"I met with your husband and his lawyer this morning. He's willing to give you the divorce if you'll agree to remove the original language in your petition. If you do, the divorce will automatically go through in about thirty days."

"If I don't?" Myron wouldn't do anything unless it was for his benefit.

"This possibly could drag on for months," he answered simply.

"Change to what?"

" 'Irreconcilable differences.' His lawyer pointed out your husband has his reputation to consider."

Rage swept through her. "He should have thought of his reputation before he hit me, treated me like dirt."

"What is your answer?"

"No," she said tightly. She knew she was being unreasonable, but she wasn't giving in to Myron ever again. For the first time in her life, she had the means and the courage to stand up for herself. Pure stubbornness or not, she had no intention of backing down.

"The burden of proof will be on us, and that will take investigation, which will take money."

Why did it always come down to money? "How much?"

"Five hundred dollars to begin with. I'll place it in an open account and draw out of that as needed."

Briefly she squeezed her eyes shut. "I'll wire the money this afternoon."

"You must have gotten a pretty good job," he said.

"Yes, I did. Anything else?"

"No."

"Good-bye, Mr. Powell."

"Where is she?" Adam asked, the phone clutched in his hand. It was past one.

"She had to go back into town, Dr. Wakefield," Odette told him. "She said she had business to take care of."

"What kind of business?"

"I'm not sure. She just asked what the address was here and left."

"Tell her I want to see her as soon as she returns." Adam hung up the phone and went to the window. He'd been on edge since Lilly left that morning. He shouldn't have snapped at her, but he had enough of people trying to get him out of his room. He was comfortable here. He knew where everything was, and it was safe.

But what if she had kept going? Samuel had reluctantly admitted he'd taken her to the bank and she'd cashed her paycheck.

Where the hell was she?

"Dr. Wakefield," came the soft voice followed by two knocks.

Lilly. He whirled. "Come in."

"You wanted —"

"Where have you been?" Silence. "Well?"

"I had some business to take care of. I told Odette."

He heard the shakiness in her voice. "What's the matter?"

"I . . . nothing. Odette said you wanted to wait for your lunch. Are you ready now?"

"Come here." He thought she wasn't going to comply until he felt her presence, smelled the fragrance of roses. "Are you crying?"

"No."

Not willing to take her word, he lifted his hand and unerringly found her face. Her skin was smooth beneath his fingertips. "You aren't going to tell me what's going on, are you?"

"No." Her voice trembled.

"Are you in trouble with the police?"

"No."

He sighed in exasperation. "Can you say any other word?"

"Sorry."

His hand fell. "Lilly, you could definitely drive me insane."

The deep grooves running across his forehead clearly said he was annoyed, but he had also gone out of his way to help her and ensure that she was safe. "I appreciate you looking after me. My mother —" She bit back the words *in-law,* quickly correcting the mistake she'd almost made.

254

"My mother was the only one who ever did that before."

"What about your father?"

"Left when I was a baby."

"That must have been hard," he said, hearing the flat inflection of her voice. "My father was busy, but he was a big part of my life."

"Your mother told me he was a wonderful man."

"He was. He had a thriving practice, but he was there when it counted. My father, Jonathan, and Mother were in medical school together."

"Your mother?"

"Top of her class until she decided to marry my father and drop out."

"She gave up her career for him?"

He shook his head. "People used to say that all the time, but Mother always said she hadn't given up anything, that she'd gained and she never regretted her decision for a moment." His face saddened. "Losing him was hard on her."

"But she has you and your sister, and memories linger."

"Yes, they do."

Lilly realized that they were having a conversation like two normal people, not adversaries. "I was going to fix chicken salad for lunch. You want me to bring you a tray?"

"Thanks, and while we eat you can tell me about what they did to your car."

Her mouth opened, then closed. "You want us to have lunch together?"

"Isn't that what I just said?"

"If I do, you aren't going to be perturbed with me if I don't know everything, are you?"

Heavy eyebrows lifted over his shades. "I promise to try."

"Good enough."

Dr. Wakefield kept his word. They talked more than they ate. Lilly wasn't sure if that was because he was still nervous about eating in front of people or because he simply wasn't hungry. Having carried his usually empty plates back to the kitchen, she felt it was more of the former.

Telling him she had to help Odette with supper and that she'd pick up his tray later, she left. She knew she had been right when she went back and only fragments of the potato chips and bits of bread remained.

Lying in bed that night, she stared up at the ceiling of the moonlit room. Life was a mystery. You never knew if misery or happiness was waiting around the corner. You just had to be ready. She hadn't been ready today when her lawyer called. She'd almost crumpled. Dr. Wakefield didn't know it, but he had helped her not to. His intervention was all the more profound when she knew he was fighting his own misery, his own demons.

She vowed again to help him fight and win his battle, if possible, just as he had helped her today.

The day was beautiful. Blue skies stretched forever, swept by a gentle easterly wind. Lilly breathed in the fresh-scented air and stepped off the back porch. It was quiet and peaceful here and filled with a calm beauty.

Immediately her thoughts went to Dr. Wakefield shut in his room. Not wanting a repeat of last week she hadn't dared mention going out again. However, if he wouldn't go out, she'd take the outside inside to him.

Seeing Samuel pruning, she walked over to him. "Samuel, would it be all right if I cut some flowers for Dr. Wakefield's room?"

Stopping, he rubbed the sleeve of his long-sleeved shirt across his perspiration-dampened forehead. "Yes'm."

"Good. Which ones do you suggest?"

"The roses, lilies, and tulips might make a nice arrangement." He nodded toward the front of the property. "The doctor and I had talked about adding a couple more beds of flowers to the front yard. Maybe some hydrangeas or tulips in all colors of the rainbow in a winding trail along the fence line. Guess it'll have to wait now."

"Why?"

"He's bl—" Samuel stopped himself and looked away.

Lilly realized he hadn't meant the words spitefully. Dr. Wakefield was more than an employer to Samuel. He was a respected friend. "I thought we agreed not to treat him any differently?" she said.

"He can't walk the grounds with me, tell me how wide or how far from the fence he wants the beds," Samuel said logically.

Before answering, Lilly glanced around the beautiful yard. It was the first week of May. Color was everywhere, drawing one's eyes and soothing the senses. She couldn't name all the flowers and trees, but some she knew: daffodils, pansies, geraniums, azaleas, dogwood, and redbud trees.

"Odette says you've been here over thirty years. How much of this design is your idea?"

"Most of it," he said, then caught her meaning, already shaking his head. "But I never do anything without discussing it with the owner first."

"Has Dr. Wakefield ever not liked anything you suggested?"

"No," Samuel said slowly. "But there's always a first time."

"Why don't we go see?"

258

Adam felt restless, bored, and trapped. He'd tried to listen to the new tape Lilly had given him that morning, but the dull monotone of the person reading the book almost made him want to commit murder. The baseball games also had ceased to amuse and entertain.

"Dr. Wakefield."

Adam whirled from the balcony and started toward his door, unconsciously anticipating matching wits with Lilly. "What are you going to badger me about this time?"

"We can come back," Samuel said hesitantly.

"Samuel?" Adam said, surprise in his voice. "I thought you were Lilly."

"I'm here," she said. "I brought you a surprise and Samuel came along to talk with you."

He smelled the fragrance. "Flowers."

"Red and yellow roses, creamy magnolia and gardenia blossoms. Your room will smell wonderful," she said, going past him. "I brought you two vases. One to go to the far right of your nightstand. The other in the middle of the vanity. Samuel, why don't you tell Dr. Wakefield your ideas for the flower beds in the front?"

"I, er . . ." Samuel faltered.

"Dr. Wakefield, Samuel said you had

259

thought of increasing the beauty of Wakefield Manor with additional seasonal flower beds along the fence line," Lilly intervened.

Adam had wanted to develop a flower garden showcase similar to those he had seen in Europe, but that had been before his blindness. "That will have to wait."

"Yes, sir. Whenever you're ready," Samuel quickly said.

"What did you want to plant?" Lilly asked, coming to stand by Adam.

"Geraniums, irises, pansies, tulips, camellias."

"That's what Samuel thought. How far back and how wide did you want the beds?" she questioned.

Adam sighed impatiently and ran his hand over his head. "I don't know."

"Would it be as far back as this room? Would the bed be as wide as yours?" she asked.

"I'm not sure." She was rapidly pushing him into snapping at her again.

"Samuel, what do you think?" Lilly asked. "I'm sure Dr. Wakefield values your opinion."

"I've always been very pleased with Samuel's work, unlike some people," Adam said before Samuel could answer, hoping she'd get the point.

"Thank you, Dr. Wakefield. Hearing you

say that means a lot," Samuel said.

"I'm lucky to have you," Adam said, meaning it. He never had to worry about Wakefield Manor or unnecessary withdrawals against the household account.

Encouraged, Samuel said, "Maybe the beds in the front could be a couple hundred feet back, twice the length of the hall, and half as wide as that wide bed you sleep in. I could border everything with monkey grass if we just did the tulips. The camellias as a backdrop for daffodils, snapdragons, and begonias for March and April. Then in the summer I could switch to begonias, impatiens, and snapdragons."

"That sounds beautiful," Lilly said.

Adam thought so, too, but he'd planned on having an active part in the planning of the garden. Even with Samuel's helpful hints, he couldn't judge distance. He wanted to "see" the placement. "It'll wait for a few months."

"Yes, sir." The disappointment in the elderly man's voice was evident.

"Thanks for coming up," Adam told him.

"No bother. I was just trying to tame those red-tipped photenias on the east side of the yard," the gardener said. "They're over six feet and blooming. We had a mild winter and the yard did well."

"Samuel, why don't you write down

what you plan and we'll discuss it?" Adam offered, suddenly anxious to make amends for his earlier abruptness.

"Yes, sir. I'll do that."

"In the meantime, have you given any thought to taming the acres at the back of the house?" Adam asked, wanting to give the man something.

"I have. It'll be kinda like little clearings of flowers so you never know what you're gonna find, short mixed with tall plants and flowers. There'll be paths wide enough for two people, so you could walk and enjoy them. No sense having flowers if you can't enjoy them," Samuel mused. "Be nice to bunch delphiniums, roses, daylilies, and variegated irises in long, curved borders. It'll take muscles, time, and money, but it'll be worth it."

Thoughtfully Adam rubbed his chin. "An iris-lined pond in a quiet nook with a series of waterfalls would add serenity to the gardens."

"Yes, sir, it would." Samuel's voice sounded eager already.

"Then get started right away. By this time next year I'll be able to see what progress you've made."

Samuel waited a second too long before he replied, "Yes, sir." Lilly knew it the instant she saw the harshness in Adam's face replace the speculation.

Outside the door, she and Samuel were quiet as they walked a few feet down the hall. "I'm sorry. I thought taking an interest in what was going on around the house would be good for him."

"Not your fault. It was mine." Samuel gripped his straw hat in his hands. "He kinda threw me off when he said he'd see the gardens. Mrs. Wakefield said the doctors weren't sure."

"He hasn't given up hope."

"A man's gotta have hope, Miss Lilly." Nodding, he went down the hallway.

Sighing, Lilly went to Dr. Wakefield's room and knocked.

"What is it now, Lilly?"

She opened the door. He stood in the exact place they had left him, his chin thrust forward belligerently, his shoulders thrown back. He was freshly shaven, wearing a melon-colored Polo shirt and stonewashed jeans. He looked fit and handsome. "You could always come outside and walk the grounds."

His lips tightened. "A waste of Samuel's time and mine."

"He doesn't mind."

"I do."

The last days had been calm. She'd almost forgotten how temperamental Dr. Wakefield could be. But at least she now realized he would never harm her. She walked to him, close enough to see her reflection in his shades when he turned toward her. "You enjoying the new tapes?"

"Not especially."

"Why?" she asked, trying to figure out where this particular mood had come from.

"The woman's voice is irritating."

Glancing around for the tape recorder, Lilly walked over and hit the PLAY button. In seconds she understood and hit STOP. "I bet Edgar Gunn wanted to commit murder," she said, referring to the author.

Adam's lips twitched.

Seeing it, she came to a quick decision. "I was planning on going into town this afternoon. Why don't I pick up the book and read it to you?"

He shrugged. "You couldn't do any worse."

"Dr. Wakefield, you are too kind."

What had seemed like a good idea to Lilly hours earlier no longer seemed that way.

"Are you going to read or stand there?" Adam asked sharply.

"In biblical times, didn't royalty throw people who didn't please them to the lions?" she asked, only half-teasing.

Adam's mouth twitched. "The only lions around here are the stone ones by the pool."

"I guess I'm safe then." Picking up a footstool that had been pushed against the wall, she placed it near Adam's feet, sat down in front of his chair, and opened the book. "Do you want me to start at the beginning?"

He frowned. "You're on the floor?"

"Footstool. I'll put it back," she quickly told him. "Mother Crawford always liked me to sit close so she could catch the words faster."

"Interesting way of phrasing." Folding his arms, he leaned back in his chair. "All right, scare me."

She did, using the inflections of her voice to show the different characters and the terror. She might have read longer, but she yawned.

"What time it is?" Adam asked.

"Twelve-thirty," Lilly answered around another yawn.

"Go to bed," Adam instructed. "We'll continue tomorrow."

Fighting another yawn, Lilly replaced the footstool. "Good night, Dr. Wakefield."

"Will you be able to sleep?" he asked.

"If you hear footsteps thundering down the hall coming this way, it will be me," she told him with a laugh.

"Maybe you should read *Silent Prey* after lunch?" he suggested.

"I don't mind an hour after lunch, but

mystery stories are best just before bed."
She opened the door.

"Leave it ajar if you want."

The offer surprised and delighted her. "I think I will. No sense being like Julia in *Silent Prey* and fumbling with a doorknob while the killer is coming."

"You're scaring yourself."

"It's all right this time."

"Why?"

"Because I have you to protect me," she answered simply and left.

Adam sat in his chair, thinking of what Lilly had said and totally unaware of the pleased expression on his face.

Chapter Eleven

Despite reading *Silent Prey*, Lilly had no difficulty sleeping that night or the next. She began to look forward to the times she and Adam had together after lunch and at night before bed. From his reaction, he enjoyed their times together as well. In a week, she had finished one book and started on *The Being.*

Samuel interrupted one afternoon a week later. His hat in his hand, he came in and perched on the edge of an armchair. "I drew up the plans for the back, and I thought you might like to hear them. But if you don't mind, I'd just like to wait until next summer and you can walk the grounds with me. There's a couple of places that the lily pond might go, but I wanna be sure. Is it all right to wait?"

"Next summer would be fine," Adam said flatly.

Samuel pushed to his feet. "I better get back to work."

"He's a good man," Lilly commented after the gardener had gone.

"Did you put him up to this?" Adam asked, his voice like chips of jagged ice.

Lilly's eyes widened. "No."

Adam came to his feet. "Wasn't that an-other ploy to give the poor old depressed doctor a way to be useful, to give him hope?"

"No."

"I don't believe you. He'd never come up here on his own."

"Why would you say such a thing? He admires and respects you."

Adam whirled, his fists clenched. "He pities me and it probably sickens him to see me this way, just as it sickens me to have him see me."

Suddenly a scream, a real one, ripped through the house. It was chilling and full of pain and fear.

Lilly and Adam froze.

"Help! Help!" Samuel's frantic yell boomed through the house.

Lilly flung open Adam's door and raced down the hallway toward the stairs.

"What is it? What happened?" yelled Adam from behind her.

She never paused. "I don't know!"

Lilly hit the stairs running. She didn't stop until she barreled into the kitchen. On the floor flat on her back Odette moaned and whimpered. Samuel, her hand clutched in his, knelt by her side. A few feet away were scattered mixing bowls and an overturned step stool.

"Lord, help me!" she cried.

The plea spurred Lilly into action. Rushing across the room, she knelt on the other side of the housekeeper and took her free hand. "Lie still, Odette. Where do you hurt?"

Tears streamed down the woman's face. "Oh, God, all over. I hope I didn't break my hip like Sister Jackson."

Lilly's frightened gaze flew up to Samuel.

"Hush that nonsense," he chided, his voice unsteady. "You just got the wind knocked out of you. You should have waited for me to put up the mixing bowl, woman."

"I hurt, Samuel. I hurt!" she cried, a stream of tears rolling down her face. "Go get Dr. Wakefield."

"Odet—"

"I want Dr. Wakefield!" she cried, cutting off her husband. "He'll know what to do."

Samuel's callused hand tightened on his wife's for a second; then he nodded and lifted his head. "Go get Dr. Wakefield."

Lilly looked from husband to wife; their eyes were pleading for her to do as they asked. "He may not come."

"He'll come," Odette drew in a deep breath. "Just go tell him. He'll come for me."

"He'll come," Samuel confirmed.

"Maybe we should just call an ambulance," Lilly suggested, trying to remain calm.

"Oh, my Lord! I want Dr. Wakefield," Odette sobbed.

"Hush that crying, woman, or you'll get your pressure up. Miss Lilly is gonna go get him, and I bet you he'll say you're just fine."

Odette closed her eyes, tears leaking from beneath the lids. "I want Dr. Wakefield."

"I'll go get him." Lowering Odette's hand gently to the floor, Lilly dashed out of the room.

"What's happening? Someone answer me!" yelled Adam.

Lilly heard Dr. Wakefield's voice the moment she rounded the corner of the hallway leading to the stairs. It appeared she wouldn't have to go get Dr. Wakefield. He was coming to them. Or so she thought until she reached the base of the stairs and saw him, both hands clutched around the newel cap.

Cautiously he stuck one foot out only to withdraw it. Even from the foot of the stairs, she could see the fear in his face. The reason that he never wanted to leave his room was suddenly answered.

"Odette fell off the folding step stool, and she's asking for you," Lilly explained, continuing up the stairs.

Adam jerked back. "Me?"

Praying she was doing the right thing, Lilly came up beside him and took his free hand so that he was between her and the stair railing. "You. She's frightened. She became worse when I mentioned calling the ambulance. Samuel is concerned about her blood pressure."

"I–I can't."

"Dr. Wakefield!" Samuel's voice called from below.

"They need your help."

His face furious, Adam turned on her. "I can't even help myself."

"Then help someone else. Forget yourself and go help Odette. Calm her enough so I can call the ambulance."

"It's not —"

"Nothing is easy. I know. Now come on and take my arm. You lead off."

For a moment she didn't think he would do it; then he took her arm, drew a deep breath, and stuck a foot out.

"We're coming!" Lilly yelled, praying Dr. Wakefield wouldn't give up. He didn't. Lilly prayed each step, giving out a progress report as they went.

As soon as they entered the kitchen, Odette cried, "I knew you'd come. I just knew it."

"Odette. I–I don't know how much help I can be."

"I've been here praying, and I know you can help," Odette told him.

Adam didn't move.

"You are going to help her, aren't you, Dr. Wakefield?" Samuel asked, his leathery brown face showing fear for the first time.

Adam lifted his hands. Hands that he couldn't see.

To be needed. He was a doctor. A surgeon. Once he had been on his way to being the best in his field.

"Please," Lilly whispered. "Please."

"Take me to her side."

Lilly complied, leading him to Odette and then stopping so he could kneel by the fallen woman. He was barely settled before Odette reached out and tightly grasped his hand.

Adam folded his other hand over hers. Slowly he moved his fingers to her pulse. Satisfied with what his fingertips told him, he ran his hand up her arm to her face. Cool. Not sweaty. "Do you hurt anywhere?"

"My back. My head. My sit-down. My legs."

"Let's start at the head and go down." His hand went to her head and felt the cloth. "Wearing your turban?"

"I washed my hair and didn't have time to press it out." Despite the situation, she sounded chagrined.

"As I recall, you always looked rather

stately in your turban." His hand gently slipped the covering off and checked her head for lumps. "Do you recall hitting your head?"

"No, but it happened fast. That's how Sister Jackson broke her hip." She sniffled.

Adam's examination moved to her shoulder. "I think we can rule that out. Hip fractures are very painful, and every movement would be uncomfortable. I'm not hearing the hitch in your voice."

Odette closed her eyes. "Thank the Lord."

"Let's see about the rest of you. Here we go. Neck. Right arm. Left arm." His fingertips followed the map his words described. "Lilly, let me know if she shows any signs of pain."

Adam waited, listening to Lilly's calm voice reporting Odette's reactions. "Move the leg that doesn't hurt first. Start with the toes, then ankle, knee, hip."

Odette had no difficulty with the left leg. She got as far as her ankle on the right leg before she cried out.

"Stop," Adam ordered. "Help me to where her leg is," he told Lilly. She did as instructed and he immediately felt the warmth, the slight distension. Without waiting for assistance, he found the left ankle, compared. "You injured your right ankle, Odette. I can't tell how badly, but

Lilly was right in wanting to call the ambulance."

Samuel was already getting up to call.

"Notify Dr. Brown, too, Samuel. Lilly, get two quart bags and fill them with crushed ice. Then, see if you can find a couple of ten-pound bags of sugar or flour to hold them in place. I don't want her ankle to move more than necessary. That should be good enough until the paramedics get here and splint it."

Samuel came back to his wife's side. "The ambulance is on the way and I called your doctor. Thank you, Dr. Wakefield."

Adam nodded. "Lilly, you better go wait by the road. This place is not the easiest to find."

"I'll go," offered Samuel.

"Stay with Odette," Lilly told him.

"And I'll stay here and let Odette hold my hand," Adam said, giving the woman's hand a gentle squeeze. "Now, what have those rambunctious grandchildren of yours been up to lately?"

It seemed forever instead of the ten minutes it took for the ambulance to come. Lilly waved them down. The ambulance stopped even with her. A young black woman jumped out.

"Hi. Where's the person needing help?"

274

"Up at the house," Lilly answered.

"Hop in."

"Thank you." Lilly scrambled inside.

"She fell off a kitchen stool?" the female attendant asked.

"Yes. Dr. Wakefield thinks she did something to her ankle."

"A doctor has already seen her?" asked the burly male ambulance driver. Unconsciously Lilly shifted closer to the door. The man had a surly bulldog look about him that reminded her too much of Myron. "He lives there. He told us to call the ambulance."

"Lucky for her," the woman said.

The ambulance came to a halt directly in front of the steps. The wail of the siren faded, but the red light continued to flash. Piling out of the vehicle, the attendants went to the back for their case.

"Lilly, what happened? Is Adam all right?" Eleanor cried, running from around the side of the house.

"He's fine. Odette fell and he had us call the ambulance."

"Adam?" Surprise flashed across her face.

"Which way?" asked the male attendant, his broad face unsmiling.

"This way." Lilly led them to the kitchen, then stepped aside.

"I think I'm about to be replaced." Adam came to his feet, reaching out his hand. "Lilly."

"Coming, Dr. Wakefield."

The male attendant stopped, the emergency case banging against his leg. "He's the doctor who told you to call?"

"Yes," Lilly answered.

"You got to be kidding. That guy is blind," the male attendant said, his voice filled with derision. "I'm sick and tired of all these false runs. This is the fourth one today."

"My son is a prominent neurosurgeon," Eleanor declared. "If he said to call an ambulance there was reason."

"Mother?" Frowning, Adam turned toward her voice. "When did you get here?"

"I —" Eleanor hesitated. "We'll talk about it later, once Odette is taken care of."

The male attendant turned to go. "This is a wash. I'm not taking the advice of a blind man."

"Samuel?" Odette whimpered in pain and fear.

Samuel came to his feet. "I called the ambulance and I'm telling you you'd better take my wife in, and you had better do it to the best of your ability, as limited as it seems to be. I already called my wife's doctor and he's expecting her and we're going in that ambulance."

"It's your money to waste," the surly man said.

"John," the female attendant hissed in warning.

"I'll go get the cart," John said and left.

"Take me to my room," Adam ordered, his voice tight and strained.

"I'm sor—"

"Now," Adam said, cutting Lilly off.

"Come on." She hooked his hand through her arm and led him out of the room.

"Adam —"

"Not now, Mother."

Her hands clamped together, Eleanor stepped aside and let them pass.

Lilly glanced around as the sound of the gurney rolling over the hardwood floor faded into silence when it reached the area rugs. His lip curled, the attendant stared at them. Lilly mouthed, *bully* and led Adam up the stairs.

Eleanor was so angry she was trembling. Too angry to stand still, she paced the length of the counter in Adam's kitchen, the telephone gripped in her hand.

"Eleanor, what is it?"

"Jonathan, I'm so angry I could spit."

"Then spit and tell me how I can help," he told her.

His calm, reassuring voice almost made her smile until she thought of Adam's face, the look of defeat, when he left the kitchen. Quickly she told Jonathan what had happened, ending with, "Please check on Odette and get me the name of that attendant. He hasn't heard the last of this."

"I'll call the ER to see who is on duty and check on Odette. As soon as I can, I'll leave here and go over there personally," he told her. "And leave the attendant to me."

Eleanor heard the tightness in Jonathan's voice, and oddly, it eased some of her anger. He was the first person she had called when the hospital notified her that Adam had been hurt. He'd chartered a plane and been there in four hours as calm and reassuring as he was now.

"How did Adam take you being there?"

"Not very well," she admitted. Jonathan always seemed to know the things she didn't have to speak. "Perhaps I should have gone as he requested."

"Adam loves you, Eleanor. He's not angry at you, but at the situation."

"I know, but it's just so hard." Tears welled up in her eyes. "Why?"

"Would knowing the answer make any difference? Would it make this any easier on any of us?"

"No," she answered softly. She forgot at times that she wasn't the only one suffering. "I'll let you get back to your patients."

"I'll be out after I leave the hospital."

"You don't have to do that. It's a long drive."

"I'll see you around seven. Good-bye."

Eleanor hung up the phone feeling better. She wasn't alone. As long as she had Jonathan she wasn't alone.

Going to the foot of the stairs, she stared up. If only Adam had someone who would stand by his side no matter what he said or did. To let him know that he mattered. Nicole certainly wasn't that person. She was an intelligent, beautiful, ambitious woman. She'd tried, but she hadn't been able to stick. Few women could have when nothing was being given in return. It took unconditional love and understanding to keep caring for someone without expecting anything in return. Eleanor had been aware of that when she walked away from a medical career and married Randolph. He'd shown his love in countless small ways: notes on her pillows, impromptu rendezvous, midnight suppers. But she'd always been aware his career came first.

Not an easy lesson, but one she had learned as any wife of a doctor must learn. Illness was seldom convenient, to the patient, to the physician's family, to the attending physician. But if the bond was strong enough, the love and the marriage would survive.

Adam needed someone. Eleanor just wished she knew who.

"Please leave."

Lilly heard the words, saw the humiliation and defeat in Adam's face, felt tears prick her eyes. She knew what it was to feel the same way. "You need to eat."

"I need to be left alone."

For the first time, something inside her didn't go still and quiet at his raised voice. She'd seen him with Odette and now understood what a wonderful and caring doctor he must have been. "That ambulance attendant was wrong."

Adam's shoulder jerked. "He was right. How could I help someone when I can't even help myself?"

Without thinking, she caught his arm when he would have moved away from her. "You did help. You calmed Odette, reassured her enough so she didn't get hysterical about going to the hospital in the ambulance. That's more than her husband or I could do."

"You said it. She was hysterical. She's probably fine."

"You didn't think that when you examined her."

His laugh was bitter. "A blind doctor. No wonder the attendant was incredulous." He pulled his arm free. "Go, Lilly. Please."

She watched him feel his way across the room. "You have to eat."

Finding the chair, Adam sat down and turned his head.

She was used to him shutting her out, but this time it was different. He had been defiant in the past, but this time there was defeat in the slump of his shoulders, the bowed head.

"You have to eat," she repeated, barely getting the words past the lump in her throat. "I'll go fix you a tray."

Leaving the room, she started down the stairs and saw Mrs. Wakefield. The older woman met her halfway.

She searched Lilly's face, then slapped the flat of her hand on the bannister. "I wish I could get my hands on that ignorant man."

"Me, too," Lilly said, anger creeping into her voice. "He had no right to talk to Dr. Wakefield that way."

For a long time Eleanor studied the usually quiet Lilly, who was now almost as angry as she was. The few occasions that Lilly had called or come to the cottage had been brief. Eleanor had gotten the distinct impression that at times Lilly was afraid of her own shadow. It didn't take much thought on Eleanor's part to figure out the reason, but now she was upset on Adam's behalf.

"Thank you, Lilly, for caring."

Lilly flushed and clasped her hands in front of her. "He was so gentle and caring with Odette. He calmed her down and made her relax. He must have been a wonderful doctor."

"He was. That's why this is so senseless and painful for all of us."

"But he can still get better, can't he?" Lilly questioned.

"I pray so, Lilly," Eleanor said, her gaze going up the stairs. "I don't suppose it would be a good idea to go up and talk to him."

Lilly saw the heartache in the older woman's face and felt helpless. "He doesn't want to see anyone."

Eleanor nodded and wrapped her arms around her waist. "Do you have any children, Lilly?"

The question caught her off guard. She had wanted Shayla and Rafe to be hers, but they never had been. "No."

"It's one of the most rewarding experiences you can have. You want them to be happy, to be loved. You'd give anything for that, pray for that to happen." Once again she stared up the stairs. "A mother should be able to help her children."

If there was one thing Lilly understood, it was the need to be needed, to know you made a difference in someone's life. She also understood how it felt to fail. Acting on instinct, she tentatively touched Eleanor's shoulder. "I was just going to fix Dr. Wakefield dinner. Would you like to help?"

"He used to love my stuffed pork chops."

"Then stuffed pork chops it is." Gently but firmly she led Eleanor to the kitchen.

The step stool was still overturned, the stainless-steel mixing bowls scattered over the tile floor. Quickly Lilly crossed the room to pick up the step stool and put it in the closet.

When Lilly turned, Eleanor had already picked up the bowls and placed them in the sink. Somehow Lilly wasn't surprised. Eleanor Wakefield wasn't a pampered woman or one who sat around waiting for others to do for her. "Do you think Dr. Delacroix could find out how Odette is doing?"

"I've already called," Eleanor said, turning on the faucet in the sink to wash the bowls. "He's going to check on her and come by later."

Lilly opened the freezer door, took out a package of pork chops, and went to the microwave to defrost them. "Then we better fix extra."

Uneasily Lilly stood outside Adam's door. It had been two hours since Odette had been taken to the hospital. Lilly thought she'd have news of the housekeeper's condition by now. She didn't.

Dr. Delacroix had called to say there had been a pileup on the freeway and the emergency room was in chaos. Eleanor had returned to the cottage after extracting a promise from Lilly that she would call her after she left Adam's room.

Propping the tray between her body and the door, she knocked. She didn't expect an answer, and she didn't get one. "Dr. Wakefield, I have your supper tray." Opening the door, she stepped inside the dark room. The light from the hallway only penetrated a few feet. The room had never before been in complete darkness since she arrived.

She shivered and flicked on the light. She saw him immediately.

He sat in the wingback leather chair. His long legs sprawled in front of him, his wrists limply hanging over the arm of the chair, his dark head thrown back as if he were staring at the ceiling.

Closing the door, she set the tray on the table. "Stuffed pork chops. Your mother helped. She said they used to be one of your favorites."

He didn't move.

She swallowed. "We still haven't heard how Odette is doing. Dr. Delacroix went thought of her marriage. "I filed for divorce."

"Why?"

"He hit me," she whispered. "I–I made excuses every time it happened. Mother Crawford wasn't my mother; she was my mother-in-law and the kindest, sweetest person I ever knew. After — after she died I packed up and left while he was at work. I was on my way to New Orleans when my car broke down. That's why I went back to town the day I got my car out of the shop. Myron is going to fight the divorce. I had to send my lawyer more money." She felt Adam's fingertips brush her arm, then slide down until his fingers entwined with hers. There was strength in his hand, a quiet gentleness. "I bet before you lost your sight you wouldn't have let anyone question your judgment."

His hand jerked. Afraid he'd pull away, her hand twisted and clasped his. "You lost your sight because of the greed and cruelty of others. Don't let anyone else take more. Please."

"Don't waste your tears on me, Lilly."

"I'm not," she said, brushing the moisture away.

"I was an arrogant bastard. I thought I made my own destiny. I was a fool." His thumb grazed the top of her hand. "My stupidity was just as much the cause of my

286

losing my sight as their greed."

"How can you say that? You don't know they wouldn't have attacked you anyway."

"No, I don't. But in my arrogance, I thought I was invincible. I had just finished a marathon surgery. Over seven hours. I was high on my own power."

"That doesn't excuse them," she said. "Myron always said it was my fault that he yelled. He said he hit me because I questioned him. That was an excuse, not a reason. I realize that now." Her hand tightened. "It took me years to realize I might not have control, but I had choices. That was the turning point for me."

"You were right to leave."

"I know that now." She swallowed. "I'm never going back."

"No, you won't."

The sound of the phone ringing startled both of them. Whoever called had dialed Dr. Wakefield's private extension.

"Take a message. I don't want to talk with anyone."

"What if it's your mother?"

"Tell her I'll call her tomorrow."

Realizing there wasn't any point in arguing with him, Lilly rose and went to answer the phone. "Ouch."

"What happened?"

"I walked into the foot of the bed."

"Turn on the light before you break your

neck!" Adam snapped.

"Yes, sir." Lilly turned on the lamp on the nightstand, then snatched up the phone on the fifth ring. "Hello. . . .

"Oh, my goodness. Wait a minute," she said, her fingers clamped tight on the phone. "It's Odette's oldest son, Samuel Junior. Odette had a fracture and he wants to thank you."

"Are you sure?"

"Come talk to him yourself," Lilly said, experiencing a strange mixture of feelings, sadness that Odette was injured but relief that Dr. Wakefield had been right.

With smooth movements that were so different from hers, Dr. Wakefield walked to the bedside table and took the phone. "This is Dr. Wakefield. She's resting comfortably? . . . I see. Put her on.

"Odette, stop fussing. Considering your diabetes and hypertension, I think spending the night in the hospital is a wise decision." Adam's lip twitched. "I don't think your doctor needs to call and discuss the management of your care with me, but I appreciate the confidence. Let me speak with Samuel.

"Samuel, take as long as you need off with Odette. I can tell she's going to be a difficult patient. . . . You're welcome. Good night. Thanks for calling." He hung up the phone, a smile growing on his face.

"I'm suddenly hungry."

"It won't take but a minute to heat up your dinner."

"This time I don't mind cold food, but you could do something else for me."

"What?"

"Call Mother's number and let her know."

Eleanor was looking out the cottage window for Jonathan when he pulled up. Opening the door, she rushed out. By the time he had gotten out of the car, she was standing there, a broad smile on her face. "Odette and her family called Adam. He called me. Isn't that wonderful?"

It was all he could do not to graze his knuckles down her cheek. "I was there when they called."

She made a face. "I might have known."

"They were hesitant to call since it was late, but I convinced them that Adam might like hearing he was right."

She hooked her arm through his and led him back inside. "Thank you, Jonathan."

"You might also be interested in knowing that even without a formal complaint filed by Samuel, the female attendant had already spoken to her superiors."

Eleanor's temper flared again. "Good for her, but it doesn't end there."

Jonathan palmed her cheeks. Immediately she stilled. "Let me take care of it. In the meantime, I smell something delicious."

Eleanor laughed despite her accelerated heartbeat, her nervous stomach. "Jonathan, do you ever think of more than food?"

Brown eyes glowed. "Frequently."

The smile froze on Eleanor's face. Her nipples actually tingled.

Slowly Jonathan's hands slid from her face, leaving in their wake heated flesh and a growing desire to feel his hands again. "But sometimes a man has to take what he can get."

"Pork chops," she managed.

"It's a start," Jonathan said.

Eleanor stared into his intent gaze and felt as if she were on a precipice and the dirt was crumbling beneath her feet. One wrong move and she'd go over the edge. "I'll fix your plate."

Jonathan watched Eleanor hurry away and almost smiled. Soon. Very soon she'd be rushing toward him and into his arms.

Hands in his pockets, he followed her into the kitchen.

A sound woke Lilly up. Lifting her head from the pillow, she listened. Music. A piano.

Reaching over, she turned on the light. She frowned, then threw back the covers and went into the hallway. It was definitely a piano, and the sound was coming from downstairs. It couldn't be.

She turned the light on in the hall and swiftly ran down the steps, the volume of the music and her surety growing with each running step. She burst into the living room with her chest heaving.

Trembling fingers clicked on the light switch. Adam sat at the piano. His fingers danced over the keys with a precision that brought the bright sheen of tears to her eyes. She brushed them away and sat in the nearest chair.

Suddenly he stopped. His dark head twisted to one side. "Lilly?"

She swallowed the lump in her throat and found her voice: "I didn't mean to interrupt."

He turned and Lilly's breath caught. On his handsome face he wore a teasing smile she'd never seen before. "You didn't."

"You play beautifully."

"Thanks. I haven't played in years."

"I always wanted to, but we never had the money," she said wistfully, glad the old pain and anger were no longer there.

"Come here. I'll teach you."

Her shoulders snapped back. "What?"

"You don't think I could do it?" He folded his arms across his chest in an obvious challenge.

"I didn't say that," she hastened to re-assure him.

He scooted over and patted the wooden bench beside him. "Then come and sit down."

Uneasiness moved through her. "Maybe we should wait for morning?"

"Why? We're both up. Neither one of us has to get up early, so why wait?"

In the face of such logic, she didn't have an answer. "All right." Her bare feet were silent as she crossed to him. She slipped onto the bench beside Adam. The instant she did, she realized her mistake. The cool-ness of the cherry wood bench and the heat of his muscled body against hers jolted her nervous system. "Oh."

"What's the matter?"

"I, er . . . nothing."

"Give me your hands," he requested, holding his out.

She didn't want to. Even now she re-membered the softness of his and the roughness of her own.

"Lilly?"

She stuck out hands that shook. "Don't be disappointed if I don't learn very easily."

He took her hands in his. "Why would you say that?"

She opened her mouth to say, "Because Myron always said so," then said instead,

"It's the middle of the night and my brain isn't functioning at top level."

He smiled and the sight did strange things to her insides. "Mine is. This is easy. I'll play the melody and you play the chords."

"What — what song are we going to play?" she asked, extremely conscious of him in a way that she had never been of Myron.

"Beethoven's 'Moonlight Sonata.' "

"What?" She tried to snatch her hands back.

Laughing, he held them firmly in his. "Lilly, I promise you can do this. You just have to trust me."

The laughter and his words caused a warm rush of feelings inside. "I trust you. It's me I don't trust."

"Then allow me to prove how mistaken you are." Taking her fingers, he placed them on the keys, three notes for each hand. "Now, when I pause you simply strike the keys. The melody is slow, a bit haunting, but the chord gives the music power. Ready?"

Lilly stared at his long, elegant fingers on the white keys, and said a little prayer that she wouldn't shake his emerging confidence. "Ready."

The movement of his fingers, the beauty of the piece, almost caught her off guard the first time he paused. The second time she was ready. She struck the notes and listened as Adam played on.

She was playing Beethoven. The music was as beautiful and as haunting as Adam had said. Laughter, free and easy, drifted from her mouth. "I'm doing it. I'm doing it."

His laughter joined in. He finished with a flourish. "Told you. Now, what else shall we play?"

Since most of the songs she knew were spirituals, she chose those, singing along with the music. She had a strong, clear voice and soon became more caught up in the words than what her fingers were playing. There were tears in her eyes when the last note of "How Great Thou Art" softly ebbed away.

"You have a beautiful voice," Adam said.

Lilly sniffed, rubbing the back of her hand over her eyes. "Thank you, but it was your playing."

"Seems we make a good team," he said quietly.

All of a sudden, she became aware once again of their thighs touching, of her being in her nightgown with nothing underneath. While playing and singing, one or both of them had scooted closer. Heat flushed her cheeks.

"This team member is getting sleepy."

to the hospital, but there was a pileup on the interstate and the emergency room is a madhouse."

Silence.

She removed the silver dome from the tray. "Meat at twelve, steamed broccoli at six. Apple pie at nine in a dessert plate."

"Take it back."

"Dr. —"

"Just leave me alone. Please."

Lilly replaced the lid but she couldn't make herself pick up the tray. Instead she pulled up another chair near his.

He straightened. "What are you doing?"

"Staying." Crossing the room, she flicked off the light switch, then felt her way back to the chair and sat down. "I didn't put Samuel up to talking to you today. I admit to doing it the first time, though. He wanted to show you he had faith you'd plan the garden together."

"A blind doctor and gardener. How interesting."

"You can't let what that man said bother you. I know about people like him who try to make others feel small so they can feel superior. My husband was just like him."

"Your husband?" He shifted toward her. "You never mentioned a husband."

Shame and embarrassment swept through her as it always did when she

She stood. "I think I'll go up."

"I'll go with you." Closing the lid, he slid off the bench.

Automatically she stepped beside him and let him take her arm. They stopped at the bottom of the stairs. "You get to lead again."

"Does this mean you're not going to badger me anymore?"

"Help," she corrected.

"Oh, yes. I forgot."

Smiling, they went up the steps.

Chapter Twelve

Adam was restless. Not the kind of restless that had kept him on edge since his blindness, but restless with the anticipation of getting the day started. Standing in front of Lilly's bedroom door, he contemplated for the umpteenth time that morning whether he should wake her. It had been after two when they had come upstairs for the second time last night. That was a scant five hours ago.

Folding his arms, he leaned against her door. Thanks to Lilly, he didn't have to live in a black void wondering about the passage of time. However, now it presented another problem. Since he was well aware of the early hour, should he wake her?

The unavoidable truth was that he missed her. He'd thoroughly enjoyed playing the piano by himself, but her shy, hesitant presence had increased his enjoyment.

She had faith in him yesterday after Odette's accident. She never doubted. Neither had Samuel and Odette. Despite his blindness, they had trusted his judgment. The male attendant had seen a blind man and prejudged him without looking for himself to see if Odette was injured. He'd judged Adam as Adam had judged himself, worthless and of no value to anyone.

But they both had been wrong. In giving reassurance to Odette, Adam knew he had received much more.

He thought of returning to his room and letting Lilly sleep, but the thought quickly disappeared and he gave in to temptation. He rationalized his decision by thinking there was no schedule to follow. Smiling, he raised his hand and knocked. The day was theirs to do as they pleased.

Lilly snuggled deeper into the pillow, but the persistent sound continued. Finally the sound penetrated. Knocking. Someone was at the door.

She jerked upright in bed. Throwing back the lightweight comforter, she scrambled out of bed, grabbing her robe from the foot of the bed as she passed. Opening the door, she was shocked to see Dr. Wakefield, arms folded, leaning against the doorjamb. "Dr. Wakefield!"

"Good morning."

"Is everything all right?" Her gaze ran over him silently. He certainly looked fit and well. He had on a turquoise Polo shirt and a pair of snug-fitting jeans that encased his long, muscular legs. Lilly shivered and pulled the lapels of the cotton robe closer together.

He tucked his head sheepishly. "I'm hungry."

Relief swept through her. She should have known. "Give me ten minutes. I'll come to your door and knock."

"Thanks."

Closing the door, Lilly quickly got the clothes she always laid out the night before and went to the bathroom to bathe and dress. In less than the time allotted she knocked on his door.

The door opened before she lowered her hand to her side. He stepped into the hallway. "You're right on time."

She smiled as he took her arm. "I may regret getting you that clock."

"That's a distinct possibility."

At the stairs, she paused and allowed him to find the railing with his left hand and take the lead going downstairs. She remained silent until they reached the bottom of the stairs. He might act casual, but his fingers had tightly gripped her arm on the way down.

"What would you like for breakfast?" she asked when they entered the kitchen.

"Surprise me."

"Since you're hungry, how about a quick omelet? You can beat the eggs."

His steps hesitated. "We might have a small omelet."

"You didn't doubt me on the piano; I

don't doubt you whisking eggs." She paused by the curved end of the kitchen counter. "Stool or the breakfast table?"

"Since you're going to make me work for my breakfast, the stool."

She took his hand and placed it on the padded seat. "Watch it when you slide on. The cabinet has gotten my knees a couple of times."

"As I recall, it's jumped out at me a time or two." Sitting, he placed his hand on the sparkling countertop. "Ready to work for my breakfast."

Lilly hoped she was doing the right thing. Finding a bowl, she cracked six eggs, picked up the whisk, and took everything to Adam. "Eggs can be slippery little devils, so I always start slow."

Silently Adam took the bowl and whisk. Lilly made herself move away and not watch. "Bacon or sausage?"

"Doesn't matter."

Lilly heard the tightness in his voice and opened the refrigerator. "Why don't I fix both?" Removing the meat, she reached for a knife and heard the scraping of the whisk against the side of the bowl. She glanced around to see Adam's stiff movements. But he was trying.

"Together, we'll have breakfast in no time. Remember, we're a team."

"I don't think you'll ever let me forget,"

Adam said, his lower lip tucked between his teeth in concentration, stirring instead of whisking, but Lilly couldn't have been prouder.

Eleanor walked briskly along the path from the cottage toward the main house. She needed a cup of coffee and had used the last of hers yesterday morning. She made a face. After seeing Adam, she was going grocery shopping. She didn't want a repeat of Jonathan checking out her food supply. Even as the thought annoyed her, she felt a little thrill of delight that he cared enough to check.

She was going up the steps to the kitchen when the sound of laughter caused her to go stock-still. Then she closed her eyes and gave thanks. She'd despaired of ever hearing Adam's carefree laughter again.

"Good morning, Adam, Lilly," she greeted them, opening the screen door and coming inside.

"Good morning, Mother," Adam said.

"Good morning, Eleanor. Have a seat. I'll get you a cup of coffee, and thanks to Adam, there's plenty of French toast and fixin's for an omelet."

Eleanor glanced at the smug expression on her son's face. "Explain."

"I had to work for my breakfast. I did

the eggs," Adam told her. "I did a pretty good job, if I do say so."

Pulling out a chair, she sat down at the round table across from her son. "I can't wait to taste for myself."

Lilly set a cup of black coffee by Eleanor. "Here's your coffee. Black."

Eleanor sipped her coffee and studied her son's happy expression. "I like that smile on your face."

Pushing the plate away, he leaned forward and placed his arms on the table. "I put you and Kristen through a lot. Thanks for hanging in there."

"What else would your family do?"

"Here's your breakfast," Lilly said, setting the plate in front of the other woman and handing her flatware and a sunny yellow napkin.

"Looks good." Eleanor forked a bite of the omelet in her mouth. "Ummm, delicious. Can I come back every morning?"

"You aren't moving back into the house?" Adam asked, pausing with his cup of coffee in his hands.

She laid her fork aside and came to a quick decision. "I rather like the cottage. Besides, you and Lilly can do whatever you've planned without having to worry about entertaining me."

His brows bunched. He took a sip of coffee, then replaced the mug on the table.

"I haven't thought much past this morning."

"If you'd like, you could get a handle on your mail. You have two boxes like the kind copying paper comes in that are crammed full. I had Kristen ship them to me last week. I went through it and discarded the junk mail, but you still have a lot of correspondence. Working together, Lilly and I could start going through it." Arms folded, Eleanor leaned across the table. "Your accountant's been taking care of most of your business, but you know your father always insisted that we know where our money was being spent."

Adam nodded. "Lilly, if you'll help me navigate to my study I'll contact my accountant first; then I have a couple of calls to place and then we can go through the mail."

Sitting behind the desk in his study, Adam listened to the phone ring in Kristen's apartment. Aware that his sister wasn't a morning person, he patiently waited for her to wake up enough to recognize the ringing of the phone and answer it. Her first class wasn't until nine. It was barely seven on the Coast.

"Hello."

Her soft, East Coast–accented voice sounded husky and gravelly from sleep.

"Wake up, sleepyhead, and talk to your big brother."

"Adam! Oh, Adam." All sleepiness left Kristen's voice, to be replaced by ringing excitement. "It's so good to hear your voice. I was hoping you'd call so I could tell you how proud of you I am."

He leaned back in the leather chair, the corners of his mouth tilted upward in a reluctant smile. "I guess Mother called you."

"Last night. You know how she is."

They both were aware that their mother had followed a predictable pattern, bragging on her children. Just as they were both aware that in the weeks following his accident his behavior had been appalling rather than heroic, but neither brought it up. "So how are the studies going?"

"They're about to get better."

He accepted her cryptic statement. She had worried and suffered right along with him. "Everything is going to be all right. Mother, Jonathan, and I will be there to see you graduate next month."

"I'm counting on it. I've missed you, big brother."

"The same goes here."

"Then why don't I come down for the weekend?"

"No way. I distinctly remember the last weeks of undergrad school. Papers coming out of the wazoo. Stay and study."

"Spoilsport."

He chuckled. "You'll thank me when exam time comes."

"It's good hearing you laugh again."

"It feels good. Now, go study."

"Bye, Adam. I love you."

"I love you, too. Bye."

He hung up the phone, dreading the next call. But there was no way around it. Getting the operator on the line again, Adam placed a call to Nicole at her office in downtown San Francisco.

Despite it being early, he knew that unless she had a business appointment, she'd be there. She believed that good work ethics and responsibility started at the top.

"Nicole Ashe." The tone was polished and smooth as silk. It fit perfectly the image that Nicole always wanted to project.

"Hello, Nicole."

"Adam?" Surprise quickly gave way to unbridled delight. "Oh, Adam, honey. It's wonderful hearing your voice. When are you coming back?"

His fingers drummed on the desk blotter. "Not for a while."

"Why not?"

He never realized until then how much it annoyed him for Nicole to question him. Usually he ignored her. "I enjoy being here."

"How can you say that? I'm here. Your friends are here." Her tone became petulant.

"I made them as uncomfortable as they made me." His fingers stopped their drumming motion and closed into a tight fist.

"What about me?" she asked, her voice deepening to a suggestive husky purr. "Don't you miss me? Don't you want to be with me?"

"Nicole," he said and sat forward in his seat, dreading what was coming next. "I don't want to hurt you, but you know it can never be as it was between us."

"Yes, it can if you'll only let it."

He hated the plaintive note in her voice. "We both know better. Cut your losses and move on."

"It's her, isn't it?"

His fingers touched a pen on his desk. He picked it up. "Her who?"

"That Lilly person."

He drummed the pen on the desk, wondering how he could quickly end the call without hurting Nicole's feelings. "Lilly has nothing to do with my decision."

"Yes, she does." Nicole's voice cooled. "Since you didn't want to speak with me, I called Kristen. She's kept me informed about the woman your mother hired."

"She helped me."

"For a thousand dollars a week, I should hope so."

His shoulders snapped back in shock. "What?"

"Didn't you know?"

He clutched the pen. He felt betrayed, used, and it came through in his voice: "No. No, I didn't."

"I'm sorry if this sounds harsh, but she did it for the money. If you're staying for her, you have no reason to."

"Yes, why else would she or anyone put up with a blind man?" Bitterness tinged each word.

"I didn't mean it that way," she hastened to reassure him.

"Good-bye, Nicole."

"No, Adam, wait. Let me expl—"

Adam carefully placed the receiver in the cradle instead of slamming it as he wanted. Anger churned through him, at himself, at Lilly. She'd been paid an exorbitant amount to care for him. He recalled her pleading the first time she came to his room. She wanted to stay for the money, not because she felt anything for him. She'd been doing a job, nothing more.

The phone rang again and he ignored it. He didn't want to speak to Nicole again, and he was positive it was her. He wasn't sure why the amount of Lilly's salary bothered him, but it did.

"Dr. Wakefield, Nicole Ashe is on the phone," Lilly said as she entered the study.

Adam lifted his head and turned in the direction her voice had come from. "How much did my mother pay you, Lilly?"

"What?"

He rose and planted both hands on the desk. "How much did my mother pay you to care for a hopelessly depressed blind man?"

The words lashed out at her. Finally she understood. "That's why Ms. Ashe sounded so upset on the phone. She told you."

Adam's lips thinned with anger. "No wonder you were so anxious to stay. No wonder no matter what I did or said you always came back. You would have taken care of the devil for that kind of money."

There was no use denying his words. He had spoken the truth. "I was desperate, yes, but I also wanted to help you."

"Spare me the humanitarianism. The longer you stayed, the more you earned. I was a meal ticket." His laugh was bitter. "To think I thought . . ." His voice trailed off, his head lowered.

"Dr. Wake—"

His head came up sharply. "You're fired."

"What?" Her eyes widened with shock.

"Get your things and get out. I want you gone within the hour. You hear me? Get out!"

She wouldn't cry. Lilly told herself that, but it didn't stop the silent tears flowing down her cheeks. Her fault again for believing, for letting her guard slip even a tiny bit. She had only herself to blame for the ache in her chest.

She shouldn't have let herself care about him as a person. Men weren't to be trusted. They played with your emotions. Shutting the suitcase, she dragged it from the bed and left her bedroom. She met an anxious-appearing Eleanor on the stairs.

"Lilly, Nicole called. She said Adam became upset when she mentioned your salary."

"He fired me."

Eleanor's eyes widened and she came to Lilly and placed her hand on her trembling arm. "He's upset. He'll calm down once he's had time to think this through."

"He doesn't want me here." That admission hurt. Hurt badly.

"Yes, he does. He's just too upset now to realize it," Eleanor said. "I had no idea he'd be so upset about your salary."

Lilly worked her shoulders. "It doesn't matter. I'll be going. Thank you for trusting me to take care of Dr. Wakefield."

"Lilly —"

"I'm not staying. I won't be treated like

this again. Myron was enough."

"Myron?"

There was no reason not to tell her. "I lied. I was married. I filed for divorce and left my abusive husband the day my car broke down. I left there with no firm job prospects, few clothes, and very little money. That's why I didn't want to have a reference check. I didn't want him to find me." She spoke past the stinging in her throat. "Mother Crawford wasn't my mother; she was my mother-in-law. She and my stepson, Rafe, were the only good thing to come out of my marriage. When I left Myron, I promised myself that I'd never be subjected to that kind of treatment again. I deserve better."

"Lilly, I'm sorry."

"Not your fault. Good-bye, Eleanor. Please tell Dr. Delacroix good-bye for me." The lump in her throat threatening to choke her, she stepped around Eleanor and quickly went down the stairs.

Eleanor went down the stairs behind Lilly, but her destination was the study. His shoulders bent, his head resting in the palms of his hands, Adam sat behind his desk. The sight tore through Eleanor, but she refused to let his dejected appearance dissuade her. "What did you say to her?"

"Not now, Mother." His voice was tired.

"Yes, now. Lilly came here afraid of her

309

own shadow and I just learned why, an abusive husband, but she stayed and stuck it out to help you. She almost didn't take the job because Jonathan wanted a reference check. Even with the offer of a thousand dollars a week, she chose to sit in a broken-down car. That took fear and courage."

"But she took the job, didn't she? The money was too good to turn down."

"It might have been initially for the money, but I saw the look on her face when she came from your room the first time. She cared and she's shown me she cares time and time again. I stayed in the cottage to ensure that I wasn't mistaken about her. Do you think for one instant that if I thought she was only here for the money I wouldn't have hired someone else?"

Adam rocked back in his chair. "Just proves she's a good actress. She annoyed me."

"And by doing so she got you to forget that you were blind and act instead of react. After she got you to eat and get cleaned up, I would have let her stay in any case. In fact, I told her as much. She had a job, regardless. But she kept trying to think of ways to help you. Everything from the tapes to the clothes was her idea. Not mine. And you just kicked her in the teeth!"

Slowly his head came up. "I didn't know."

"And you didn't ask. You just struck out the same way you've been doing since your blindness. I've been disappointed, even hurt, by your actions, but I've never been ashamed of you until this moment."

He flinched at the cutting remark but knew it was deserved. "Mother, I'm sorry."

"I'm not the one you should be apologizing to." Eleanor wasn't in a forgiving frame of mind.

For an endless moment, Adam sat there; then he stood and hurried around the desk and straight into the Chippendale armchair.

"Damn!" He and the chair both toppled.

"Adam!" Eleanor rushed to him, then hesitated. In the past he had never wanted help.

"Mother, could you please help me up and show me to the garage?" He reached out his hand to her. "I think it's time I became the man you raised me to be."

Brushing tears from her eyes, Lilly opened the door of her car, tossed her suitcase on the front seat, and slid in beside it, chastising herself as she did so. She had no reason to cry. She had money in her pocket; her car was running. She had nothing to cry about. It had just been a job.

And she had come to care about Dr. Wakefield more than she should.

Tears fell harder. Clutching the steering wheel, she leaned her head against it and cried.

"I thought I told you not to waste tears on me."

Stunned, she jerked her head up to see Adam standing beside the open door of the car she had forgotten to close. "How . . ." she began, then saw the answer to how he had found his way to the garage. Eleanor stood a short distance away. "Go back inside, Dr. Wakefield."

"Ordering me around again." It was more of a statement than a question.

"I never ordered you around," Lilly told him, wishing she didn't recall when that had been a joke between them. "Please move so I can close the door."

He moved closer. Reaching out, he touched her shoulder, then slid his hand down to grasp her hand and tug. "Come on; let's go back into the house."

"No, I'm leaving."

"I'm sorry, Lilly. Sorrier than you'll ever know."

"Some hurts can't be mended with words."

His breath hissed in sharply. His mouth tightened. "I'd never abuse you like he did."

"You hurt me," she said softly, her voice thick with unshed tears. "Don't you think I know how it feels to be used? How it feels not to be wanted for yourself? Myron did that to me for six years."

Anger shot through Adam. "I'm not that slime of a husband."

"Then you think I'm a user like he was?"

"Never. You've got to believe me." Adam raked his hand over his head in growing frustration. "Oh, hel— heck, Lilly. Never that. Never that."

"Do you have any idea how you made me feel?" she asked, her words so quiet he had to bend his head to hear them. Then he wished he hadn't.

She sounded defeated, lost. Guilt ate at him. His only defense was the truth, a truth that would leave him as defenseless as she.

"Do you think I wasn't hurt? No matter how much I pushed you away, you always came back. No one ever did that, except my family. Besides Jonathan, you're the only person who never caved in or acted differently. You never treated me as if my blindness diminished my intelligence." He paused and drew in a deep breath. "I thought it was more than a job. I thought you . . . hell, I thought you cared about me like I care about you."

He cared.

His words rushed through her like a healing balm. He cared. He'd cursed, but it was out of frustration, not hatred or disrespect.

"Please stay," he continued, his hand gripping hers tightly. "You haven't finished reading *The Third Degree*. I doubt if Mother will read it to me, as upset as she is with me."

The joy spiraling within Lilly took a nosedive. "That's what you want me for, to read, cook, and clean?"

"No. I could hire someone to do that," Adam told her. "I want you for what no amount of money can buy. As a true friend. Please stay."

Lilly sniffed and brushed the last lingering tears from her eyes. A true friend. She'd only had one in her entire life. "On one condition?"

"Name it."

"You teach me to really play the piano."

"It's a deal."

Eleanor was waiting for them when they emerged from the garage arm in arm. "I'll just go to the cottage and get the mail."

"You can't carry that much by yourself," Adam protested. "I'll go with you."

Both women traded worried glances. Lilly spoke first. "The path is smooth, but I don't think you should carry a big box."

"I didn't intend to. Mother probably has a handled shopping bag or two that we can use."

Eleanor glanced at Lilly for guidance. Getting Adam out of the house and down the steps to the garage had been awkward for both of them. The winding path to the cottage was twice that distance.

Adam, his jaw clenched, spoke into the growing silence: "I'm not helpless."

"We never thought you were," Lilly said, praying she was making the right decision. The worst thing they could do was discourage Adam's emerging confidence with their own fears. "While you two are getting the mail, I'll take my things back upstairs."

"Come on, Mother," Adam said, reaching for his mother's arm and feeling her tremble. He leaned over and whispered, "Think of this as helping me take my first baby steps. I might have fallen, but I got up and I learned."

"You certainly did," Eleanor said, her voice steadier. "Lilly, we'll be back in a little bit."

Lilly watched them trying to find a rhythm to their steps and knew they were going to be all right when Adam bumped into his mother and almost fell. Instead of reacting with embarrassment or anger, he had laughed. He wasn't afraid of trying and failing. He'd come a long ways from the angry, frightened man she'd met when she arrived.

And she'd helped. No one could take that away from her. She was good at something.

Grabbing her suitcase, Lilly went inside. She was passing the telephone stand in the hallway when the phone rang. Pausing, she picked up the receiver. "Wakefield residence." The line clicked dead.

Shrugging, she hung up the phone and continued upstairs to her room. Deciding unpacking could wait, she came back downstairs and went to the kitchen and started to finish cleaning up. She wanted all the household duties out of the way so she could help Adam if he needed her. She'd just finished when the phone rang again. "Wakefield residence."

There was no answer, but she could tell there was someone on the line. Myron? Her stomach knotted in fear. "Who's there?"

"I want to speak to Adam."

Nicole. Lilly recognized the silky voice and the bad attitude immediately. "Why do you dislike me?"

"I asked to speak with Adam."

Lilly's fingers flexed on the phone. Nicole had the same demanding way about her that Myron had. "Unless you answer my question, you aren't going to."

Nicole's quick intake of breath echoed through the phone. "Why, you. You're just the hired help!"

"If I were just that, I wouldn't bother you so much," Lilly said, sure she was right.

"Don't give yourself more importance than you have," Nicole said tartly. "Adam admires sophisticated, beautiful women. Even blind, you can't possibly think he'd want you."

"You're jealous," Lilly said, the unbelievable thought taking root in her brain and sprouting like a dandelion after a hard spring rain. She laughed at the absurdity of it and the undeniable pleasure it gave her.

"I'd be a fool to be jealous of you!"

"You won't get an argument from me," Lilly said. "Those things you think so highly of don't mean squat to Adam now, and although you may not be aware of it yet, he's a better man for it. Surface means nothing to him, and that's what worries you, isn't it, Nicole? You're all show."

"How dare you speak to me that way. Wait until I tell Eleanor and Adam."

"After you hurt Adam, do you think either of them will want to speak with you? You tried to paint me in a poor light, not once thinking of how it might make Adam feel. You might be beautiful and sophisticated, as you said, but you're selfish and unsure of yourself with Adam."

"You —"

"Instead of calling me names, Nicole, your time would be better served trying to think of a way to apologize to Adam and his mother for causing trouble. They're nice enough to forgive you and think you acted out of love and concern for him." Lilly's tone cooled. "I know better. I've known someone just like you who gave everyone the impression of being kind and generous but who was actually mean and spiteful. I'll tell Adam you called." She hung up the phone, feeling proud of herself until she felt a presence behind her and turned.

"Dr. Delacroix!" Her heart threatened to beat out of her chest.

This time it wasn't his build that intimidated her but the sharpness in his brown eyes. "What was that all about?"

Nervously Lilly rubbed her hand against the side of her leg. She and Dr. Delacroix were on better terms now, but she was well aware she had no right to speak to Nicole that way. "Nicole and I had a difference of opinion."

His long legs carried him too quickly from the doorway to within a few feet of her. "What about?"

"I think you should ask Eleanor."

"I would if she were here."

So that was the reason for Nicole's re-

318

peated phone calls, Lilly thought. She hadn't been able to reach Eleanor at the cottage, so she had called the main house. Lilly glanced at the back kitchen door. "She and Adam went to her cottage. They're probably on their way back. You could take the path and meet them."

Instead of taking the hint, he said, "If Nicole did something to upset Adam or Eleanor, I want to know and I want to know now."

Lilly started to step back from him as he advanced purposefully toward her again; then she stopped. He wasn't Myron. He wouldn't abuse others to make himself feel important. She'd seen the tender way he stared at Eleanor, the love in his eyes for Adam.

"All right, I'll tell you. But I'll do it while I marinate the roast for dinner."

"Whatever it takes."

In clear, concise words she related what had happened after Adam spoke with Nicole on the phone. Lilly ended by saying, "Instead of hurting me as she intended, she hurt Adam."

"You're right about one thing," Jonathan said from where he leaned negligently against the counter, his legs crossed at the ankles, his arms folded.

Lilly glanced over her shoulder as she bent to place the marinated meat inside the refrigerator. "What?"

"She's jealous."

Lilly flushed and turned toward the refrigerator. "I-I didn't mean it the way it probably sounded." Closing the door, she went back to clean up the countertop and busily began putting away the spices for the marinade. For the first time in a long time, she wished that her hands weren't callused and worn, her face so angular, her clothes faded.

"Then you wouldn't care that Adam and Nicole had a very close relationship before his blindness?"

There was no mistaking his meaning. Her hands shook as she picked up the plastic wrap and placed it back in the cabinet. "I'm just the hired help."

Strong, gentle hands closed around her shoulders and turned her toward him. Jonathan stared deep into Lilly's sad wide eyes. "Take some advice from a man who's been there. Lying to yourself only makes it harder."

Her heart boomed in her chest, but not from fear. "I don't know what you're talking about."

Jonathan's face filled with despair. "I'm afraid you do. Soon you'll have to stop and admit it to yourself, and then, Lilly, you'll learn what true heartache really is."

The door behind them slammed.

Chapter Thirteen

Jonathan glanced over his shoulder and saw Eleanor and Adam with two handled bags in his hands. The look of shock on Eleanor's face caused Jonathan to drop his hands and quickly step away from Lilly. As soon as he'd moved, he realized his mistake. He'd acted as if he'd been caught in an indiscretion.

Lilly, not sensing the undercurrents, went to them and took Adam's arm. "Dr. Delacroix is here to see you and Eleanor, Adam."

"It must be Wednesday," Adam said, allowing Lilly to lead him farther into the room.

"Yes," Jonathan said, his gaze going behind Adam to Eleanor, who remained unmoved. "I didn't get a chance to take *Lady Lost* out last weekend; I thought I'd take her for a run on my day off."

"You have a horse?" Lilly asked.

"A speedboat," Adam said, wistfulness in his voice. "But she can't beat mine."

Jonathan cut his eyes to him. "You'll never let me forget that race. You want to come with me?"

Adam shook his head. He might have

climbed a hill or two. He wasn't ready for a mountain. "Maybe another time."

"How about you, Eleanor?" Jonathan asked, his gaze going back to Eleanor. She wouldn't meet his eyes.

"I have to help Adam," she said quietly.

"Lilly can do that, Mother." Adam held up the bags. "This will keep us busy for most of the day. Go on. You need to get out."

"Maybe Lilly would like to go in my place," Eleanor said, aware of the brief spark of jealousy she had felt when she saw Jonathan staring down into Lilly's eyes, his hands on her shoulders. She fought hard to dispel it.

Lilly shook her head. "I've never been on a boat before. I'm not sure I'd like it."

"Looks like it's you and me, Eleanor," Jonathan said.

Eleanor tried to tell herself she hadn't heard the possessive note in Jonathan's voice and, if she had, that she shouldn't feel pleased. There was nothing between him and Lilly. Jonathan didn't practice duplicity. He wouldn't pay court to two women at the same time. The instant the thought materialized, Eleanor stiffened. She was teetering on the edge of that cliff again. "Perhaps some other time, Jonathan. I planned to go see Odette today."

"I'll drive you," Jonathan offered. "I

called before I left. She was being discharged this morning."

Adam smiled. "I bet Dr. Brown is thrilled."

Jonathan had to smile with him. "I've never seen him so harried. Last night he was ready to pull out the few strands of hair left on his head."

"Odette is strong-willed," Adam said.

"Just like another woman I know," Jonathan said, his gaze back on Eleanor.

"Please give her my best," Lilly said. "Eleanor, could you please take her some flowers from me? If it's all right, I'll repay you when you get back."

"That's a marvelous idea, Lilly," Adam said. "Pick up an arrangement from me, too."

Eleanor, who was trying to think of a gracious excuse to go in later by herself, felt trapped. From the pleased look on Jonathan's face, he was well aware of her predicament. "Of course."

"We better get going." Jonathan crossed the room and lightly took Eleanor's arm. "It'll take time for Eleanor to pick out the right flowers."

She arched a brow. "I am not that indecisive."

"Never said you were, but you have always known what you wanted and you've never settled for less."

"I've never seen the sense in settling when you can have what you want," she said with asperity.

"I couldn't agree more."

Eleanor felt her stomach roll as he stared down at her, felt the unexpected heat generated from their close proximity, the exciting feel of his hand on her bare forearm, the brief flare of the heat in his dark eyes.

A woman wouldn't have to settle with Jonathan.

She quickly banished the unsettling thought from her mind. Jonathan was just a friend.

Jonathan had seen the quick flare of interest in Eleanor's eyes. He hid the knowledge in his heart. Walking beside her to her cottage through the quiet garden, he felt again the rightness of his love for this woman who loved so strongly. His patience was slowly being rewarded. He realized that he had to let her come to him.

Walking up the steps, she opened the door to her cottage. "It won't take but a moment to change."

Jonathan watched the nervous flutter of pulse in the base of her throat and wanted to press his lips against it to soothe her. Her eyes were wide, wary, watchful. She expected him to pounce. Now that he knew she was awakening to her feelings for him, he could wait.

"I'll just sit here on the porch. It isn't often I get a chance to do that."

The relief in her eyes was instantaneous. "Of course."

Jonathan sat down and draped his arms on the back of the wooden bench, trying to calm the desire churning through his body. Soon, very soon, Eleanor would be his and he could give free rein to all the ways he wanted to love her.

In thirty-nine years of wanting he'd had a lot of time to fantasize.

Her back pressed against the door, Eleanor tried to calm her racing heart. Her palms were actually damp. Annoyed with herself, she pushed away from the door and went into her bedroom to change. She'd never been frazzled. There wasn't a time in her life she hadn't known what she wanted or how to get it.

Reaching into the closet, she took out a white sheath and laid it on the bed. When Mary and Alfred Delouth's only child chose to follow in her father's and grandfather's footsteps into medicine, no one doubted she'd carry on the family tradition. She had the brains, the guts, and the drive. She finished high school at fifteen, with twenty-five acceptance letters to the most prestigious universities in the country and enough scholarship money for ten students.

Then, in her second year in medical school, she'd looked up into the brownest eyes she'd ever seen and fallen head over heels in love with Randolph Wakefield, a senior medical student. Thankfully, he had felt the same way.

Pulling off her blouse and skirt, she reached for the linen dress. Poor, sweet Randolph hadn't known what hit him. She could have returned to medical school after Adam's birth. But after she held him in her arms, looked into his bright eyes, she had realized that medicine was no longer where her heart lay. Her family was.

She'd always known what she wanted and how to get it.

Her lipstick poised, she stared at her reflection in the mirror and critically assessed herself. She wore her fifty-nine years well, thanks to a good metabolism and good genes. High cheekbones were still distinguishable; the skin on her face and beneath her neck was smooth and firm.

Her eyebrows might be shaped professionally, but everything else was as God had given her. Proof of that was the faint streaks of gray hair at her temples, which she refused to dye. Her gaze dipped to her reasonably firm breasts, then lower to her waist. She frowned on seeing the faint rounded outline.

And reality hit.

Capping the lipstick with an irritated flick of her wrist, she picked up her bag. She wasn't twenty, with legs as long as a gazelle's and a figure that turned heads. It had been so long since she had paid any attention to how men viewed her that she had probably read too much into the way Jonathan had looked at her. Perhaps she should cut back on her estrogen dosage.

He stood up when she stepped onto the porch. The sun shone over his broad shoulders, silhouetting him. Her breath snagged. There was no denying that Jonathan was a formidable man.

"That didn't take long." His big hand lifted to rest on the small of her back as they went down the walk.

His hand felt like a brand upon her skin. She said the first thing that came into her scattered mind: "Randolph hated to be kept waiting."

"But seeing you, I bet he didn't mind," Jonathan said easily, leading her past two giant stone urns of impatiens and moss roses.

She flushed at the compliment and sucked in her stomach. "He said he didn't."

"For the right woman, a man would wait

a lifetime. I know I would." Jonathan opened the door to the Mercedes.

The words were spoken with such quiet passion that Eleanor felt them all the way to her soul. She and Randolph had shared passion and so very much love and happiness. She missed him, but she also realized how blessed they both had been. "I had my one great love, Jonathan. I pray you find yours." She slid inside the car.

Jonathan closed the door and slowly walked around to climb inside. He commended himself on not slamming either of their doors, then speaking in a normal tone when he asked Eleanor if she had a special florist shop in mind. He glanced over when she didn't answer.

"Eleanor?"

She lifted her head and tears shimmered in her amber eyes. His gut clenched.

"What is it?" he asked, afraid he knew the answer.

She sniffed and reached for a tissue in the tiny black purse that couldn't have held much else. "I just felt sad for a moment, that's all."

"Randolph?" he asked, hating himself for the jealousy and unable to do anything about it.

"I . . . no. I just felt sad." She gave him a watery smile. "I should be tap-dancing on the ceiling. Adam is coming back to us."

The pad of his thumb, the only safe way of touching her, brushed the tears away from her smooth cheek. "The past weeks haven't been easy. All the tension has finally caught up with you."

"I suppose." She sniffed one last time and reached for her seat belt. "We better get going. If I tear up again you have permission to shake some sense into me."

"How about if I kiss some sense into you?"

She jumped and whirled around to face him. "What?"

There was such affront in her eyes that he had to laugh. The sound got tangled in his throat when her eyes strayed to his mouth with open speculation. He started the car. It was that or grab Eleanor and satisfy both of their curiosities. "I use a florist by my office. We'll try there first."

Odette and Samuel Tucker had lived in their neat frame house since the first day of their marriage fifty years ago. They'd raised their seven sons, welcomed their wives, and doted on their fifteen grandchildren. In their opinion, God had blessed them.

"Thank you, Eleanor and Dr. Delacroix. These flowers are beautiful," Odette said, her eyes going once again to the two bouquets of roses and mixed cut flowers that sat in the living room amid family portraits and her collection of black angels.

"We all wanted to wish you a speedy recovery."

"She will if she stops trying to tell the doctor what to do," Samuel said from a straight-back chair pulled up to the couch on which Odette reclined.

"He wants me to stay off work for six weeks. What kind of nonsense is that?" she asked, obviously incensed and with no intention of listening.

"Considering your medical history, I think it's a wise decision." Jonathan eyed her distended ankle propped up on two pillows. "They won't be able to put the cast on until the swelling goes down. Getting around Adam's house on those hardwood floors and rugs might be unstable with a cast on. The stairs are certainly out."

"Told you." Samuel nodded emphatically.

Worry swept across Odette's face. "I'm not used to idleness. Besides, I need to get back to work."

"Odette, if it's your salary you're concerned about, please don't worry. It'll continue. And don't worry about Adam. Thanks to your faith in him, he was in the kitchen this morning eating breakfast and laughing with Lilly," Eleanor told her.

Odette's eyes brightened. "You don't say?"

"I do say." Eleanor smiled. "You made him remember the wonderful doctor he was."

"Praise the Lord," Odette said, with a nod of her turban-covered head. "Not that I don't trust the Lord, but I was wondering why I had this accident. The Lord certainly works in mysterious ways. Dr. Wakefield helped me get the help I needed with my diabetes. My falling down helped him the same way."

"Odette, you mentioned last night you haven't been able to spend much time with your grandson. After the cast is put on and you're up and about, you could spend more time with him if you didn't go back to work," Jonathan suggested. It was no secret that Odette doted on her latest grandchild.

"He's such a honey. This morning he had a little bit of my biscuit and smacked his lips."

"If Dorothea sees you feeding Cameron solid food, she'll have a fit."

Odette harrumphed and crossed her arms. "Won't hurt him none. Just look at his daddy and uncles. You sure Lilly and Dr. Wakefield can get along by themselves?"

"Positive," Eleanor said, recalling their laughter.

"Well, then, I guess I stay here and

worry this old man."

"Old?" Samuel pushed to his feet with an agility that belied his seventy-one years. "I better go get your medicine before I become too feeble to move."

Odette just smiled.

Eleanor watched the interaction between Odette and Samuel. Their love for each other showed clearly with every word, every gesture, every glance. They were among the lucky people who were blessed to find that one person in all the universe who made their life complete. Jonathan hadn't been that fortunate. That was the reason she had cried, the thought that he might never find such happiness. He had so much love to offer.

"Here you go," Samuel said, handing Odette her medicine and holding the glass of water until she had put the pills in her mouth.

"You make an excellent caregiver, Samuel," Jonathan said.

"It ain't hard when you care about the person." He took the glass. "Even if they are as stubborn as a mule."

"I couldn't agree more," Jonathan said. He and Samuel completely ignored the outraged expressions of the women.

Adam had come to a decision. It hadn't been an easy one to make. His hands outstretched, he bent from the waist and "patted" the air on the way to his desk in the study. He felt the solid walnut wood, then followed the smooth edge of his desk until he could sit in his Chippendale swivel-tilt chair.

The feeling of accomplishment he'd felt when he helped Odette three days ago was slowly ebbing away. Each time he had to wait for Lilly or his mother to take him farther than the living room, it chipped away at his self-esteem bit by bit.

Yesterday he'd tried to find his way by himself to the kitchen and had tripped on a bench against the wall in the hallway. Thankfully, when he'd fallen he hit his head on the padded seat and not the exposed wood on the arms or on the hardwood floor, but the incident had frightened him and caused him to pull back.

For the rest of the day he'd gone no farther than his room and his study by himself. Fear was creeping over him again. He could feel it. If he didn't get a handle on it and gain some real independence, he'd revert back to the way he had been.

He couldn't have that. He'd hated his life and had begun to hate others.

Reaching out, he picked up the phone and punched in the first two numbers. The phone would ring on every phone in the house except his private line in his bedroom.

"Yes, Dr. Wakefield?"

Somehow her voice always reached through his fear. He eased back in his seat. "Lilly, could you please come to my study?"

"Yes. Do you need me to bring you anything?"

He had to smile. She continuously tried to fatten him up. "No, just you."

There was a slight pause, then, "I'll be right there."

Hanging up, he tried to figure out if he had imagined that breathless catch in her voice and why it pleased him to think he had not.

"Yes, sir?"

The pleasure of moments ago evaporated. He frowned. "From now on call me Adam."

"But —"

"We can argue about this, but I'll win, and there's another matter I want to discuss with you," he said.

The spark of annoyance Lilly felt at Dr. Wakefield's imperious tone was short-lived. That was who he was. She perched on the end of a chair. "What matter?"

"I want you to understand that I appreciate everything you've done for me, but I need more." The fingers on his right hand fiddled with a gold pen. Since she was reasonably sure he wasn't working his way up to firing her, she asked, "In what way?"

"I'm tired of depending on you and Mother to get me where I need to go, tired of bumping into furniture, tired of fanning the air," he finished, his voice tight.

"If you took Orientation and Mobility classes you'd be able to go where you want without our help," she suggested, holding her breath for his reaction.

He rocked forward in his chair. "How did you know about that?"

She barely kept from squirming. "Your mother was able to get a social worker by the name of Harriet Parker to come out and talk with us about the best ways to help you. One of the things she mentioned was Orientation and Mobility classes."

"Could you please call Mother and ask her for the phone number?" Picking up the phone, he set it closer to her, then shoved the gold pen and a pad toward her.

Breathing a sigh of relief, she stood. "Of course." In seconds she had Eleanor on the phone and the information. "Do you want me to dial it for you so you can speak to Harriet?"

"Thank you." No one but Lilly seemed to understand his need to do as much for himself as possible. He thought the reason was probably because they were both fighting to turn their lives around.

"Mrs. Parker, please hold. Eleanor

Wakefield's son, Dr. Wakefield, would like to speak with you."

Adam's fingers circled the phone, feeling the lingering heat of Lilly's hand and its calming influence. She never doubted him. "Mrs. Parker, thank you for taking my call. I'd like to inquire about taking O & M classes." There was a long pause. "Tomorrow at one here would be fine."

Lilly tapped his shoulder and whispered in his ear, "You need to send a car for her."

The warm breath against his ear caused his mind to race in an entirely different direction. "What?"

"She has a guide dog."

Adam nodded his understanding. She hadn't described the social worker as blind but had let him know just the same. "I'll send a car for you. . . . All right. I'll expect you and Mr. Dillion at one. Goodbye."

"I better go find the tea service," Lilly said when Adam hung up the phone. "Do you think finger sandwiches and lemon cookies will be all right to serve? Maybe I better ask Eleanor."

"Whatever you prepare will be fine, Lilly." Adam's mind was on trying to figure out why his body had reacted so oddly to the breath of a woman. His body hadn't wanted sex since his accident.

Nicole could testify to that.

"I don't think Odette would agree with you," Lilly said, worry in her voice. "I'm going to call your mother. I don't want you embarrassed."

Adam came out of his musings. "Lilly, you're making too much of this."

"You can't tell me you haven't always served your guests the best."

He had, but that was before. Then he realized that, to Lilly, before was no different from now. "Perhaps you should ask Mother."

"I will."

They hadn't discussed the menu with Adam, but judging from the compliments of his two guests, they had done well. His mother sat beside him, serving and keeping the conversation flowing. Lilly, off to the left, was quieter. He'd asked her to sit, but she'd refused.

"You have a beautiful estate, Dr. Wakefield," Harriet said.

Caught off guard by the comment, Adam was unable to hide his astonishment. "Th-Thank you."

Laughter erupted, followed by a voice aged by whiskey and smoke: "He's too polite to ask how you know, Harriet."

Adam frowned in the direction the voice had come from, directly across from him.

Since Brent Dillion's hands were the size of dinner plates, Adam thought he was probably bigger and broader than Jonathan. There the resemblance ended. The man had none of Jonathan's smooth manners or tact.

Adam was beginning to wonder if Harriet had been right in her high praise of the O & M instructor. "I don't think that comment was necessary, Mr. Dillion."

"I disagree and so will Harriet. Blindness demands two things: honesty and trust. Without them, you're heading for trouble," he said. "And call me Brent."

"Brent's right, Dr. Wakefield. I may not agree with his methods, but he gets the job done," Harriet said. "As for how I knew, he described the grounds to me as he drove in. The echo in the room, the feel of the tapestry chair I'm in also helped."

"How long did it take you to learn that?" Adam asked, leaning forward.

"Weeks, perhaps months, but as I explained to your mother, it depends on how much effort the person is willing to put into it," she told him.

"I'll be seeing by then." Adam firmly crossed his arms and sat back on the sofa.

Brent Dillion's gaze narrowed on Eleanor as the cup rattled in the saucer in her hand. "In the meantime, you want to get around by yourself, is that right?" Brent asked.

"Yes." Adam had no idea why the man irritated him.

"You don't like me, do you?"

Eleanor opened her mouth, but Brent held up his hand.

"No."

"I can imagine. I'm big, bold, brash, and worse, I can see."

Unfolding his arms, Adam surged to his feet. He felt Lilly touch his arm and caught himself in time to keep from jerking away. "I didn't invite you here to insult me."

"Ladies, can you please excuse us for a bit?" Brent asked. "Doc and I have some talking to do. Go on. Don't come back unless you hear something breaking."

"Very funny," Adam said, clearly not amused.

"Yeah, I'm a riot." Brent sat back down. "Since the ladies have left I'm sitting, so you might as well take a load off."

Adam sat. "I heard them leave and since the angle of your voice changed, I'm aware you're sitting."

"Do you know how many people in the world couldn't have made that deduction? Sighted people depend too much on their eyes and forget their other senses. They let their sight distract them. Doc, I'm proud of you."

His expression one of bored indifference, Adam said, "Yes, I can tell by your voice."

Rough laughter rumbled. "I guess you can tell why I've gone through two wives and countless meaningful relationships. You have a special lady?"

"No." The word was clipped and didn't invite conversation.

"This is good tea. You sure you don't want any? No? Well, where was I? Oh, yes. Dating for the visually impaired." He took a loud sip of tea. "I have unsighted buddies on my golf team who get more ladies than I do. At first they were hesitant to approach a woman, but they soon got over it. Now they listen to what and how it's said instead of looking at face and body measurements."

"They play golf and they're blind?" Intrigued in spite of himself, Adam unfolded his arms.

"Yep. I have to sight the ball, tell the direction, but they do the rest by themselves." Brent placed his cup on the table. "The only things an unsighted person can't do are drive and read."

Adam's hands flexed. "Lilly says there is a computer program that can read print."

"Sure is. Various programs run from about two-fifty to over a thousand bucks; then you have to figure in the optical scanner and if you need to upgrade your computer. Shouldn't be hard for a stepper like you."

"That's condescending."

"Yeah, maybe, but I see you sitting there, rich and successful, looking down your nose at me, angry at me because an uncouth guy like me can see and you can't. Well, let me tell you about what pisses me off," Brent said, his voice taking on a hard edge. "It's a single working mother whose out-of-control diabetes takes her sight, a hardworking steelworker who forgot to flip his helmet down when he fired up the blowtorch and now can't support his three children. You don't know how fortunate you are, Doc."

Adam felt the anger sweeping through him. "I was a neurosurgeon. It takes skill, courage, and finesse to incise into the brain. You have to know where and how to approach the lesion, especially if it's in a delicate or eloquent area. And you sure as hell better know what you're looking for and what to do when you get in there. Do you possibly have any idea how long it took to learn?"

"No, Doc, but I got a feeling you're going to tell me," Brent said mildly.

"I studied sixteen years after high school. Only two-thirds of the doctors that go into medicine finish. That number is cut in half for neurosurgeons. Intelligence is rarely the problem. What gets you is the emotional stress. The long hours. At a little over two thousand, we're probably the smallest of the surgical specialties. I was on my way to being the best. Now, I can't cut into a damn piece of meat without making a mess." His hand fisted the front of the Polo shirt he wore. "I'm reduced to wearing these because I have trouble buttoning a damn shirt correctly."

"And you have the money to buy as much meat or as many of those shirts as you want. You won't get any sympathy from me," Brent shot back.

Adam's head snapped back. "I wasn't asking for any."

"The hell you weren't. Your blindness was a bump in the road to you; for some it's careening off a cliff. You can still pay the rent and live large. Your children aren't going hungry; the wolf isn't at your door. You don't have to worry about what do you do when the people who've always depended on you can't." Brent ticked off each word with biting precision. "*That* takes your pride."

"That's where you're wrong," Adam said just as heatedly. "Money has never been the measure of what my family and I feel for each other. I know about lost pride. I've been so far down I didn't think I'd ever get up again, but I have. To you, because I have money, that makes my blindness livable. I'd give away every cent to be able to see again." He came to his feet, his chest heaving with anger. "That's not an option. I have to start where I am and go from here. I plan to stay up and stay a man. With or without your help. Good-bye and thanks for coming." He retook his seat. "Please see yourself out."

"Do you still want to work with me?"

"Do *you* want to work with *me?*" Adam countered. He could tolerate the obnoxious, outspoken man; he couldn't tolerate being lost.

"The way I see it, we can only go up from here. My hand is directly in front of you if you want to shake it."

Adam came to his feet and reached out. A large hand firmly enclosed his. "By the way, I was ticked that you could see. How did you know?"

"Occupational hazard and your body language," Brent explained, withdrawing his hand. "If I eat a quick lunch, I can fit you in between two and three, Monday, Wednesday, and Friday."

"Can't we increase the hours?" He wanted to learn as much as possible as soon as possible.

"Not unless we clone me. I came out here as a favor to Harriet. I'm squeezing you in as it is."

The man and woman, Adam thought. "I'd like to offer financial assistance to the young mother and the steelworker."

The unexpected slap to his back almost toppled Adam. "You've got heart, Doc. Sally is now a court reporter and Simon is the top salesman for his insurance company."

"Was that little story a prod or test or motivation?" Adam asked, irritation creeping back into his voice.

"All three. I don't have time for temperamental, stuck-up, snooty people. Too many others need my time," Brent said.

"If you're as good as you are arrogant, you must be amazing."

"I am, Doc; believe me, I am. Now, let's go take a look at your computer to see how quickly we can have you searching the Web."

Lilly was all thumbs. She couldn't seem to concentrate on the piano keys. No matter how much she tried to block out the pressure of Adam's thigh against hers, she couldn't. If she scooted over, he'd invariably reach over to guide her hands and their bodies would connect again.

His touching her hands only increased her nervousness. She'd started putting Vaseline on them at night and wearing her church gloves to soften them, but she couldn't tell any difference. They remained callused and rough from six years of keeping her house spotless. Adam's hands, like his mother's and Nicole's, were smooth, the nails short and rounded. Lilly had searched for a nail file in one of the seven bathrooms and hadn't found one yet.

Her thoughts elsewhere, she hit D instead of C, B when it should have been A. Finally she drew back her trembling hands and folded them in her lap. She'd humiliated herself enough for one night. "I guess I'm tired. Why don't we stop for tonight?"

"What's the matter? You've been tense all afternoon."

"I guess I was worried about you and that man. I thought you were going to fight."

She had paced the entire time. It had surprised her to see them walk into the kitchen together, unharmed and talking cordially.

"Try again. There has to be more to it."

She fidgeted. "There isn't, Adam."

"That's the first time you've called me by my first name," he said gently.

She swallowed and tucked her head. Like a child, she had practiced so she wouldn't stumble over it and reveal how being near him made her feel strange and excited at once. "I–I should go upstairs."

Before she could move, he took her hands in his. "Talk to me. Is it something

I've done or said? Did Nicole call again?"

"No."

"Your lawyer?"

"No."

"Lilly, we aren't going to go through the one-word answers again, are we?"

She glanced up. He wore a teasing smile on his face. Despite herself, her heart skipped a beat.

"Your pulse is racing."

"I–I must be coming down with some kind of bug," she said, skirting around the truth.

"Why didn't you say something sooner?" Rising, he pulled her to her feet. "Let's get you upstairs and to bed. Don't you dare get out of that bed tomorrow. I should have thought of this sooner. You need help. Odette won't be back for five more weeks. I'll have Mother call an agency to-morrow."

The consequences of her duplicity were quick and unsettling. "I'll be fine. There's no need to call the agency."

He must have heard the frantic note in her voice, because he stopped halfway out of the room. "You don't think I'd hire anyone over you or fire you because you're sick, do you?"

She hadn't. Fear of losing her job no longer kept her awake at night. Her growing feelings for Adam did. She'd

346

thought Myron had killed any possibility of her caring for another man. She'd been wrong.

"I'll be fine after a good night's sleep. Tomorrow I'll call Odette and see when the cleaning crew is scheduled to come."

"We'll see. Now go to bed."

"Good night, Adam." She escaped to her room.

The next morning, Lilly chatted gaily with Adam while she cooked breakfast. She made sure she acted no different. Adam was getting too good at distinguishing her emotions and moods.

Finished, she called Odette and, after chatting for fifteen minutes, learned the crew was due the next day. Happy, Lilly told Adam the information while she was going through his mail with him. Whatever it was that had caused her to forget dreams were highways to unhappiness, she now had it under control. Adam was an employer, nothing more. She had dreamed foolishly before and reaped the bitter consequences. She didn't plan on repeating her mistake.

Brent arrived exactly at two Monday afternoon. Lilly led him into the study and took a seat beside Adam.

"I prefer that my student and I get to

know each other alone," Brent said without preamble.

Lilly was already rising. Adam's hand on her arm stopped her. "I'd like her to stay."

Brent rocked back on his booted heels. "Afraid I'll let you walk into a wall or one of these fancy chairs?"

"She stays." Adam was relatively sure that wouldn't happen, but he wanted Lilly there just the same.

Laughter rumbled from a deep chest. "All right, Doc. Let's get to work and see if I can earn that trust of yours."

Adam stood and listened to Brent talk about reference points, naming hallways and corners, landmarks, and positional terminology when all he wanted to do was walk upright like a man. He told him as much.

"Do you let your patients tell you how to diagnose and treat them?"

Adam's tight lips were his answer.

"Thought not. Let's talk about clues, any auditory, tactile, kinesthetic sense that will help you determine location, position, or line of direction. You smell anything?"

"Roses." As soon as the word was out of his mouth he wanted to call it back. He was sure Lilly wouldn't understand, but he wasn't so sure about Brent.

"Roses, huh? Doc, I'd say your kinesthetic memory is working just fine."

"Can we get on with this?" he asked.

"What do you smell, Lilly?" Brent asked, grinning.

"I — er, nothing," she said, a foot away from Adam, and flushed. She wasn't about to admit she smelled Adam's citrus cologne, that she had to catch herself a couple of times to keep from leaning closer to the enticing scent.

Brent grinned. "Imagine that. Two people a foot apart and totally different noses. And might I say, Lilly, that you have a pretty nose."

"Are you going to teach or flirt?" Adam asked, annoyed with Brent. He had no right to flirt with Lilly.

"Teach." With that, Brent began moving through the house. Adam could do nothing but hold on and trust him not to run into a wall.

Chapter Fourteen

The fourth time Brent came, he brought the optical scanner and the read-print program to install on Adam's computer. Adam was awkward in using the arrow keys instead of the mouse, but after a while he was doing fairly well, since the program "told" him when he went wrong.

His confidence that he had overcome all his bumps in the road grew until Brent handed him a cane. To Adam's profound disappointment, he was awkward and off-balance with the black five-foot extension of his arm that came to the middle of his chest.

"Slow down and think, Doc."

"I am," Adam said impatiently, his right hand clenching the rubber grip of the sturdy aluminum cane.

"I understand that you were quite a renowned neurosurgeon," Brent said in a conversational tone.

"Yes," Adam answered, his words clipped as he made his way around the sofa and a chair on his way to his destination, the fireplace.

"Tell me, then, the first time you made an incision, was it as good as the hundredth time?"

"Of course not." Adam barely kept himself from snapping the answer.

"Then how did you learn?" Brent asked mildly.

Finally Adam reached the fireplace and turned toward Brent. "By not giving up, by practicing every chance I got."

"Practice. Ah, yes. Then why on earth did you think the first or second or even the third time you tried to use your cane you would be perfect?"

Adam rubbed the back of his neck "I don't know; I guess because I was ready to learn."

"Good. That's what I wanted to hear. Learning comes from doing. In this case, by using your cane." Brent glanced at the silent Lilly. "Could you please get me something to drink? I'm as parched as a tick on a dead dog."

"Of course," she said, rising from sitting on the sofa. Her hands had been clamped so tightly together they ached. Every step Adam took, she took with him. Every defeat he experienced, she experienced with him. "What would you like?"

"A margarita, but since I'm on duty, anything fruity, and I'll pretend."

"Would you like something, Dr. Wakefield?" She had decided not to call him Adam when guests were present.

"No."

"I'll be right back."

"Take your time," Brent advised.

Frowning, Lilly said, "All right."

Adam listened to the fading sound of Lilly's shoes on the area rugs, then the hollow sound indicating she was on the hardwood floor in the hallway. "Now that you've gotten rid of Lilly, what's next?"

"Figured you were smart from the first. And to answer your question: what's next is that you begin to learn."

"I thought that's what I was doing already. Was it necessary for her to leave?"

"Yes. Whether you like to admit it or not, she's a distraction. You tense up when she's in the room."

"That's ridiculous. I want her here."

"Exactly, and you have high expectations of yourself when she's looking. You don't want to flounder or fall or bump into furniture. You want to be the self-assured man you've always been. Just like you learned to be that man, you must learn again."

"I told you I'm willing to learn." Brent would try the patience of a saint, and Adam had never been a saint.

"I know what you said, but I'm watching what you're doing and it's piss-poor." Brent crossed to him. "To teach you, I must have your complete concentration. To learn, you must have the same concentration. I don't have it with Lilly here.

From the beginning, I told you that I preferred to work without an audience because the student works best that way. It wasn't a whim."

"Here's your drink."

Brent took the glass from Lilly and sipped the fruity concoction of pineapple and orange juice, then handed it back. "Delicious. Dr. Wakefield, are you sure Lilly can't get anything for you?"

Adam arched a brow. He didn't think it was by accident that Brent had addressed him professionally for the first time. He'd wanted to remind Adam that he was the expert here. Not Adam. And as irritating as it might be, Brent was right. Adam had had Jonathan check on the outspoken man, and he was the best. "Lilly."

"Yes?"

He heard her move across the room, smelled the light scent of roses. "Brent feels I'm too macho when you're watching. So I guess you have the rest of the afternoon off. But don't you dare read *The Third Watch* without me."

First came worry that she wouldn't be there if he needed her; then, as what he had said sank in, a smile worked itself across her face. He wouldn't, as he had put it, be macho if he only cared for her professionally. Her heart sang.

"If I did, I'd be too scared to go to sleep

tonight. If you gentlemen will excuse me, I have some phone calls to make. I'll be in the kitchen."

As soon as Adam heard the last faint sound of her shoes he said, "Now that she's gone we can start. Or do I get my knuckles rapped?"

"Good one, Doc. I'm strict, but when I turn you loose, I could set you down in the middle of Times Square and you wouldn't hesitate to orientate yourself and find where you need to go."

Adam shook his head and reluctantly grinned. "You certainly don't lack self-confidence."

"Neither do you," Brent said. "Once you have the cane down pat, you might consider a guide dog."

"A guide dog takes too long to train. Besides, when my sight returns, I won't need him."

"Logical, but what if your sight doesn't return?"

Adam's jaw hardened. "It will."

"Then let's get started."

Assured she'd have privacy for a while, Lilly placed a call to her lawyer. His secretary put her through to him immediately. "Hello, Mrs. Crawford."

"Evening, Mr. Powell. How is the investigation going?"

His impatient sigh echoed clearly through the line. "Nothing new. I told you I'd call if there was."

She barely kept from biting her lip or bowing her head. "Yes, but I was hoping he might change his mind about going to court."

"Unfortunately, no."

"You still can't find anyone to testify against him?" she asked, half sitting on the stool at the counter.

"To everyone I've spoken with, across gender and race lines, Myron Crawford is a kind, generous man who loves his family and never let a friend down."

"What about Rafe?" Her one chance was finding her stepson. He'd suffered more than she had at Myron's hands.

"No luck on locating him. But I'm not sure he'd help our case."

"What do you mean?"

"People here characterize him as a smart but undisciplined and ungrateful trouble-maker who left the day of graduation and almost broke his father's and grand-mother's hearts," the lawyer told her. "The same people all say Shayla is a sweet young woman who is devoted to her father. By the way, she's going to testify for her father."

Lilly closed her eyes. *There are never those as blind as those who will not see. Myron and Shayla only let you see what benefited them in the long run.* "You couldn't find anyone to testify for me?"

"So far I haven't," the lawyer slowly told her. His tone didn't indicate that he held out much hope that things would change in their favor. "You can always change the reason for your petition for divorce and skip going to court."

Her eyes snapped open. They gleamed with anger. "No! I backed down enough from Myron."

"You may lose."

"But the bottom line is that I wouldn't have backed down and I'll still have my divorce." Too angry to sit, she slid off the stool and began to pace the length of the cord.

"But it'll cost more emotionally and financially. His lawyer is going to come after you, and it won't be nice," he warned.

She suddenly realized that her mother's reputation and what people thought Lilly's was would be the lawyer's key weapons. Her mother might have been loose, but Lilly wasn't. Myron was the only man she'd ever slept with, but no one knew that other than Myron. How long would she have to live under her mother's shadow and shame? "I imagine he will," she finally said.

"You also have to consider that if you lose, you'll have to pay court costs and his lawyer's fee. Hutchinson is a crafty and shrewd devil. It wouldn't surprise me if he's already come up with a figure that's way over the usual amount because his case looks unbeatable," Powell warned. "Whatever the amount, you'd have no recourse but to pay."

She stopped and leaned her head against the base of the curved cabinet at the end of the counter. She'd put back every extra cent she earned. She'd bought nothing that wasn't a necessity. She had more money now than she ever had in her life. Being poor didn't scare her; backing down from Myron again did. "We go to court."

"All right." His tone didn't inspire confidence.

"Good-bye, Mr. Powell." Lilly bowed her head and wrapped her hands around her waist. Would she ever be free?

"Was that your lawyer?"

Lilly spun around sharply. "You move quietly."

He came closer. "And you're being evasive."

How could he know her better than anyone ever had, even Mother Crawford? The thought comforted and frightened her. "Myron is going to fight the grounds of my divorce petition," she said and explained that finding her stepson, Rafe, was her only chance of winning the case. "If I lose I show off to Brent."

Lilly walked beside him. "I think you like him."

Adam paused and stepped around the settee against the wall in the hall. "Why would I like an arrogant, overbearing, opinionated man?"

"Maybe because he reminds you of someone very close to you?" Lilly said, going through the front door Adam opened for her.

"Why, Lilly, I thought you liked Jonathan."

Laughing, they went down the front steps together.

Brent proved to be as good as he prophesied. After three weeks, Adam could go through the main rooms of the house without help or difficulty. Reference points and landmarks, those initially irritating terms, enabled him to move freely, avoid objects, and find what he wanted. To celebrate he invited Jonathan to dinner.

Lilly wanted the occasion to be a memorable one. She pored over recipe books and checked twice with Odette and Eleanor about Adam's favorite foods before settling on honey-glazed ham as the main course. The slices would be big enough for Adam to find and cut without difficulty, and there was little likelihood of the meat falling off his fork. She chose baby asparagus and roasted red bliss potatoes for the same reason.

Dessert had to be special. No matter how much Adam teased her about her high-cholesterol, calorie-laden cooking, he usually asked for seconds and often thirds.

Grinning, Lilly sat back in her chair at the table in the breakfast nook, listening to the faint strains of music. Beethoven again. Adam usually played after lunch. Twice a week, on Tuesday and Friday, she'd join him then or after supper for her lessons. She was still learning to "sight" her keys. Adam was patient but firm. He intended her to learn to play the piano. She understood it was his way of saying he was sorry, but it was also to give her confidence.

Lilly went back to flipping through the cookbooks. Odette had at least a dozen and had admitted ruefully to Lilly when she called that she didn't use any of them. She cooked from scratch. The more Lilly flipped, the more she realized she wasn't going to find the answer for a dessert. She didn't want a mishap. Perhaps she should take Odette's rule and cook from scratch a dessert she was familiar with.

Her hand clutched the hardbound book. There was only one that she considered fancy enough to fit the occasion. The dessert she wanted to prepare had been taught to her by Mother Crawford and handed down through four generations of Crawford women, although Lilly didn't consider herself a Crawford woman. The last time she had cooked the pie had been at Myron's insistence two weeks before Mother Crawford's death. Just thinking of Myron angered her.

Closing the book, Lilly went outside. Still restless, she started walking. The sight of the rosebushes in bloom stopped her. They were Mother Crawford's favorite. The kind woman had given Lilly more love than anyone else before or since. Thinking back, she recalled what Mother Crawford had said when she was teaching Lilly the recipe.

"This is given to only one Crawford woman in each generation to hand down to the next. It's an honor and a trust. You make sure you know who you're giving it to." Then she had looked Lilly straight in the eye and said, "I never taught anyone else this and I don't aim to. Crawford or no, I would have picked you."

At the time Lilly hadn't thought anything of her words except her happiness that Mother Crawford had that much trust in her and that, for once, she wasn't standing in line behind Carol, Myron's first wife.

Mother Crawford had given the family recipe to her, Lilly. She had loved her and had faith in her. Turning, Lilly went back to the kitchen. She knew what she wanted to prepare for dessert, a family recipe based on love and trust.

"Show time."

Adam opened the door to his bedroom and walked into the hall. Lilly had offered to accompany him to dinner, but he wanted to do it by himself. It wasn't pride that ruled his decision but his increasing need to regain as much of his independence as possible. He wore a white shirt, a gray silk tie, and a herringbone two-button suit for the occasion. Now all he had to do was get downstairs.

From experience, he knew navigating the hallway wouldn't be much of a problem. He'd practiced numerous times by himself without a mishap. With the cane repeatedly making an arch above the floor, he made his way to the top of the stairs. Here things would get a little trickier, but nothing, Brent had assured Adam, he couldn't handle. He'd gone up and down several times, but never without Brent being there to guide and warn him.

"Pretend I'm there," Brent had said.

Adam anchored the cane to the back of the first step and moved up diagonally with it, then drew in a fortifying breath and stepped into nothingness. As always, his